UNTRULY
with *You*

Untruly With You
Florence Fields

florencefields.com
@authorflorencefields

Untruly With You is a work of fiction. Names, characters, places, and incidents either are the product of the author's imagination or are used fictitiously. Any resemblance to actual persons, living or dead, events, or locales is entirely coincidental.

Copyright © Florence Fields, 2025

IBSN 979-8-9885725-3-4 (e-book)
IBSN 979-8-9885725-2-7 (paperback)

First Edition: February 2025

For the dreamers who leap before they look,
and the planners who pack a parachute—
this one's for finding love somewhere in the middle.

1

LAINE

I WANT to enjoy every nugget of delightful chaos that life has to offer.

My first—and only—ex saw that in a much less idyllic light.

"I can't keep watching you zig-zag around without a destination," he once told me.

I looked up at the road signs, double-checking myself. I never got lost in the city. Sure enough, we were going down Houston Street as planned. "I thought we were headed to Lombardi's for lunch?"

He threw his hands up, halting in the midday sidewalk traffic. Like true New Yorkers, those around just rushed by us like a stream along a jutting rock. "I don't mean it literally."

"So, we aren't getting pizza?"

"No. We aren't getting pizza."

I crossed my arms over my growling stomach. "What destination do you want, then? Sushi?"

"Laine." He said my name with so much weight, I prepared myself for the oncoming monologue. Then those big blue eyes peered into mine, glistening on demand, in search of connection. He was a Tisch student through and through, never one to avoid the dramatics. "I need a destination, a commitment. I can't keep up with the constant uncertainty of our journey. It's like being on a rollercoaster without knowing when it will stop."

"Is this about the movie thing?"

"No," he huffed. "It's about everything."

I got pizza alone that day.

∪

I HAVEN'T LEARNED whatever lesson he was trying to teach me. That much is clear.

My finger hovers over the trackpad of my laptop for no more than two seconds before I press down, the "Drop Class" text highlighted in yellow for a split second.

It's not that I wasn't enjoying the class; it's just that I wanted to be sure I made the most out of my last elective at NYU. After all, the whole reason of life is to enjoy every little minute of it. Plus, my dad has been begging me to take up an interest in Shakespeare ever since I could read.

I have over an hour until class, but, as usual, it takes me twenty minutes to decide on an outfit, ten minutes to pick the right music for the commute, and five minutes to decide on the right shade of red lipstick. (For what it's worth, I choose a hot-pink turtleneck and matching beanie, brown leather coat, oversized plaid scarf, the new Harry Styles album, and a classic scarlet shade that makes my black bob hairstyle look all the more French.)

My phone buzzes as I lock my door behind me, and I find my twenty-odd group chats piling up endlessly.

Once on the street, I race across the February slush and make it onto the A train just before the doors close. As we pass through each station, I tap my foot against the floor, trying to will the train to go faster. Even Harry Style's smooth, sweet voice serenading me through my headphones isn't soothing me today. When the train finally arrives at the West Fourth Street station, I sprint out of the turnstiles and up the escalators.

The lunch traffic is already in full force. People are rushing from one side of the street to the other while honking cabs and buses zoom past them. I weave in and out of pesky tourists that don't seem to understand why everyone else is in such a hurry. As I move, the cold air bites my nose and dries my eyes. When I get to the last block of my commute, my eyes begin watering. I wipe them, smudging eyeliner and mascara on my fingers.

Unlike most other colleges, NYU doesn't have a campus to itself. Instead, a collection of buildings houses NYU's classes. Thankfully, because I've been working on my bachelor's degree for six years—and have joined (and dropped out of) *many* classes and social groups in that time—I know most of the university by heart. I find my building easily, running under the ever-present scaffolding along the street to get there.

Once inside, the elevator draws me toward it like a magnet. It's already full of students, but I squeeze into the pack, hunching my shoulders and ignoring the dirty looks thrown my way.

"Hey, Laine!" a girl says from the back of the elevator.

I vaguely remember her from the acting class I took as a freshman. And though I can't remember her name, I wave back at her as if we're best friends.

I check my watch. Seven minutes past noon.

When the elevator finally arrives at my floor, I shove into the crowded hallway and run to the door to my lecture hall, slamming it open without wasting a second. It sounds with a

3

loud clang, and all eyes in the room fall on me. A few students snicker, and I brush my bangs into place. I wipe at the mascara under my eyes, trying to appear at least halfway presentable.

The professor stands at the front of the small room, wearing a stern expression that's exaggerated by his very Eugene-Levy-esque eyebrows. "I hope you have an excellent reason you've come to interrupt our class?"

I clear my throat and steady my adrenaline-laced breaths before responding. "I joined your class this morning, taking the last spot, I believe." Despite the fact that I was able to add the class to my schedule, a quick scan of the room tells me that there isn't a seat left—not one.

"We're two weeks into the semester," he says, turning back to the projected slide behind him—Cultural Context of *The Tempest*. "You're two weeks too late. And not to mention," he pauses, checking his watch, "seven minutes late today."

Sorry, bud, I think to myself. *You're not getting rid of me.*

I don't think I could survive yet another semester at school after this. I didn't mind taking my time when my tuition was covered. Thank you, Mom, for giving me the benefit of being a professor's daughter. But now that I've aged out of that perk and student debt is piling up, I am far more motivated to graduate.

"Actually, sir," I say, startling my professor. Clearly, he isn't used to being contradicted. "NYU policy says students can join a class up to two weeks into the semester if there is still an available spot, which there is in this case. One last spot. So, if you don't mind, I'd like to stay." And honestly, I don't care if he *does* mind. I'm here.

He looks at the front row, and someone—I think the guy with the brown curly hair—speaks up, barely loud enough for me to hear. "She's right, technically."

The professor harrumphs. "Name?" he asks, raising his thick eyebrows at me.

"Laine Rodriguez," I say in my best, bubbly, Laine Rodriguez voice. I flash the smile that has won me countless friendships over the years.

"We have an exam next week," he says. "You will need to catch up on what you've missed on your own time."

I lift my chin. "Understood!" It could be the onset of nerves, or it could be my winter layers covering me indoors, but either way, my skin crawls with warmth.

He gestures at me to sit. I glance around the room again, but sure enough, there aren't any seats.

"She can take my seat," the same curly-haired guy from before says.

"I need you up front," the professor responds, going back to his lesson without another word to me.

As quietly as I can manage, I slide my jacket off and unwind my scarf from my neck. But no matter how silent I am, there are a handful of students who look back at me, studying the fresh addition to their class. I try to ignore them, but when I catch the eye of the curly-haired guy in the front row, I freeze for a moment.

Even from across the room, his expression catches me off guard. While the others eyeing me seem thoroughly entertained by my less-than-ideal entrance into the class, his gaze is soft and steady. I stare back at him and try to discern that gentle expression on his face. Apologetic, I suppose. Maybe a dash of pity.

"Miss Rodriguez?" At the sound of my professor's voice, I straighten, my cheeks webbing with heat.

"Yes?" I say, hoping my grimace looks something like a smile.

"I suggest you take a seat and learn what you can before next week's exam."

How long was I staring at that guy?

Before I can get distracted again, I plant myself on the floor and crane my neck to see the projector screen. For the rest of the hour, I scramble to copy every slide into my notebook, trying to ignore the occasional glance from the guy in the front row.

2

SUTTON

EVEN WITHOUT HER bright-pink sweater or the fact that she barged into class ten minutes late, Laine Rodriquez would stand out. Her hair is in a classic style that reminds me of 1920s flapper girls and she's wearing red lipstick, the kind I've only seen girls wear to formal events—never to class. Throughout the hour, I peek back at her periodically. Her bangs stick out from her beanie in wild angles, and her eyes are wide, fluttering between the slideshow and her notebook as her hand flies across the lined paper. Those thick, dark eyebrows wrinkle with worry.

Laine fidgets constantly. She straightens her sweater. She rolls to sit on her knees. She twists the small pendant on her necklace from side to side. I've never seen someone so restless.

When class ends, Laine wastes no time running to the front of the lecture hall, sticking her hand out to Mr. Hirsch. He stares at it for a few moments before taking it, shaking once. Meanwhile, I'm frozen in my seat, petrified on Laine's behalf.

Mr. Hirsch doesn't wait for Laine to speak before airing

his grievances. "I don't like tardiness, Miss Rodriguez. As if it weren't enough for you to wait until the last possible day to add my class, you then choose to show up ten minutes late."

Laine smiles despite the criticism, her entire face joining in on the expression. It's a miracle that Mr. Hirsch can resist smiling back at the brilliance. "I'm very sorry. It won't happen again. I will be taking this class seriously. You see, I need to pass in order to graduate at the end of the semester."

Mr. Hirsch raises his eyebrows and begins packing his messenger bag. "You may have been able to join our class," he says, not bothering to bring his eyes to hers, "but that doesn't mean you'll be passing. This is an upper-division class, and the workload is evidence of such. Being late to my class shows a lack of discipline and propriety."

"I'll do anything," Laine says, nodding as if to convince herself of her own words. "Do you have office hours?"

"No."

Laine winces before fixing a smile across her face again. "Okay," she says, letting out a single, breathless laugh. She swallows hard. "Are there any tutors?"

Now it's my turn to flinch. I move my gaze to my laptop and type away gibberish on the keyboard, trying to signal to them how busy I am these days.

"For that, you should talk to Mr. Sutton Davis," Mr. Hirsch says, closing his briefcase with a thud so forceful both Laine and I straighten. "Good day, Miss Rodriguez."

He gives me a curt nod on his way out of the room. And then it's just me and Laine.

She rocks back on her heels a few times before plopping down in the seat beside me and leaning her chin down on her palm. For a minute, she doesn't speak. Instead, she waits for my eyes to meet hers. Despite myself, they do.

She leans over to see what I'm working on. I slam my laptop shut before she can see that my typing has been utter nonsense. "Hi," she whispers, the corners of her mouth lifting a touch.

"Hi," I echo.

Please don't ask me to—

"Can I schedule a tutoring session with you?" Laine asks, as if she can read my mind.

"No."

"No?"

"I don't have any availability. All my tutoring appointments are booked," I explain. It didn't take long for Mr. Hirsch's students to realize how tough he is. Laine opens her mouth, but I quickly add, "For the whole semester."

Laine's rich olive skin takes on a pinky tint, a subtle wash the same color as her sweater. When she looks at me, I can almost see my reflection in her eyes, which are so dark the irises and pupils blend. She has a scar above her lip, not unlike my own.

It's never easy for me to turn a student down. I remember what it was like to be drowning in schoolwork, looking for any sort of life preserver. But I can't be that life preserver for every student, or I won't be able to stay afloat myself. Still, with those big, dark eyes and bright smile, there's an even stronger draw than usual that's begging me to help Laine.

"I need to pass this class," she says, her chest rising and falling with quick breaths. "I need to graduate. And something tells me next week's exam is going to kick my ass. And maybe every exam after that. Don't you have *any* open sessions?"

I study Laine for a few moments, and she fidgets, uncomfortable with the silence.

"No," I force out again. The thought of taking on yet another student makes my anxiety climb. Heat gathers under the collar of my button-down. "I'm sorry. Aside from my own classes, I have dozens of students I'm working with, my TA responsibilities, a job, and my internship. So, no. I don't have any availability." My words come out colder than I intended.

Laine pulls back a few inches, shocked by my frankness. She pushes a stray lock of hair under her jaw. "Well, if anyone cancels…"

Her defeated expression is almost enough for me to add another thing to my plate.

Almost.

But not quite.

Not when I'm so close to finishing school, closing the end of a hard-fought chapter in my life. "I'll put you on the wait-list for tutoring," I offer.

"Thanks. See you next week."

I nod, and she accepts defeat, taking sluggish steps out of the room. I feel so bad about turning her down I nearly call out to her. Instead, I check the calendar on my phone again, something that has become habitual. I'm met with a screen chock-full of colorful little squares that will dictate my life for the coming months.

School. Work. School. Work. Tutoring. Counseling. Repeat. Repeat. Repeat.

I double-check the room to be sure everything is tidied before sloshing through the remnants of snow outside. Though I should be thinking about my endless to-do list, my mind circles back to Laine. To the furrowed brows as she copied notes down. To the deflated look when I told her no… three times.

When I get to my next appointment, a one-on-one with the professor overseeing my thesis, I'm welcomed by the *Althea Carr* etching on the frosted glass door. Thanks to the cold, my nose is running and my lips are chapped. Feeling— and likely looking—worse for the wear wouldn't be so bad except for the blur of bright pink I see through the frosted glass.

Ms. Carr's voice, sharper than usual, is muffled by the door. "Do I even want to know why you're not in class right now, Laine?"

"Do you?"

"Do I need to remind you that if you drop a single class, you won't be eligible to graduate this spring?"

"My sixty grand in tuition is reminder enough. Thanks, Mom."

"It's not my fault you didn't take advantage of your four years of free school. If you had graduated on time—"

"You pushed me into school before I had any idea what I wanted to do. It's no wonder I had to change my major."

"Fine. But *most* students don't switch majors four times."

My instinct tells me to wait to knock so I don't interrupt, but the accidental eavesdropping seems almost worse. Before I have the chance to back away from the door, I hear Ms. Carr's voice again, louder than before—loud enough to be directed at me, hiding behind the semi-private glass.

"Yes?"

Even though I know Ms. Carr already saw me, I knock.

"Come in," she says with a sigh.

I try—really try—to make my eyes land on Ms. Carr when I open the door. But Laine is like a bright-pink billboard I can't tear my eyes away from. She's perched on the arm of the chair opposite Ms. Carr's desk. The second I peek my head in, her wide smile is back, giving no indication of the argument she was in seconds ago.

"If it isn't Sutton," Laine exhales, her cheeks reddening a touch. She quirks a questioning eyebrow up. "Please tell me you came to say there's a tutoring appointment open."

"You know Mr. Davis?" Ms. Carr asks, her eyes narrowed. She always calls her graduate students by their last names.

"He's the TA of my *new* elective. He's the one that will

11

ensure I do, in fact, get my degree this semester. Right, Sutton?"

"As long as you can show up to class on time," I say.

Laine's smile pinches. "Thanks for the tip."

"Laine, Mr. Davis and I have an appointment to talk about his thesis." Ms. Carr flicks her eyes to the open door behind me.

When I look back at Laine, she is staring up at me through her eyelashes, a mischievous lift at the corner of her lip. "Sure, sure. I was just going to ask my mom about Miranda in *The Tempest*. And…"—Laine pauses to look down at her notes from class, rereading a copied slide word for word in a monotone voice—"what Miranda can teach us about feminism both in the seventeenth century and today."

"Are you trying to turn this into a tutoring session, Miss Rodriguez?" I ask.

"No, no." Laine waves her hand. "I'm just trying to make casual, organic conversation. What do you think, Sutton?"

I fight the urge to give in to Laine's playful personality. *You don't have time for this*, I remind myself. "I think you should read the play," I tell her.

"You're such a brilliant tutor. I can see why you're booked solid."

"I thought this wasn't a tutoring session?"

She crosses her arms over her chest. "Not with that kind of attitude it isn't."

"Laine," Ms. Carr prods, impatience hardening her voice again.

3

LAINE

I PULL two armfuls of hangers from my tiny closet. "What does one wear to a date auction?"

"That depends on if you're the bidder or the one being auctioned," Macy says, leaning over her stack of homework.

"Does Paul know you're going to a date auction?" Jeanie asks.

Paul? I rack my brain, and Jeanie must be able to read the confusion written across my face. "Paul...Paul, your boyfriend," she says flatly.

Oops. "Of course I remember Paul!" *Barely.* We dated for two months, but we tired of each other quickly. He hated that I couldn't make up my mind on anything, and I hated that he insisted we always have a plan for every little thing. He actually started drafting a three-month schedule of the movies we should watch together. When I suggested we watch *Little Women* rather than *The Godfather* on December fifth, as was his plan, I knew by the look in his eyes that we were doomed. Soon after, we had the whole your-life-is-a-rollercoaster-that-I'm-not-tall-enough-to-ride talk. "It didn't work out," I say. "Didn't I tell you about that? I'm taking a break from dating. A *long* break."

Jeanie's disappointed expression isn't because she actually likes Paul. She barely knew him. Rather, her downturned lips are the result of her belief that most of my relationships are surface level.

Maybe she's right. After almost six years at NYU, I can't go be out near the university for more than a couple of hours without seeing someone I know. It's always a simple connection: Sadie who took me to my first karaoke bar, Mike who dragged me to the school's abysmal baseball opener last year, Carrie who modeled for me during my brief stint as a photography major. I know dozens—no, *hundreds*—of other students. I've made countless memories.

However, there's not a single person at school I would bare my soul to or who I would call in an emergency. I don't have anyone I'd consider my "best friend." Not Jeanie, not Macy. They're just two of the many friends I have on rotation. They both work with me at *Washington Square News*, the student newspaper.

"Is there anyone specific you're trying to score a date with?" Jeanie asks.

"I'm writing an op-ed on the Zeta Psi auction and whether date auctions are a reasonable way to fundraise. I don't suppose either of you wants to come? I'm not bidding —keeping it professional and all—but there's bound to be some guys worth going for."

Jeanie and Macy agree immediately, both almost as spontaneous as I am.

U

THANK goodness I dressed in my usual abundance of layers. But even with my patchwork coat, plaid sweater vest, button-down, and green beret, the evening chill begins to set in. Only a fraternity would plan an outdoor *rooftop* fundraiser in February. Still early on in the semester, there are more people than I usually see at an event like this. Everyone bops between the keg and the DJ, who is really just one of the members of the frat with his iPhone hooked up to the Bluetooth speakers. And apparently, he has an affinity for mediocre house remixes of Rihanna songs.

Despite arriving almost thirty minutes late, we came at the perfect time for the betting to start. A guy in a backwards hat, a Vineyard Vines shirt, and giddy, glazed-over eyes takes the microphone. "Alright, alright, everyone!" he says, a constant chuckle bubbling under every word. "Welcome to our annual Zeta Psi date auction. We've got a *fire* selection for you all tonight. Some nerds, some jocks, some romantics. No matter your taste, there's gotta be a Zete for you."

The crowd claps and hollers as the influence of the cheap beer works its way into everyone's bloodstreams.

"Now remember," Jake says, putting on his best serious face, "either person on the date can end it at any time. But whether you're only together for the party or if you keep the party going all night, it's for charity. So. Don't. Be. Stingy!"

The betting begins with the leadership of the frat. The president is dressed in a full suit and carries a red rose, the treasurer comes out dressed like Tom Cruise in *Risky Business*, complete with black Ray Bans and boxer shorts, and the secretary strums a guitar, serenading each girl who raises a hand to bid on him.

Every guy has a shtick, and I work frantically, taking as many pictures and notes as I can.

After almost an hour, I start to lose interest—and the feeling in my fingertips. I take a break from pictures to ask one-off questions to those around me, hoping for good snippets I can throw into the article.

But then, he takes the stage.

I almost don't recognize him. A big, black cowboy hat sits atop Sutton Davis' head, and he dips his chin down to try to avoid drawing attention to himself. Aside from the hat, Sutton is dressed simply, in a sage-green sweater and tan pants, not much of a cowboy. While the other guys were sure to make a show of commanding the stage, Sutton hardly moves. Even so, the crowd chatters in excitement.

"*Hello*," Macy says in a singsong voice, giggling as she grasps my elbow.

"Next up," the announcer shouts into his microphone, somehow still just as energetic as he was at the start, "we have Sutton Davis, a Zete alum! Sutton is a *sexy* cowboy, hailing from the small town of West River, Montana. After this semester, he will be graduating with his master's degree in English and American Literature. If you're interested in learning about riding bareback, Sutton Davis is the guy for you."

Even from across the rooftop, I can see Sutton's cheeks glow red. Clearly, he didn't approve of the double entendre.

"Let's start the bidding at twenty!"

Immediately, six hands shoot into the air.

"Thirty?"

Even more hands.

"Forty-five?"

I push through the crowd to get closer to the stage. Jeanie and Macy follow at my sides. "One hundred!" I yell, cupping my hands on either side of my mouth.

The announcer catches my eye and says into the microphone, "One hundred to—is that you, Laine Rodriguez?"

I smile, not bothering to figure out where I know the announcer from.

Sutton looks up, his eyes connecting with mine, and his eyebrows immediately furrow low.

"One-fifty!" someone behind me says.

"Two hundred!" I yell back. I can practically hear my wallet cursing at me.

"Who is that?" Macy asks me.

"My TA for Shakespeare. This could be my only shot at a tutoring session."

"Two-twenty-five!" another person yells.

"Tutoring," Jeanie hums. "*Right*. Doesn't hurt that he's drop-dead sexy."

"So much for your new no-dating rule," Macy adds.

Looking at Sutton on the makeshift stage, I can see why I am needing to bid so high. With how overwhelming my entrance to class was, it was hard to see exactly what Sutton Davis looked like. But objectively speaking, he *is* good looking. He has a square, sharp jaw and a strong nose fit for a Greek statue. He's tall—*very* tall—and broad, and all at once I can actually see him as a Montana cowboy. Though, admittedly, my knowledge of the cowboy life is minimal, so in my imagination, Sutton is at a high-noon duel, backdropped by twirling tumbleweeds.

"We can do better than that!" The announcer laughs, wrapping an arm around Sutton's shoulders, which are more rigid than a piece of plywood. "Come on, you know what they say. Save a horse, ride a cowboy!"

Immediately, Sutton covers his face with one hand. I don't think I've ever seen someone look more like the embodiment of *kill me now*.

"Two fifty!"

I curse and rifle through my Mary Poppins bag of a purse, shoving past loose hair ties and crumpled receipts. I count out all the cash I can wrangle, even desperately resorting to digging for coins.

Looking back up, I find Sutton's eyes already on me, and I

swear I see a hint of disappointment shadowing his features. I shrug and mouth out the words: *I'm out.*

"Two fifty going once...twice..."

Just then, Macy and Jeanie both shove bills into my palm. After a quick squeal, I add all the cash up.

"Two hundred eighty-seven dollars!" I yell, thrusting my cash into the air. "And thirty-seven cents!"

The announcer whistles into the microphone. "That's our biggest bid of the night, folks!" He counts down the longest three seconds of my life until I finally hear, "Sold!"

It's impossible not to smile when I see Sutton walking down the stairs of the stage, hunching his shoulders in a failed attempt to disappear into the shadows.

I flick the brim of his hat. "This is a good look."

"I'm not supposed to go out with students I TA for," Sutton says, still blushing.

I shrug. "That's no problem."

"And you won't be saving any horses, if you know what I mean."

"Now *that* is a disappointment."

Instead of answering him, I say a round of thank-yous and goodbyes to Macy and Jeanie, who promise to snag some more quotes for the article on my behalf.

"Come on, cowboy." I grab Sutton by the elbow and lead him inside. Once the door closes behind us, a tense silence fills the hallway. I release him, clearing my throat.

"Where are we going?" he asks, looking like I might say something like "to harvest your organs."

"We're going to study."

"How do I know you're not planning on something sinister? Like torturing the exam cheat sheet out of me."

"Do I seem like the kind of girl that would do that kind of thing?" I raise an eyebrow. "More importantly, would that actually work? Because I'm pretty desperate."

As we wait for the elevator, I turn to face Sutton head-on, needing to crane my neck to look up into his eyes. This close, I can smell his cinnamon gum, which he chews anxiously. "I promise I won't torture you for sensitive information." I hold my pinky out. After a few seconds, he wraps his pinky around it, and the warmth of his hand travels up my entire arm. "I must say, you don't strike me as a frat boy, Sutton."

"Frat boy *alumnus*," he corrects, a hint of a smirk at his mouth.

I snort. "Like that's much better."

"It wasn't really my scene. But rent was way cheaper if I stayed at a frat."

"Fair." I know all too well the struggles of New York rent.

I don't waste any more time. The entire walk and subway ride to my apartment is filled with questions for Sutton about the first two weeks of class I missed. By the time we get to my front door, he has already explained the major bullet points from the first week of class.

I was lucky to find any apartment I could afford on my own, even if that means my life is constrained to four hundred square feet. My micro apartment is small, but what it lacks in size it makes up for in *stuff*. Sutton walks along the front wall of the room slowly, overwhelmed by the disorganization and clutter. Each step is hesitant, as if he will detonate a bomb with one wrong step. I swear his face pales when he looks at the whiteboard calendar on the wall, half finished, half covered with Post-it notes. It's the perfect representation of the way my brain processes.

I take my coat off and throw it on one of my two barstools.

Sutton's gaze moves to my bookshelf, the one my dad named The Hobby Graveyard. There's an unfinished piece of embroidery, still on its hoop, a tackle box of bracelet beads, and film canisters on the top shelf.

When Sutton looks back at me, I shrug. "I like trying new things." Having him here, looking at my belongings, feels more intimate than I anticipated, and my skin prickles with that realization. "Come on. No time to waste."

With no couch and limited options, I sit on the edge of my bed. Sutton takes the open barstool.

For three hours, Sutton and I hardly look up from my homework. We read through the first two acts of *The Tempest*, and I'm struck by how naturally Sutton delivers the lines. Reading the play on paper makes my head spin, but hearing him read it out loud makes everything fall into place. He takes on a confident air, expressing exactly what I imagine the characters are feeling in every scene. It's almost enough to keep my full attention, but I still end up tapping my fingers or twisting my rings around here or there to try to keep my hands occupied.

By eleven-thirty, all fragments of my attention span have shattered, and I collapse onto my bed belly-first, facing Sutton sitting on my desk chair. He couldn't stand out from my room more if he tried. While everything around us is busy, colorful, and loud, Sutton is calming.

"Are you really from Montana?" I ask him, interrupting the monologue he was reading.

He nods.

"Are you really a cowboy?"

For the first time, Sutton smiles—*really* smiles—and it takes me off guard. Dimples dig into his cheeks, and his piercing eyes soften. "*Was* a cowboy is a more fitting, I think."

"Why aren't you anymore?"

"Long story."

"Make it short, then."

Sutton straightens, his smile fading. "I never wanted to stay at the ranch forever."

"Why not?"

"Family complications. Why were you and Ms. Carr arguing?"

"Family complications," I mimic, smiling in hopes that it will lighten the mood. Sutton stays quiet, patiently waiting for more. "She hates that I am indecisive. That it is taking me six years to finish my degree. That I can't commit to much of anything, at least in her eyes."

"I'm sure that's not true," he says.

"It is. And really, it's pretty ironic of her to be so judgmental, to call *me* a quitter." At Sutton's raised eyebrow, I add, "Long story."

One side of his mouth lifts. "Make it short."

"On the day of my high school graduation, my mom told me that she left my father. It came out of nowhere. They said they didn't have a big fight or anything. They didn't even try to make it work. Even though they were high school sweethearts, they apparently woke up one day and realized they weren't in love."

Sutton nods slowly. He clearly doesn't know what to say to that story, because he changes the subject. "I hope I didn't distract you from bidding on a real date tonight."

"I was just there to cover it for the student paper."

"You're a writer?" he asks.

I shrug. "I guess so. I bounced between majors for a long time. *Not* because I'm a quitter, but because I wanted to try everything out. I loved chemistry and dance and statistics. Eventually, I got a job at the paper and realized that journalism was my ticket. When I'm interviewing people, writing their stories, I get to live through them." I smile to myself. "I want to experience everything life has to offer. Since that's impossible, experiencing things through the stories of others is the closest I can get."

Sutton makes a little hum.

"Does that make sense?" I ask.

"Complete sense. It's the same reason I want to be an editor."

Even though my instinct drives me to want to speak, I follow Sutton's style and stay silent, hoping it will prompt him to continue.

"Growing up, I loved feeling like I was living a thousand lives through the books I read. I could float the Mississippi River or survive a plane crash or befriend a wolf. And now I want to bring books that are full of life to other kids."

"So why not write yourself?"

He narrows his eyes a bit, as if to discern if I'm joking. Finally, he says, "No. I don't think I have any stories worth telling."

I shift a bit, tense in the thick silence between us. "Thank you for helping me tonight. I owe you."

Sutton gives me a smile just big enough to hint at his dimples. "Anything for charity."

I walk the five steps to the front door and open it for him, watching as he leaves down the hallway. Just as I turn to go back into my apartment, Sutton calls my name out, stopping me. When I spin back to him, his jaw is clenched and his lips are tight, as if he's trying to stop himself from talking.

"This class is important enough for you to spend three hundred dollars for a few hours of tutoring?" he asks.

"Absolutely. I need to graduate. I need to prove to my parents that I can do this. And...I want to prove it to myself."

Again, Sutton tightens his mouth before releasing a slow breath. "What is your schedule like next week?" By his expression, it looks like he is actually in physical pain from his words.

I glance over at my whiteboard calendar. "Work, then book club Monday, cookbook club Tuesday—"

"You have *two* different types of book clubs?"

"Yes. I'm interviewing a group of soon-to-be graduates on Wednesday. A friend has their art studio debut Thursday…" My voice trails as I try to remember any other commitments I might have forgotten.

Sutton shakes his head, looking like he's holding in a laugh. "I'm guessing you usually have plans on Fridays, but if you ever need another tutoring session, those are the one night a week I sometimes have off."

"Really?" I ask, my limbs feeling lighter than they have in weeks.

"Really."

4

LAINE

THREE MONTHS LATER

AT THIS POINT, I think Sutton could find his way to my apartment blindfolded. It's been over three months since our first tutoring session. The week after the date auction, we met once. The next week, twice. And now, it's rare that I go more than a couple of days without seeing him. At first, it was strictly for tutoring. That eventually evolved. We grab coffee before class. We meet for study sessions. We help each other rework our resumes, over and over again. Sutton often joins me at my random events and social groups.

After he came to my end-of-year party at the student paper, he told me that I had more friends than anyone he's ever met.

"And I'd bet not one of them knows my middle name," I told him.

"It's Althea," he responded immediately. "Like Ms. Carr's name."

I didn't expect to become friends with Sutton. He's a gentle giant, though, and it's hard not to love his goodness.

I'm not the only one who couldn't resist befriending him. Our mutual endearment toward Sutton is the first thing

Mom and I have agreed on in recent memory. In fact, she's made it a habit to come around my apartment more, just on the off chance that she might see us both. She invites Sutton to networking events at different publishing houses, introduces him to other editors, and wrote him a glowing letter of recommendation.

"She likes you more than she likes me," I told him one day after a particularly long drop-in by Mom.

"That's not true. You're her daughter."

I rolled my eyes. He dropped the subject.

Even Dad bonded with him after learning that Sutton was a TA for my Shakespeare class. Dad, a playwright himself, exhausted my knowledge of the stage long ago. He started inviting Sutton to our bi-monthly dad-daughter dinners to revive the conversation. Not long after that, we started following those dinners up with movie nights dedicated to Shakespeare, including, at my request, the derivatives like *She's the Man* and *Ten Things I Hate About You*.

When Mom and Dad learned that Sutton didn't walk at his bachelor's graduation and isn't planning on walking for his master's either, they were in an uproar, which is why I'm now walking along the street with a massive garment bag folded over my arms.

One of Sutton's roommates lets me in as soon as I knock, greeting me by name. Sutton's door is slightly ajar, but I tap a knuckle against it anyway.

"Come on in," Sutton says, sounding as exhausted as I would expect this late in the semester. He's lying across his bed in gray sweatpants and a white shirt, one arm behind his head, propping it up so he can read from his beat-up copy of *Where the Red Fern Grows*.

In that position, his shirt is lifted just enough for a strip of skin to show between it and his waistline. I move my eyes away and around the room, my face hot. Despite us spending so much time together this semester, there has always been a line of professionalism, a reminder that he was still my TA, and I was still his student. I'm taken aback seeing him in such a casual way now. It feels like I'm intruding.

I fumble with the garment bag and drop it across the foot of the bed. Sutton stands, rustling a hand through his curls. He started the semester with a clean-shaven face, but slowly, as he got busier and busier, that turned into a short-trimmed beard. His curls grew out too, almost kissing the neck of his shirt now.

"A graduation robe," Sutton says after unzipping the bag open. A smile tugs at the corner of his mouth.

"You're walking in graduation with me. Tomorrow." I lift my chin up, and Sutton grins, those dimples flashing.

"Maybe..."

"My parents demand it." I wave an ushering hand at Sutton. "Go try it on."

He does as I request, grabbing suit pants and a button-down on his way to the bathroom to change.

Not daring enough to sit on Sutton's bed, I perch on the edge of his desk. As always, Sutton's room is perfectly neat. His calendar on the wall is color coded, and his laundry basket is divided into three sections. Even his ever-growing collection of books is stacked neatly along his shelves. Everything in its place.

Almost as soon as I hear the bathroom door click closed, Sutton's phone, laying on his desk, goes off. The name "Frankie" shines up at me from the screen.

"Hey, Sutton!" I yell, grabbing his phone. As I do so, though, my thumb grazes the green button on the screen, and the call connects.

A voice, higher than I expected, comes from the phone. "Sutton?"

He never mentioned a Frankie, and there's nobody in our class by that name he could be tutoring.

"Hello?" the voice says again.

Without thinking, I hold the phone up to my ear. "Hi?"

"Oh, sorry," Frankie, whoever she is, sounds surprised. "I was trying to call Sutton Davis."

I should probably bring the phone to Sutton, but instead I say, "This is his phone."

"*Oh!* Sure. Really? Right." She tumbles over her words. "Will you just—just have him call me back? As soon as possible. It's important."

"Do you want me to go get Sutton now? He's just in the other room."

"No, no. Just ask him to call Frankie. Thanks."

The line goes silent, and I lay the phone back down on the desk, feeling a bit nauseated. I'm still trying to remember if Sutton has ever brought up "Frankie" before, but my thoughts are interrupted by Sutton's reentrance into the room in his full graduation attire. The robe accentuates his towering frame. Some of his dark curls peek out from the bottom of the cap, and even though he's trying to stay cool, I can see a whisper of an excited expression.

I can't help but smile back at him as I marvel at how he looks so fully...*Sutton* in the getup. He stands tall, confidence radiating from him like a beacon. His face glows with an inner light that is all his own, and I feel like I'm seeing Sutton anew. He's proud of himself—as he should be—and it's quite the sight.

"One last thing," I say, pulling a small black box from my tote.

Sutton takes it from me carefully, opening the top. A gold cord is wrapped up inside. I take it out, unfurling its length, and drape it around Sutton's neck, letting it cascade down his front. "An honors cord for Mr. Summa Cum Laude. Technically, you should have worn this at your bachelor's graduation, but it's better late than never."

Sutton's smile grows when he looks at me again. "What do you think?"

I tuck my cropped hair back under my jaw. "I think you're going to show me up tomorrow."

"I doubt that very much," he says, taking his cap and gown off. "Come on. Let's head to your exam."

I'm not worried about my Shakespeare final. It's the last test of the semester, and thanks to the best tutor, I could still pass the class even if I fail this one. Still, Sutton—in true Sutton fashion—takes advantage of our commute by quizzing me from the study guide. I give my answers automatically, most of them deeply ingrained in my mind by now, but my thoughts are still circling around the phone call. As soon as we're in front of the door to the lecture hall where we first met, I can't hold my question in any longer.

"Who's Frankie?"

Sutton takes a step back, his eyes widening slightly.

"Someone named Frankie called you back at the apartment," I explain, moving my eyes to the floor so I can avoid looking directly at Sutton. "She wants you to call her back. ASAP. I don't remember you talking about a Frankie," I say, hiding my anxiousness with a weak laugh.

If Sutton is suddenly dating this "Frankie" girl, that would mean our time together would end. After all, even if assured there's nothing going on between us, even though I've sworn off dating, there's no way she would be happy about us spending so much time together. Already, I'm imagining the loss of my first best friend.

Sutton runs a hand through his hair, grinning. "She's my sister."

I'm quiet for a few moments, feeling like I'm walking a tightrope. One on hand, I'm relieved to hear I won't have to worry about Frankie in *that* way. But on the other hand, in all the time we've spent together, I can only remember a few times Sutton has talked about his family. I've gone into dangerous waters. While I know Sutton has a brother and sister, that's about *all* I know.

He doesn't like to talk about his family.

And I like to keep him happy.

So even now, when a hundred questions are firing in my mind, I squeeze my lips together.

"You shouldn't be thinking about my sister right now, though. I'll call her back after the graduation dust settles." Sutton grabs me by both shoulders, his massive hands squeezing me gently. "You'll do great," he says, leaning down so he can look me directly in the eyes. His face softens, and those dimples flash as if carved just for me.

A flutter in my stomach stirs. I must be more nervous about the test than I realized.

5

SUTTON

"JUST A FEW MORE PICTURES!" Ms. Carr gushes, grabbing me by the elbows and manually scooting me right next to Laine.

In the midst of the graduation excitement, I almost forgot about the missed call from Frankie. The weight of it feels like a distant cloud in the sky, currently outshined by the radiance of Laine and her parents.

"Come on, act like you know each other," Cyrus prods, smiling at us from behind his camera.

Laine obliges, tightening an arm around the middle of my back, and I follow suit, laying mine over her shoulders. It's strange how a simple touch can hold so much significance. Even as we started to spend more and more time together throughout the semester, I was careful to keep boundaries between us, especially when it came to physicality. Now that I'm no longer Laine's TA, the barriers that restrained me from getting too close have vanished, leaving possibilities that both excite and terrify me.

As we pose for the pictures, I wonder if my feelings are transparent to those around us. I wonder if Cyrus and Ms.

Carr have noticed the way my smile is always bigger, my laugh always louder when I'm with Laine. Even if they haven't guessed my feelings yet, how much longer can I conceal them when I can no longer carefully hide behind the walls of professionalism?

I can't help but notice the softness of Laine's skin beneath my hand and the way she leans in slightly, as if she's reveling in the closeness just as much as I am. Maybe it's wishful thinking, though. After all, Laine has always made it clear that she could never dream of settling down. She relayed her failed college relationships early on in our friendship and swore that she doesn't want a serious relationship until she's thirty. Even if she changes her mind, surely it would be for someone more like her. Fun, energetic, *alive*.

Not some guy on antidepressants who works fifty-hour weeks so he can avoid thinking about anything else.

"We should go find our seats," Laine says, showing her palm to the camera. She gives my torso a squeeze before letting go.

"Fine," Ms. Carr says, snapping one last picture. "We are *so proud* of you," she whispers, pulling Laine into an embrace. When she draws back, holding Laine at arm's reach for one more look at her, both of the women's eyes glisten. They're a far different pair than the one I accidentally eavesdropped on just mere months ago.

"No tears!" Cyrus says, butting between them so he can give Laine a bear hug. "This is a day of celebration."

My breath catches in my throat as I watch the three of them. Laine isn't as close with her parents as most people I know. She claims that she's seen them more in the past few months than she has for the past few years. But still, they love her, even if they don't always show it.

My parents don't even know I'm graduating today.

As if reading my mind, Ms. Carr pulls me into her thin

arms. "We're proud of you too." She's at least a foot shorter than me and has to weigh half what I do, but she still manages to wrap her arms around my middle. Cyrus piles in on the hug, dragging Laine with him, until all four of us are packed together.

"I'm sorry your family couldn't be here," Cyrus says, his voice almost a whisper.

In our tight huddle, I see Laine's eyes flick to me nervously. "Okay, I love you both. I really do," Laine says, a bit breathless from Cyrus's continued squeezing. "But Sutton and I need to go to our seats, or we'll be late. Let's go, cowboy."

"Look at you, being a stickler for time." Cyrus laughs, breaking the group hug. "Never thought I'd see the day. Sutton really *is* a good influence on you."

Graduation is being held at the center of the Yankee baseball stadium, and as Laine and I make our way through the crowd of cap-topped grads, we can't go more than ten feet without someone stopping Laine to talk to her. She has that effect on people. Everyone who meets her sees her as a friend. She claims I'm one of the lucky few for whom that is actually true.

"How weird was that?" Laine asks me once we're seated. "My parents haven't spent any time together since their divorce, and now they're doing a *group hug*?"

"They're excited for you," I insist. "As they should be."

"They're excited for you too, you know."

During the ceremony, I can't focus on the words much. My gaze, as usual, is drawn to Laine, studying her smile, appreciating the proud tilt of her chin.

"You did great," I whisper to her once we're standing in line for the stage.

Laine turns back and flicks the gold cord around my neck, grinning. "*Me?* You're the one with the perfect GPA. Besides,

I'm convinced I only passed Mr. Hirsch's Shakespeare class because you're the one in charge of grading homework."

"Are you accusing me of cheating in your favor?"

"Maybe my parents paid you off," Laine says, shrugging playfully.

I roll my eyes. "You're not waving off your accomplishments that easily, Laine. I'll have you know that I haven't graded a single assignment of yours."

Laine's brows furrow. "What do you mean? You always graded homework for Mr. Hirsch."

"Yes, but never *yours*."

She scoffs. "Why not?"

"Because I am..." I pause, inhaling sharply. "I'm a bit biased toward you. You earned that A."

"You didn't have to do that, you know. It's not like we were dating or—"

"I know," I interject, my face warm.

"Right. I know you know." Laine spins her rings around her fingers, beaming. "So, I actually did it? Fair and square?"

"Fair and square."

Laine's dark eyes shine. "How am I *ever* going to pay you back for all your help?" she asks.

"I'm sure you'll think of something." We walk in silence for a few moments until I ask, "Why *did* you need my help?"

She scoffs. "I'm surprised you need to ask me that. After all, *I'm* not the one with the perfect GPA. Far from it."

"I mean, why didn't you ask Cyrus to tutor you? He knows more about Shakespeare than I ever will."

Laine shrugs, a rare downturn of her lips showing. "We haven't talked much since the divorce. Not until he met you. I think he's proud of me just for having a friend like you."

"They would be proud of you whether or not I was here," I say. "I'm sure he would have been happy to help. But I'm glad you decided to ask me instead."

She nods, smiling at her shoes. "I'm glad too."

U

"WHEN ARE you going to tell me what the plan is for tonight?" Laine asks after we drop off our caps and gowns at her apartment. For weeks, I've been planning the perfect celebration for her. Originally, her parents were going to join, but they backed out, last minute, encouraging us to celebrate, just the two of us.

I lead Laine in the direction of our first location. The sun is starting to dip lower, a warm breeze carrying pink clouds through the sky. "First stop is The Trestle," I say, grinning in anticipation. We went there, an American bistro in Queens, during one of our first study sessions we had over dinner. Since then, it's been a staple. In fact, everywhere we're going tonight is a place we've already been together and loved.

"Ooh, truffle cheese fries?" Laine asks, her dark eyes sparkling.

"Of course. But as much as you love The Trestle, I know you'd still end up wondering what dinner would have been like somewhere else. So, after we have our appetizer there, we're going to Marufuku for ramen—"

Laine squeezes my arm excitedly.

"Then to Maison Pickle for their twenty-four-layer cake." I can't help but smile, satisfied at her reactions. "A little taste of everything."

Laine holds her belly, already imagining our oncoming feast. She's practically drooling. "You know what the only thing is that would make this better?"

"Karaoke. Already planning on it. Much to my chagrin."

"You know me well, Sutton," Laine says, walking even faster toward our first spot. "Maybe better than anyone, if your plans for tonight are any indication. But if we're going to karaoke, you're going to have to actually sing this time."

"Do you want to invite anyone else? The reservations were all for four because Cyrus and Althea were going to come."

"No." Laine sighs. "I'd rather just spend it with my best friend." She grins up at me, and the breeze stops for a moment, like the world itself is reverent at the sight of Laine's smile. For another moment, I forget about my family. I forget about the missed call from Frankie I have yet to return. I allow Laine's expression to be a balm for my worries, lightening that ever-present sinking sensation in my stomach.

The night goes off without a hitch. As if knowing how important our celebration is, every restaurant delivers perfect dishes and atmospheres. We take our time at each spot, enjoying the freedom to talk about everything aside from school. When we arrive at karaoke, we're over three hours deep into the night, bellies full and feet tired. But still, our questions haven't slowed.

"Well, you've worked your ass off all semester to become an editor," Laine says after ordering us our first drinks. "Still think that's the career for you?"

"I've been working my ass off for six years," I correct with a laugh. "Yes, I'm sure."

"But *how* can you be so sure?" Laine shakes her head in disbelief. "I mean, I think I could have been happy in dozens of careers, dozens of lives. How do you know you're choosing the right one?"

I scratch my beard, wondering how detailed to be. On one hand, I've made a habit out of not sharing personal things with anyone. On the other hand, Laine doesn't feel like just anyone. "Sometimes it feels like there is this heavy fog around me. Things can feel so distant, so dull."

Laine nods, her eyes wide as she soaks in the rare scene of me opening up on this level.

"It was like that when I was little, too. I think my mom knew that I was depressed. So, she would read to me. We would climb into my bottom bunk bed and read under the covers together. And when I was engulfed between the pages of a story, some weight was lifted, at least for a moment. It felt like…like finding a secret oasis in a harsh desert. A little sanctuary. I want to bring that to other people. To kids, if I can."

The bartender slides our glasses to us, and I take a long sip, studying Laine. She doesn't speak. She doesn't drink. She just stands, absorbing my words. Near the back of the room, someone at the microphone is giving us a particularly rough rendition of "You Can Call Me Al."

"When I checked in with you last week, you were still wanting to be a journalist," I say. "No changes since then?"

Laine glares at me playfully. "Probably to your surprise, I haven't changed my mind. I think journalism will be a good fit. I'll get to work on new stories constantly, so it should keep me engaged. *Should*."

"Any update on the job search?"

Laine huffs. "No. And I don't want to talk about it. Tonight is all about celebration. I'm going to go sign us up to sing."

I'm watching her flip through the song choices on the other side of the room when my phone goes off. I check it and decline the call, but it immediately rings again. Not wanting that to continue all night, I hit the green button.

"Frankie?"

"It's about Wells," she says in lieu of a greeting.

6

LAINE

UNSURPRISINGLY, it takes me ages to pick a song. When I finally decide on one ("Cowboy Take Me Away"), I head back to the bar. But Sutton isn't there. After a minute of searching, I see him outside the front windows, talking into his phone with his jaw clenched. Everything about his face is tense, strong, and angular. It's not a look I've seen before—at least, not with such intensity. I didn't know Sutton even had that kind of emotion in him.

Not wanting to intrude, I stay at the bar and turn back to the stage. There, a drop-dead gorgeous couple has taken the stage. The woman has long chestnut-brown hair cascading in loose curls, and the guy has a short-trimmed beard, not unlike Sutton's, and dark hair that is pushed back, hanging to the collar of his shirt. Even without them being on the stage, they would both tower over me like Roman gods. They're singing a folksy song that I haven't heard before, but it sounds old and romantic.

I'm enthralled by them. Not because they're particularly gifted singers, but because they look at each other with smiles so full and contagious, laughing through the lyrics, everyone in here smiles in return. The young woman looks so familiar, though I can't put my finger where I recognize her from.

When the couple is done, they walk, intertwined, toward the bar, leaning into one another.

"You two did great," I say to them, leaning closer so they can hear me over the tone-deaf rendition of "Total Eclipse of the Heart" that just started.

"Thanks!" the woman says, smiling at her date yet again. After she orders a drink, she asks me, "Are you here with someone?"

I gesture outside to Sutton, who is still talking on the phone, pacing in tight circles.

She nods and looks my purple tiered and ruffled dress up and down. "You're celebrating tonight?"

"We just graduated from NYU today."

"*Exciting!*" she gushes. "I'm Ophelia Brooks. And this is Adam Abrams."

"Oh!" It all clicks. "You're in fashion, right? Don't you write for *Atelier Today*?"

Ophelia beams. "I used to, yes! But Adam here,"—she pauses to wrap her arm even tighter around him—"started an independent magazine, *Wonderings*, and I joined the team."

"What are your plans now that you've graduated?" Adam asks.

I wince. "Good question. I majored in journalism, but I'm still looking for the right job."

Ophelia and Adam exchange a knowing look before she looks back at me. "Have you written anything before?"

"I worked at NYU's student newspaper, but that's it." I shrug.

"Do you have any articles I can read?" Ophelia asks.

"Um, sure..." I grab my phone and pull up the website for

the *Washington Square News*, navigating to my most recent article.

Ophelia holds her hands out eagerly. "May I?"

As Ophelia reads, I ask Adam about their magazine.

"It's all about culture," he explains. "Travel, food, art, and —thanks to Ophelia—fashion. We have seasonal issues every three months, plus online articles in between. Our team is small right now. Everyone works from home. But it's fun."

"Your writing is unique—in a good way," Ophelia interjects, handing my phone back. "It feels so natural." Her lips curl. "Have you ever thought about freelancing?"

As always, when I think about my career, or lack thereof, my skin crawls. "I haven't—not yet, at least," I admit. I slump down a bit, leaning my elbows on the bar. "To be honest, I'm still figuring this out."

"I get that," Ophelia says, taking a sip of her drink. Behind her, Adam nods.

"Really?" I say in an exhale. "You felt directionless after graduating? Like...there are so many options out there you don't know which route to take?"

Ophelia tilts her head a bit. "Well, no. I've always known I wanted to write about fashion. But it took me a while to get there. And during that time, it felt like my life was at a standstill." She drums her fingers on the bar, pursing her lips. "Freelancing can be a nice way to make some extra money while you search for something more permanent."

"That *does* sound nice," I say, sneaking a peek outside to Sutton. He's still on the phone, his free hand balled into a fist.

"We like to work with a lot of freelancers," she says. "And the ones who are a good fit sometimes end up joining our team on a permanent basis. If you ever decide you want to give it a try, email me." She hands me a white linen-textured business card: *Ophelia Brooks, President of Wonderings Magazine.*

"Really?" I ask again, feeling like my heart might fly out of my chest. My face stretches into a wide smile as I imagine Sutton's face, my parents' faces, when I tell them the good news.

"With you writing like *that*,"—Ophelia points at my phone—"yes, really. You'll just need to find something worth writing about."

7

SUTTON

"WELLS IS GETTING *MARRIED?*" I ask for the fifth time.

Frankie's shallow breaths sound as distorted as they always do when she's calling from the ranch. But even spotty reception didn't warrant this news to be broken over text.

Frankie has filled me in on all the basic details aside from one. I know the date (twenty-two days from now), location (the Davis family ranch), the groom (my brother), and my role (best man, for some who-knows reason). What Frankie has conveniently left out is the detail of the bride. Her omission is all I need to know, however.

"It's her, isn't it?" I ask, my chest tightening with each syllable that I force through gritted teeth.

"I'm sorry, Sutton," Frankie murmurs.

For the first time in years, I allow myself to think back to Cassidy Clark. Her curly red hair. Her full face of freckles. Her doe-like, emerald eyes. Her lips, perfectly symmetrical between the top and bottom, which seemed to always be in a pout.

Like most of the kids in West River, Cassidy and I both lived there from the time we were babies. With only thirty-five students in our entire grade, we were in the same classes every year from kindergarten on. In third grade, we were married under the big oak tree at recess with dandelion rings. In eighth grade, we had our first kiss. And then, just after my first year at NYU—

"You okay?" Frankie asks, pulling me from my runaway thoughts.

I clutch at the hammering in my chest, wondering if Frankie heard my racing pulse over the phone. "I'm fine," I force out.

"You'll come to the wedding, won't you?" There's something different in Frankie's voice. *Hope.* I can't remember the last time I heard it from her. "It would mean a lot to everyone. Even Wells. Even Dad."

The pounding sensation moves from my chest to my head, and I lean back against the side of the building. Ice shoots through my veins at the mention of my father.

"Sutton?" Frankie asks, her voice distant now behind the sound of my mind working overtime. "*Sutton?*"

"I'm here," I say, choking on my words.

"Will you come?"

"I don't know," I say, which is my much more polite way of saying *hell no.*

The door to the karaoke bar opens, music pouring out onto the sidewalk. I try to turn my head, but my body feels frozen in place. Only her voice can pull me ever so slightly from my mental whirlwind.

"Hey, cowboy! Guess who just got offered a freelance gig that could turn into a real big-girl job?" Only a moment goes by before Laine is right at my side, tiptoeing up to see my face. "What's going on?" she asks, her voice laced with some of the emotion I'm feeling.

"I'll—I'll talk to you later, Frankie," I say into the phone, my hand shaking as I slide it back into my pocket. The motion draws my whole body down until I'm doubled over, hands on my knees.

Everything spins.

Laine places one hand on my back and the other on my chest. "I think you're having a panic attack. Focus on your breaths." She does the same, exaggerating them so I can focus on the sound and match mine in line. When it's clear that isn't working, she brings my hand to just under her collarbone so we can both feel each other's breathing. We do this for a few minutes until the hammering in my head calms and the pressure around my chest loosens. I sink to the ground with closed eyes, still tuned in to our synchronized breaths.

"Let's go back to my apartment," Laine suggests.

I nod, even though nothing sounds better than going to my own room right now. There, I could lock myself in solitude while I pretend I can resolve my thoughts on my own, even when I know that's not the case. But Laine will want to keep an eye on me to be sure I'm okay, and I'm too tired to argue over which apartment to go to.

We take longer than usual to get through the city and back to Laine's place. She trips a few times on the trek and runs into three people and two light posts, all because her eyes are trained dutifully on me.

"I'm fine," I whisper to Laine as soon as we're inside her front door. She ignores me, sitting me down on the edge of her unmade bed and returning in a flash with a glass of cold water.

"Drink," she orders.

Once I've emptied the glass in a three gulps, Laine pushes me back against the pillows, letting my head rest on top of them. For a while, we stay silent. I assume Laine is listening in on my breathing, making sure it stays steady. My relief at her comfort outweighs any embarrassment I might feel.

"Can we talk about what happened?" Laine finally asks once my pulse returns to normal. There's still a hint of red across her lips, even after visits to three restaurants and a bar.

"Do we have to?"

Her fingers brush against my knee before she retreats to a barstool, giving me space. "I think so. When you're ready."

I groan, taking in a heavy inhale. "My little brother is getting married."

"That's a bad thing?"

"I haven't spoken to him in six years. I haven't even been *home* in six years. And now he wants me to show up there and be his best man."

"This could be a great opportunity to fix things between you two," Laine says, eyes sparkling at the thought.

"Did I mention he's marrying my ex-girlfriend? That I dated for five years?"

Laine makes a face that I've never seen from her—or anyone, really. It's the expression someone might make if they saw a monkey flying an airplane: utterly bewildered, slightly fearful, yet strangely entertained.

"Did I *also* mention that—six years ago—my father told me I wasn't welcome back home?"

"Your life is absolutely Shakespearean," Laine says, letting out a dry, disbelieving laugh. Then, it bubbles into one that's livelier. She claps both hands over her mouth to stifle her laughter. "I'm so sorry. It isn't funny. It's just...this sounds like a story I'd hear on *Dr. Phil*."

"I can't go, right?" I ask.

"It's still your brother's wedding," Laine says. "Isn't that pretty important?"

Laine doesn't have any brothers or sisters. And she has made it clear before that she's convinced that all siblings should act like they're in an episode of *The Brady Bunch*.

44

I glare at the ceiling. "In theory, yes, it's important. But in theory, it might also kill me."

"Sutton, I know your family is…complicated."

"Clearly."

"But I still think you should go."

"And not only face my estranged father and brother, but also show up with nothing to show for the past six years. A mountain of student debt, no career to speak of, no place of my own, certainly no *wedding* of my own coming up." I sink into the tangle of blankets, wishing they would swallow me up. "My dad always said coming to New York would be a waste of my time. I wanted to prove him wrong. And to show up to *their* wedding, single? As if I'm still hung up on her all these years later?"

After a few minutes of tense silence and lip-biting, Laine perks up and taps her fingers on the countertop. "I may not be able to get rid of your student debt, or hire you as an editor, or buy you an apartment. *But* I can help you with that last problem."

I scoff. "You know someone who wants to go out with a guy with depression and panic attacks and who spends money he doesn't have on books?"

"I know a girl who owes you a big favor, who wouldn't be half-bad company on a cross-country flight, and who happens to be enthralled by the idea of seeing you in full cowboy form."

For a few seconds, I try to imagine Laine in West River, Montana. Would she still wear her trademark red lipstick? Would she still insist on accessorizing every outfit beyond belief? Would she like lying in the tall grass of the ranch like I used to as a boy?

"So, what do you say?" Laine asks. She moves to the edge of the bed, grabbing me by my elbow. It occurs to me we've touched more today than we have in the past three months combined.

"I don't know…"

"Oh, come on! We're already best friends, right? How hard could it be to pretend that goes beyond platonic?"

Not hard at all, I think to myself as I study Laine's face for the thousandth time.

"I'm sorry, am I not a suitable enough fake girlfriend for you?" Laine jokes.

"I couldn't ask you to do that, Laine."

"It'll be *fuuuuun*," she insists. "Wedding aside, you can teach me how to ride a horse. We can go fishing. I can finally stargaze for the first time in my life. It sounds amazing. Besides, you can't run away from your past forever. You need to reconcile with it."

"But I have work."

"Screw work!"

SCREW WORK—FOR today, at least.

It's hard to focus on the tasks when the imminent marriage of your brother and ex is looming overhead. Laine spent all of Sunday trying to convince me to go back to Montana for the wedding. And now that I'm alone in my gray cubicle, my mind goes back to Laine's many, many arguments in favor of a trip to Montana.

She's right, I know. I need to cross the chasm between my family and me. The prospect of returning home is both daunting and enticing. Part of me wants to face my past, confront my father, and mend broken relationships. Mom and Frankie have taken the occasional trip to the city to see me. Once a week, they each call me to catch up. Still, I miss

Mom's warm hugs and the sound of Frankie's echoing laughter.

However, another part of me is in shambles at the thought of pretending Laine and I are a couple. Sure, I've imagined how it would feel to walk hand in hand with her, to curl her hair around my fingers, to touch those always-red lips. But I hadn't imagined it as part of a ruse.

When the clock hits five, I check my phone. As usual, there's a text from Laine. This time, she sent a picture of worn, red cowgirl boots.

Found these thrifting. It's kismet.

Another text is waiting for me. This one from Frankie.

Wells is convinced he can wear his wranglers to his wedding. See why I need you here on my side?

I groan, stretching my back as I stand, as if I can physically push the stress right out of my body. Right as I'm about to shut my laptop, a new email pings in my inbox. Never one to leave an email unread, I slump back down in my chair, and I swear I can actually feel the stress piling back on me. When I read the subject line, though, I stand back up from shock, practically jumping into the air.

Job Offer: Assistant Editor at Imagineer Books.

There's a big difference between an editor's assistant and an assistant editor, and for a few minutes, I'm sure my eyes are betraying me. I read through the email four times over. Suddenly, I feel like someone has thrown me a lifeline amidst a sea of uncertainty.

8

LAINE

"I HOPE you bought those cowgirl boots."

I sit up from my bed, my mouth popping open. "Are you toying with me right now?"

Sutton's laugh is a delight, even when I can barely hear it over the sounds of the city backdropping our call. "Not this time."

"What changed?"

"I got a job offer..."—he pauses for dramatic effect—"at Imagineer Books." I can hear Sutton's smile through the phone.

"*You're lying!* Sutton, that's amazing." My grin is so wide it actually hurts. Even if Sutton thought it was a long shot to get his dream job right out of college, I never doubted him for a second. "I'm so proud of you! Everything is falling into place for us."

"I can't believe it. And..." He pauses, and I can picture him furrowing his brow as he thinks out what he'll say next. "I figured if I can step forward in my professional life, maybe I can do the same in my personal life."

I click the heels of my thrifted cowgirl boots together, like a western Dorothy. "Please tell me I get to come too."

"Laine, I would be honored to have you join me as my fake girlfriend."

"Hurry over so we can work out the details!"

"I'm already on my way," he promises before hanging up.

First things first. I find Ophelia Brook's contact information on my phone and text her.

> How would you feel about a collection of articles painting the lives of a quaint Montana town?

She replies quickly.

> Go for it. With your writing voice, you could do a piece on the invention of shoelaces, and I would love it.

My entire body feels the effects of the respite. After months of stress, I have my golden ticket. Go to Montana, write some stellar articles, get hired as a full-time journalist at *Wonderings*, and help Sutton in the process. It's foolproof. And when I am hired on, I'll finally be able to prove to my parents—and to myself—that I can have a real career, a path.

Next up: find some way to keep Sutton riding this high wave.

I rifle through my dresser and find the most cowgirl thing I own to accompany my new (to me) boots. Luckily, I still have my cutoff denim shorts from freshman year. They're two sizes too small now, but I squeeze into them, trying to ignore the way my love handles spill out over the top. It's worth it for the bit. Next, I add a white eyelet lace tank top. To finish the look, I fish out my pink bedazzled cowgirl hat I wore to a Harry Styles concert years ago.

With a minute to spare, I pull up a classic country playlist from Spotify on the Bluetooth speaker. The song is unfamiliar to me, but it has a steel guitar and an opening line about a pickup truck, so I think it's fitting enough.

I wait by the front door, opening it at the first knock by Sutton. He eyes me up and down, his smile erupting into a full laugh. I do a spin, kicking a leg up at the end to show off my boots. "Howdy," I say with a twang in my voice, tipping the brim of my hat. "I'll fit right in, huh?"

"Absolutely," he says, wrapping an arm around me in a sideways hug that pleasantly surprises me.

"So, when will you officially become Mr. Cowboy-Slash-Editor?"

"Mr. Cowboy-Slash-*Assistant*-Editor." He returns my grin. "I start in three weeks."

I clasp my hands together under my chin. "Perfect timing with the wedding. And at your dream publisher. How do you feel?"

"Great. Anxious."

"Sweatin' like a whore in church?" I ask.

Sutton scoffs. "I don't know if that's something you're allowed to say these days."

"Probably not," I agree. "I've been googling country phrases, and that one really stuck out."

"The crass ones always do. Well, I've been gone so long I might need a refresher." One side of Sutton's mouth lifts. "What are some others?"

"Let's see…" I size him up. "I'd say you're looking finer than frog's hair. But you look as nervous as—oh, what was it —as nervous as a long-tailed cat in a room full of rocking chairs."

"Not bad, Rodriguez. What other research have you done?"

"That's as far as I've gotten. So, you need to help me. I need a crash course on the Davis family."

Sutton sinks onto the floor, leaning back against the bed, a faraway look in his eyes. "Let's do that another day." I open my mouth, but he must already know what I was going to say, because he adds, "I promise we'll talk about it. I'll get you caught up. But tonight, I want to pretend that our trip to Montana is just a celebratory one. I don't want to think about my brother or my ex. And I especially don't want to think about my father."

"Deal." I sit beside Sutton and turn the TV on, scrolling through our options. "But we have to watch a movie that will give me some kind of insight into cowboy living. *Brokeback Mountain, Tombstone, Legends of the Fall—*"

Sutton coughs. *"Legends of the Fall?"* His mouth spreads into a disbelieving smile. "Do you know the premise of that movie?"

"Not really. But I know it takes place in Montana."

"In it, brothers fall in love with the same woman," Sutton says, raising his eyebrows at me.

"A bit too close to home, then," I say, clicking my tongue.

"A bit. How about *The Man from Snowy River?*" Sutton suggests, dropping his gaze to his hands. "I haven't seen it in years. But it's a cowboy movie. And it was my brother's favorite."

I search for the movie with the remote. "I'm surprised you would want to watch *his* favorite movie tonight."

"Not Wells," Sutton says, his voice a near whisper. "My older brother. Duke."

"Oh," I say, matching Sutton's quiet tone. His brow furrows low. Sutton has never mentioned a second brother. "What's he like?"

Sutton shakes his head. "I'll tell you about him another night. Not right now."

SUTTON WAS SO tired last night he fell asleep on a pile of blankets on my rug thirty minutes into the movie. He didn't even wake this morning when I prodded him with my finger, so I wrote him a note telling him I would return with a meal. In a surprising turn of events, Dad invited me and Mom out to a "family breakfast."

"How's Sutton?" Dad asks, his mouth downturned in anticipation of bad news.

I already told them about the upcoming wedding.

"Sutton is doing *amazing*. He just got a job offer yesterday at his dream publishing house, where he'll be an assistant editor for children's and middle-grade books."

My parents' faces are the perfect representation of how I feel. Their eyes widen, glinting with delight, and the creases that were forming between their eyebrows soften.

"Aaaand," I say, fanning my hands out like a cheerleader, "I just agreed to do some freelance work for this amazing indie magazine, *Wonderings*. If all goes well, they could hire me on full-time."

"Laine!" they shout in unison, mirroring each other's disbelieving expressions.

"It's perfect, because if I get hired to write for them full time, I'd have fresh assignments constantly, which would really hold my attention. Guess what my first assignment is?"

"You're doing an article on the *coolest* English professor at NYU," Mom says, deadpan.

Dad nudges her. "No, it's going to be on the most talented—and criminally underrated—playwright in the city."

"Solid backup choices," I say as the two of them argue over who is more deserving of a magazine feature. "But I'm actually going to be writing articles all about the culture of West River, Montana!"

"Sutton's hometown?" Dad asks.

"Home of Mr. Cowboy," I affirm. "We're leaving for Montana this weekend."

Mom raises her eyebrows. "You're going to the wedding?"

"Not only that, but I'm going as Sutton's fake *girlfriend*." My laugh fades out as I process my parents' body language.

Dad straightens and glances over at Mom, trading a worried look. They have a silent conversation between the two of them in a matter of seconds. Apparently, their years of separation haven't impeded their abilities of parent-to-parent telepathy.

Mom is the first to speak. "Laine, are you sure about this fake-girlfriend plan?"

I frown, caught off guard by their reaction. "Of course I am. It's just for fun. So he doesn't have to show up alone."

Dad sighs, no whisper of his proud smile left. "I understand you want to support Sutton, but pretending to be in a relationship can...blur the lines. It can complicate things. What if emotions get tangled up? What if it becomes more real than you intended?"

"That's ridiculous," I insist, narrowing my eyes. Their concern washes over me like a cold, chilling wave. "I appreciate your worry. I really do. But Sutton and I are best friends. We know this is just a silly thing to make the wedding easier for him."

Dad's face softens, and he reaches out to grab my hand. "Just...be mindful of genuine emotions."

We talk for a while longer about the trip's details, but I can still see hints of worry in my parents. Not wanting to let their hesitation rub off on me, I rush through my meal, eager to get back to Sutton and his calming presence.

When I get back to my apartment, to-go box in tow, Sutton lifts his head off his pillow on the floor, giving me a crooked smile that shows off one dimple. He ruffles his brown curls with one hand. "Good morning," he says, his voice raspy. Looking at him now, dimly lit by the TV, I can understand a bit more why my parents are concerned.

Now that Sutton is no longer my TA, it's easier to see him objectively. And objectively, he's...I don't know. *Handsome* is too simple of a word. Gorgeous, I guess. A strong bone structure and nose, piercing eyes, and those rare but endearing dimples.

"Are you sure you want to come to Montana with me?" Sutton asks. "Now that you've had a night to think it over?"

I hand over his food, the smell of the fresh pancakes and bacon filling my tiny apartment. "I've already been watching YouTube videos to learn how to lasso. Can't let that go to waste."

Sutton chuckles, leaning his head back and smiling at the ceiling. There's a moment of silence between us, but it's not the comfortable kind we had during our study sessions. Now, I feel the weight of my parents' warning hanging in the air like a bad omen. But when Sutton turns his head, directing his smile back toward me, the coiled tension between my shoulder blades releases.

I wouldn't dare ruin our friendship, not for the world.

9

SUTTON

THE WEEK PASSES TOO FAST. Before I can get my feet under me, it's Friday, and Laine and I are spending our last evening in the city on her fire escape, sitting cross-legged. The scattered gleams of the city lights dance like fireflies—yellow, white, and red. The sounds of New York are lively, even though it's past sunset, from honking horns to the discordant music of a street busker and the rumble of traffic. I inhale, noting the scent of nearby restaurants, exhaust from cars, and Laine's perfume. I want to remember every detail of the city when I go back to Montana.

Beside me, Laine is going through her packing list, triple-checking everything on it before handing it over to me. "Are you sure there's nothing else I need?"

I glance it over. "You're bringing six dresses?" I look up to see Laine nodding enthusiastically. "You know we're going to a ranch, right?"

"To a *wedding* on a ranch. I need options. I packed plenty of casual clothes, too."

I shake my head slowly, fighting a smile. Laine has casual clothes, sure, but she never *looks* casual. Her style is so unique, with bright colors and patterns and plenty of texture. I never know what to expect from her, and I don't think I've ever seen her wear the same exact outfit twice.

Looking back at the list, I ask, "How are you going to bring five different hats?"

"I'll pack the beret and baseball caps in the suitcase, and I'll wear the two brimmed ones on the plane." She folds her arms over her chest. "There's no rule against wearing two hats in an airplane."

"Six pairs of shoes?"

"My red cowboy boots, ballet flats, two pairs of heels, Mary Janes, and sneakers."

"Laine…"

"Sutton…" she says, mimicking my exasperated tone. "You know I can't make up my mind on much of anything. Are you really that surprised to find out that I'm a chronic overpacker?"

"Fair."

"Besides," she continues, "how many books do you have packed up for the trip, even though you have a fully-stocked Kindle?"

I laugh. "Alright, another fair point."

For a while, we sit in the silence—at least, the relative "silence" of the city. Laine fiddles with the raw-edge hem of her pants. When she looks at me, I can see the questions behind her wide, dark eyes.

"I need to hear about your family," she murmurs, reaching over to squeeze my knee reassuringly, her fingers brushing across my skin. I clear my throat, momentarily lost in the gentleness of her gaze.

I close my eyes for a few slow seconds.

"If we're going to pull off the fake-dating thing, we need to talk about things that a couple would," Laine insists.

"Well," I begin with a heavy breath, "my father, Hank, is the epitome of a tough cowboy."

"And you two don't get along?"

I shake my head once, squeezing my eyes shut against the memories that flood back. "He's not a bad guy. Rough around the edges, sure, but he's not violent. He's like…quiet thunder. A bit scary and rugged, but not dangerous like lightning. He thinks about the ranch—Silver Ridge—all day, every day. It's his entire world. It isn't a job for him—it's a way of life. He's poured his heart and soul into that land, and he taught all of his kids to do the same. But there were moments when I felt like I was suffocating, like the vastness of the ranch was closing in on me."

I turn my gaze back to Laine, my voice softening even more. "That's when I knew I needed to step away. I wanted to experience something beyond the endless solitude. That's how I ended up in New York."

Laine nods, and I can see her fighting to stay quiet. It doesn't come naturally to her, but she tries.

"I'm closer to my mom," I explain, and Laine's mouth shifts into a smile. I can practically hear her thoughts: *finally, some good news.* "Her name is Magnolia, and she's a total sweetheart. We used to love reading together…or cooking, or gardening, or riding horses. Really, anything relaxing was right up her alley. She used to own the dance studio in town before Cassidy took it over." Laine's eyes widen. "Yes," I confirm. "*That* Cassidy."

"Do you miss her?" Laine asks. When my face twists up, she clarifies her question. "Your mom, I mean."

My lips pinch into a tight smile. "Definitely. She and Frankie come out a couple of times a year to visit me, but it never feels like long enough."

"And Frankie? What's she like?"

I sigh, wondering how I can sum her up. "Frankie

is...*amazing*. She's outgoing and fun and has the most contagious smile."

"Does she have your dimples?"

"Hers are better."

"Impossible," Laine says, her eyes reflecting the city lights. "Does Frankie work at the ranch?"

"Part-time. The rest of the time, she's at the local radio station. She bought it right out of college. It's small, but she's always loved music, so it's a good fit."

"Is Wells as much of a jerk as I imagine him to be?" Laine asks, bumping her shoulder against mine to try to make me smile.

"Probably more," I joke. "He's outgoing, like Frankie, and was a total flirt in high school. And a troublemaker. He used to get into all kinds of trouble. Maybe he still does. I don't know. He wants to take over the ranch, last I heard."

"Is that a bad thing?"

"More power to him," I scoff. "So long as it's not me."

Laine nods again and opens her mouth before closing it. She repeats that motion three times, and I already know what she wants to ask.

"You want to know about Duke?" My voice is soft, catching on his name.

Laine scoots closer to me, tipping her head down so it rests on my shoulder. As usual, my initial reaction is to shirk away from the physical touch. It's been so long since I've had someone show their care in that way. But I settle in, leaning my head down atop hers. Warmth spreads across my face. I forgot how nice it is to be close to someone like this.

"Duke was the golden boy of our family," I say, my words thick. "It was like all the best traits of the family got blended into him. Hardworking like Dad, kind like Mom, outgoing like Frankie, charismatic like Wells—"

"Smart like you?" Laine interjects.

"I think it's more like I'm smart like him. Duke was the one everyone thought would take over the ranch—the one my father had high hopes for. He was the oldest, after all." I pause, struggling to put the weight of what I've been pushing away for six years into words. My chest tightens, and my pulse races. Laine, likely hearing my breaths quicken, sets her hand back on my knee, a silent source of comfort. I inhale slowly through my nose. "He had this way of lighting up a room when he walked in. People were just drawn to him. It was impossible not to like him…kind of like you."

"Sounds like you two had more in common than you think," Laine says.

"I wish. He loved the ranch, spending countless hours there, training and bonding with the horses. It was a part of him, you know? Then…apparently, one day, he didn't come back from a ride. He got bucked off and hit his head, and…I had just finished up my freshman-year finals when I got the call."

Laine's hand tightens around my knee, and I hear her let out a shuddering breath.

"Losing Duke…it unraveled our family," I say, my voice barely above a whisper. "My father…he blamed himself. Then he started blaming everyone else, too. And I—I was angry at everything, at the world, at myself for not being there to prevent it."

Laine is silent for a few beats. "Sutton, what happened was not your fault."

"Logically, that makes sense. But it doesn't feel like that. Maybe I could have helped him after his fall. Maybe things could have been different. I think that's why I'm so anxious about going back home. Like, if I'm back at the ranch, all those feelings of guilt will bubble back up."

"It's a good thing I'm excellent distraction," Laine says. "Whenever you start to feel down, just tell me, and I'll do something ridiculous to get your mind off it. I don't know—ride a mechanical bull or something."

I try to laugh.

She lifts her head to look at me, her eyes full of mischief. "Anything to keep your mind off the heavy stuff. Plus, I've always wanted to try one of those things."

"Why settle for a mechanical bull when we'll have the real thing? I have a feeling you'd conquer it with your usual enthusiasm," I reply, the heaviness of the conversation momentarily lifted by Laine's lightheartedness. As always.

"And you can cheer me on, just like you have been since we met."

There's a warmth in her words that resonates within me. Despite the weight of the past and the uncertainty of the future, Laine has been a bright spot in my life that I didn't expect.

10

LAINE

I PROBABLY SHOULD HAVE FOCUSED on doing research for my articles this week. Instead, I spent most of it listening to The Chicks, thrifting for the trip, and watching an obscene number of John Wayne movies. Unsurprisingly, there was no direct flight from New York City to Missoula, Montana, the nearest airport to West River. Instead, we flew from New York to Seattle and finally backtracked to Montana.

I've never been out of the New York area, so I don't truly know what to expect from Montana. As we descend below the clouds, I understand why Sutton insisted I take the window seat. I'm glued to the glass, mesmerized by the stunning landscape unfolding beneath us. The transition from the concrete jungle of New York City to the vast expanse of Montana is almost surreal. Rolling hills, open fields, a winding river, and rugged, evergreen mountains stretch out as far as I can see, painting an impossibly beautiful scene.

"Wow," I breathe, unable to keep my smile off my face. "I can't believe this is real. It looks like a screensaver."

It's been a long travel day—we got to the airport at six this morning, and now it would be six in the evening in New

York—but I feel more and more energized as our plane flies lower and lower.

"It's quite the change from the city, huh?" Sutton asks, leaning over me a bit to peer out the window with me. As soon as he does, though, he retreats and closes his eyes, pushing his hands through his curls.

"You all right?" I ask, squeezing his hand.

"Thank you for being here," he mutters. "I don't know how I would have done this alone."

The mountains grow closer, the very tips of their peaks dusted with snow even in early summer. The rich, earthy colors of the landscape create a tapestry that's both soothing and awe-inspiring to me.

Sutton, apparently, doesn't feel the same. His grip on my hand tightens as the plane descends farther, and I can see a conflict playing out in his eyes. I lean closer to him, my voice gentle. "Still okay?"

He hesitates for a moment before meeting my gaze. "Yeah, it's just...a lot of memories coming back."

I nod in understanding, remembering that this trip isn't about me having a vacation or Sutton showing his hometown off. It's about him confronting his past, his family, and everything that comes with that.

"It's okay, you know," I breathe, tracing circles on the back of his hand. "You don't have to carry everything on your own. I'm here to support you, no matter what. That's what fake girlfriends are for."

The plane rattles a bit as we land, and Sutton exhales sharply.

"We're here," I say, offering him a supportive smile. "A new chapter begins."

"A new chapter," he repeats, forcing a smile.

Sutton must be able to sense my excitement over being somewhere new, and it even seems to rub off on him a bit.

When we walk outside the small, five-gate airport, we're hit by the crisp air. It carries the scent of evergreens and wet earth. I take a deep breath, trying to imprint it into my memory. I didn't imagine a place could smell so...clean. It's only vaguely similar to the pine candles I've bought before.

We walk through the parking lot, stopping at an old, sky-blue Chevy truck.

"Sweet ride," I say, chuckling at the size of it. It's boxy and bulky and wouldn't stand a chance in bumper-to-bumper New York traffic.

"It was my pride and joy when I bought it in high school," Sutton says, smiling at the memory. "Frankie dropped it off for us."

After loading our bags into the back, Sutton opens the passenger door, which is already unlocked, for me. When he gets into the driver's seat, he flips the visor down. The truck's key falls into his lap.

"And with a hiding place like that, it's a wonder that this thing didn't get stolen," I say sarcastically.

"I'm shocked Frankie didn't just leave the keys in the ignition. So paranoid," he jokes.

Our drive to West River is over an hour long, and I stare out the windows for almost all of it, often with my mouth agape. Before us, the Montana landscape unfolds, each passing mile revealing an additional layer of its natural beauty. The road winds through valleys and trees, passing by rustic barns, quaint towns, and *lots* of cattle. The charm of the scenery is unlike anything I've ever experienced—far better than any Hallmark movie I've seen—and I find myself utterly captivated by it all. Sutton, meanwhile, spends most of the drive white-knuckling the steering wheel, his shoulders held high and tense.

Distraction time.

"So," I say, "what can I expect from you as my fake boyfriend?"

The corner of Sutton's mouth lifts. "What do you mean?"

"I mean, what would it look like to date Sutton Davis? Are you the kind of boyfriend to hold hands in public? Are you going to start calling me something cheesy like *honeypot*? Are you going to finish my—"

"Sentences," he interjects. Sutton's smile grows across his cheeks, showing off his dimples. "I'm not sure what it would be like to date me. It's been a while since I dated," Sutton says.

"How long?"

Sutton winces, and I know the answer before he says anything.

"You're not telling me it's been..."

"Six years," he confirms. "Cassidy was my last relationship—my last serious one, at least."

"Well," I say, trying to act unfazed by that news, "you'll just have to follow my lead, then."

"As if you have so much experience in relationships," Sutton says, grinning. I feign offense, and a laugh rumbles in Sutton's chest. "Laine, you're the one who said relationships 'just aren't for me right now.'"

Sutton turns off the highway, and we come upon a small and spread-out town nestled against the backdrop of the downright majestic mountains. As we drive through the outskirts, a mix of excitement and nervousness dances in my chest. Here, Sutton's memories and emotions are deeply ingrained. I'm about to step into his world.

Quaint storefronts line West River's main street, each with its own unique character. There's a rustic beauty to the architecture and hand-painted signs outside of every store. There's only one lane of traffic in either direction. It only takes us a few minutes to get through the "city" of West

River. From what I can see, there's only one stoplight, one grocery store, and not a single chain restaurant.

We cross a small bridge over the fast-moving river and drive higher and deeper into the mountains. The road turns from asphalt to gravel, and the truck bobs over the washboards. Even with the windows up, the smell of the forest fills the cab of the truck, thanks to the trees that hug either side of the road.

After twenty minutes on the gravel, we arrive at a massive arch with stone and log pillars and a black iron gate between them. Sutton slows to a stop, waits a moment, and the gate opens slowly. As we pass under it, I peer up, marveling at the sight of the grand entrance, and see an S with a curved line above and below it.

Silver Ridge Ranch.

The trees widen, allowing a valley to come into view. Though it feels like we've already climbed high into the mountains, there is still a backdrop of peaks beyond the ranch, their frosty tips piercing the pale-blue sky that seems to go out forever and forever.

"This is it," Sutton says, his eyes locked on the buildings ahead. The main building on one side, like the archway, consists mainly of stone and logs. Across the impossibly green yard, there are four white barns, each one facing in toward a central point. I crane my neck to view out every window of the truck and spot three more cabins on the outskirts of the private valley.

I laugh is disbelief. "This is…gargantuan."

"So open, so big…but so suffocating," Sutton saying, a grim smile curving his mouth. "One hundred and fifty thousand acres in all."

"It's cute that you say 'acres' as if I have any sort of gauge for what that means."

"To put it in perspective, New York City is just under two hundred thousand," Sutton says.

I whistle. "Do I need a passport to get in here? Do you have your own governing body? A militia?"

As we get closer to the main home, more details come into view. Warm light pours out from the windows. A wraparound porch borders the front and sides, with lights strung between its columns. Flowerbeds in front of the house bloom in brilliant shades of pink, orange, and purple. A woman about my age with long, curly blonde hair sits on the front step. When she hears the crunch of gravel under our tires, she snaps her head up.

I can hear her yell through the closed windows of the truck. "Sutton!" She runs toward us, her smile so big it must be hurting her cheeks. She hits Sutton's driver's side window with her palms. As soon as Sutton cuts the engine, she opens his door, dragging him outside and into a hug.

"Frankie," Sutton says in an exhale, both of them squeezing their arms around each other. They stand like that for a long time, but I don't dare disrupt their moment. I've never, *ever* seen Sutton be so openly affectionate, and it makes me feel like my chest got pumped with helium.

I'm not sure how much time passes before the two separate, but just as quickly as she found Sutton, Frankie brings her gaze to me. She has the same brown eyes as Sutton, with that same bright sparkle in them. I like her already.

"Holy hell, she's real," Frankie whispers, a bubbly laugh slipping out.

"Am I?" I look through the windshield for dramatic effect. "Because it feels like I'm in a dream right now. This place is breathtaking."

Frankie dashes to my side of the truck, opening the door for me. She lunges forward but pulls back at the last second. "Uh, sorry, can I hug you?"

A single nod is all it takes before I'm being yanked from my seat. I'm five-foot-four, a perfectly average height, but Frankie must be half-a-foot taller—more, probably. Beyond that, she's a little curvy and *very* strong. When she releases me, I feel like I need to catch my breath. Sutton is close behind her, watching us with knit brows.

With Frankie at arm's length, I see that, beyond those brown eyes and golden tan skin, she and Sutton don't look similar in the least. While he's all sharp angles and squared features, Frankie has full cheeks and a heart-shaped face. She must not be wearing much makeup, because the freckles across her nose are in full view. She looks like an angel, or maybe the love child of Florence Pugh and Jennifer Lawrence. So, basically an angel.

"I'm so excited to finally meet you," Frankie says.

"Finally?" I repeat. It's only been a week since Sutton told his family about our so-called relationship.

"Yes, finally. For months I've been—"

Sutton groans. "Very smooth, Frank—"

"What?" Frankie asks, laughing again. "If she's dating you now, it's clear your months of pining have paid off."

My heart drops to my stomach, and my breath catches in my throat.

I'm not sure what my face does, but I must have enough of an alarming expression for Frankie to feel the need to clarify. "Not in a creepy way or anything!" she says, pulling her hands back to wave them in the air. "At first, it was 'This girl paid three hundred dollars to go on a date with me.' But later, it turned into—"

"Where is everyone?" Sutton interjects, a scarlet wash across his cheeks.

"Mom is inside, making your favorite pie. Wells is out with the cattle. Dad had some sort of appointment in the city."

The news of the delayed reunion with his father causes Sutton's shoulders to loosen a bit. They relax even more when Frankie adds, "And Cassidy already had plans for tonight, so you'll have to meet her later, Laine."

I try to look disappointed.

"Ready to meet my mom?" Sutton asks me.

Frankie nudges me. "Ready to meet that pie she's baking?"

I grab my backpack, but Sutton takes it off my shoulder, slinging it over his own. Then, he grabs our two suitcases from the bed of the truck, lifting them by their top handles. *Has he always been so strong?* I had to pay an overweight fee for my bag, but Sutton carries it like it's lighter than a single Trader Joe's grocery bag.

"So, you pined after me?" I whisper to Sutton, sneaking him a devilish smirk.

"It was all a part of selling the story," he says, his gaze straight ahead.

"Which reminds me," I say, linking my elbow around his arm.

He looks down at me, a crease forming between his eyebrows.

I shrug. "It's all a part of selling the story."

11

SUTTON

THE RANCH FEELS SMALLER than I remember. I haven't gotten taller in the past six years. Even so, the house seems less towering, the land less expansive, the air easier to breathe. Maybe I've matured. Maybe counseling is paying off. Or maybe with Laine by my side, everything feels easier to stomach.

Even if Frankie humiliates me in front of her.

Inside the house, hardly anything has changed. The couch has new throw pillows. I think the lamp on the side table is an addition from the past six years. But otherwise, it's the same. Two massive elk mounts sit on either side of the two-story fireplace. Four flower arrangements from Mom's garden are scattered around. The same painting as always sits on the mantel, showing two riders on horseback in front of a wall of aspen trees. It looks so similar to the view off the back deck, I could be convinced the artist used Silver Ridge Ranch as a reference.

It even *smells* the same, like wooden log walls and the unmistakable scent of rhubarb pie wafting in from the kitchen. We follow the latter like hound dogs hot on a trail.

Mom's back is to us as she stares out the window over the sink. She still has the same shoulder-length honey blonde hair curled in perfect ringlets.

I look down at Laine, and her eyes are already on me, her gaze soft. She squeezes my hand, and the thumping in my chest takes on a new meaning.

Clearing my throat, I call out, "Mom?"

Every time I've seen my mom since Duke's funeral, I've worried that she might harbor some anger toward me, like Dad or Wells do. But as always, when she sees me, there's nothing but a joyous smile. Just as quickly as Frankie had, Mom closes the distance between us, colliding into my chest and tightening her arms around my back. Laine drops my arm so I can return the embrace.

"I've missed you," she whispers. I can hear the broken shards in her voice. Guilt swells in me.

I pull back and wrap an arm around Laine, trying to make it look natural and hoping I can hide how the simple movement makes me more anxious than I was for my interview with Imagineer Books. "Mom, this is Laine Rodriguez. Laine, Mom."

"It's great to meet you, Mrs. Davis," she says, smiling her perfect Laine smile.

"Magnolia," Mom says, extending a hand out to Laine. When Laine reaches out, Mom doesn't shake her hand. She just holds it. "Or you can call me Maggie." Mom pauses, looking over every inch of Laine's face. "You are every bit as beautiful as I imagined." Her eyes flick up to Laine's head, her lips curling into a humored grin. "And I like your hats."

Laine laughs dryly, taking off the two brimmed hats she's been wearing all day. "Oh, right. I didn't want to jam them into my suitcase."

"Brilliant idea," Mom says, her gaze dancing between Laine and me. "You two look…"

Phony?

"Worn out from traveling?" Laine finishes.

Mom shakes her head, and I spot a few silver hairs woven into the blonde. *When did she get those?* "You two look perfect together." Her eyes glisten with unshed, hopeful tears. The room seems to hold its breath as Mom's sentiment hangs in the air.

Laine steps closer to me, wrapping both arms around one of my biceps and leaning her head down onto my shoulder. *Selling the story.* "Well," she hums, "Sutton *always* looks perfect. I guess I'm just an added bonus."

Heat courses through my veins at the whisper of Laine's breaths on my arm. Her soft laughter, the warmth of her touch, the scent of her hair—it's a potent combination that makes it challenging to focus. My brain knows it's a part of the farce, but my body doesn't seem to get that memo.

12

SUTTON

"I THINK THAT WENT WELL, don't you?" Laine asks, balancing on the windowsill of the guest bedroom window so she can look out at the view yet again. The orange sunset bounces off her cheeks, making her olive skin glow. She looks back at me, and I avert my eyes to my suitcase, open on the mattress. I refocus on my unpacking efforts and pray she didn't catch me staring.

Laine walks toward me and plops down on the bed, right beside my suitcase. I haven't seen her reapply any makeup all day, but her lips are still a perfect, subtle shade of red. "We have one problem, though," she says, biting back a smile.

"That problem being my brother is about to marry my ex-girlfriend?"

"Okay, two problems."

As awkward as the situation is, I can't help but laugh. "What's the second one?" I ask.

"You're not selling the whole 'dating' thing." Laine crosses her arms. "We're supposed to be in a fresh relationship, the honeymoon phase."

I try to ignore the sudden galloping in my chest. "What do you have in mind?"

"You know, hand-holding, snuggling, heart-eyes, forehead kisses…" Laine trails off and moves her gaze back out the window, her cheeks tinted pink. "I mean, we should make it convincing, right? We need to act like a couple that's head over heels for each other."

Shouldn't be too hard.

Before I can respond, she's on her feet and heading for the bathroom. "I'm just going to freshen up a bit before dinner," she says, her voice holding a hint of nerves. Maybe she's creeped out about what Frankie called "months of pining."

The guest room has an attached bathroom, and I hear the water turn on almost immediately. While Laine showers, I change out of my travel clothes and into a new outfit, trying to focus on anything aside from the feeling of Laine's arm around mine. It's a fruitless effort.

Well, at least it's better than thinking about the rest of the mess in my life.

I glance around the room, taking it in. Thankfully, we didn't get assigned to my childhood bedroom, which has apparently become a place for random storage boxes and Christmas decorations. In here, it looks like the rest of the Davis house, with a western-print rug and cowboy-centric art along the walls. It doesn't carry the same pressured feeling my old room would. I read the spines on the bookcase in the corner and pick out the first familiar title, *Peter Pan*, sinking into the leather reading chair.

Just like I when I was young, I get so wrapped up in the story I lose track of time until Laine is standing directly in front of me, hands on her hips.

As usual, she dressed unapologetically in her own unique style. This time, she's in a mid-calf dress with thin straps at the top. It hugs the curves of her chest and torso before fanning out into a full skirt with vibrant splashes of color.

She quirks an eyebrow at me, her lips curving into a mischievous smile. "Are you planning to read through the whole bookshelf, or are you going to join me for dinner?"

I close the book with a soft thud and meet her gaze, feeling the corners of my mouth twitching involuntarily. "Maybe not the *whole* bookshelf."

Laine holds a hand out to me, pulling me to stand, but keeps her fingers intertwined with mine even after I'm up. "Honeymoon phase, remember?" she says, combing through her bangs one last time with her free hand. "How do I look?"

"I'm worried Wells is going to try to steal yet another girl-friend from me."

I lead Laine down the stairs and to the dining room. Three of my family members are already at the reclaimed wood table. Mom. Frankie. Wells. Laine tightens her grip on my hand, trying to dissolve my tension before it even has a chance to bubble up.

"Wells, right?" Laine asks, her voice even more bubbly than usual. She reaches her free hand out to Wells, who takes it and shakes it once. "It's wonderful to meet you."

"Ditto," Wells says, an edge of harsh sarcasm in his voice. He doesn't look at me.

My younger brother looks more or less like he always has —pale-blue eyes that are as cold as ice and dark, wavy hair. But instead of the cocky grin I grew up seeing from him, Wells now touts a sharp, narrowed stare and a flexed jaw. All signs of his boyishness disappeared over the years we spent apart.

Mom gestures for us to sit, but before I do, I glance at the empty seat at the end of the table opposite her. Just as I'm about to ask where my father is, the front door opens behind us. Heavy, tired steps approach.

In the six years it's been since I've seen him, my father seems to have aged twenty. Sunspots dot along the leathery surface of his skin. Deep wrinkles emphasize the downturn of his mouth, as if pointing his frown out like a blinking neon sign.

After two deep breaths, I hold my hand out. My father takes it hesitantly. Neither of us shakes. Instead, we just look at one another, hands clasped together. His silver-speckled eyebrows furrow low over his watercolor eyes—those eyes that reflect years of disappointment and disapproval.

We exchange quick not-so-pleasantries, and I introduce him to Laine.

"Food's getting cold," Mom says, her voice shaky.

After pulling Laine's chair out for her, I take the last seat left—the one between her and my father, the one directly across from Wells, who still won't look me in the eye. Laine reaches over to grab my hand, and I wonder if it's more so to keep up with appearances or to reassure me under my father's glare.

"How was your appointment, sweetie?" Mom asks my father from across the table, a halfhearted smile tipping her mouth.

He shoots her a look I've received countless times, Wells even more, but *Mom*? He usually looks at her like she's holding up the sun in the sky just for him. Now, there's a warning in his eyes. His voice is even colder than his expression as he gives his monosyllabic answer. "Fine."

Laine squeezes my hand tighter.

Mom clears her throat and smiles at Laine. Despite her grin, I can see the hurt dampening the edges of it. "I can't let this moment go by without saying how grateful I am that you're both here," she says to Laine and me. "For years I've been dreaming of having all of my kids together and…" Mom pauses to sniffle. I can practically see Duke sitting in Laine's chair. "I'm so happy to have Sutton back. And Laine, we feel lucky to have you in our home."

Laine smiles up at me, leaning over to rest her head against my shoulder. "I think I'm the lucky one," she says with all the magnetism in the world. "Thank you for having me."

Mom encourages everyone to dig in, and Laine takes a bit of everything. Mom and Frankie fill her in on all the dishes. Laine's eyes widen when she hears "elk steak" and "wild huckleberry glazed trout." Mom and Frankie are clearly going all-out to make a good impression on Laine, and it's working.

"Laine, Sutton told me you're a writer," Mom says, taking it upon herself to slide a huge portion of fish on Laine's plate.

"Freelance journalist—at least for now," Laine says. "I'm not sure if it'll be the right fit, but it'll be good to try. I'm not like Sutton, who has always known exactly what he wants." She pokes me in the ribs playfully. "And he's about to get it, too!"

Everyone's eyes slide to me, and Laine's smile slowly fades when she sees their varied expressions.

"You got the job?" Frankie asks, bridled excitement in her voice. "You're going to be an editor?"

"Assistant editor," I say. "At Imagineer Books."

Dad mutters under his breath. I only catch a single, insincere word: *perfect*. His eyes stay trained on his plate, but I can see his brow furrow and the grip on his fork tighten.

Laine, eager to direct the conversation away from a sore subject, asks Frankie about what it's like to own the local radio station. Then Laine asks Mom about her time as a dance teacher. Mom and Frankie ask Laine about her degree and her new freelancing gig with *Wonderings*. The three women hardly stop talking and seem more and more enamored with each other with every passing minute. But I know that—at least in part—their constant talk is also meant to cover gaps of awkward silences.

By the time the meal is halfway over, it's clear that Hank and Wells aren't planning on breaking their apparent vow of silence. Not that my father has ever been particularly good at carrying on a conversation. But he and Wells don't know how hard it is to resist Laine's charm. She angles toward them, scooting closer to me so she can again lay her hand on my thigh. I jump a bit from her touch, as if electrified.

"Wells," Laine says, "I bet you're feeling very excited about the wedding."

My brother looks at me for the first time tonight—the first time in six years. Flatly, he says, "Very excited."

Laine laughs. "You certainly sound it," she says sarcastically.

Mom, always the peacemaker, chimes in. "We're all very...excited."

I catch Frankie making a face that looks like the bite of trout she got was rotten.

The tension in the air is so thick I could pierce it with one of those elk antlers on the wall. Laine, ever determined, presses on. "What's been the *best* part about planning the wedding?"

Wells' expression turns into a wicked grin, and he flicks his eyes at me for a second before answering. "Probably planning the wedding night."

Mom chokes on her water, Frankie lets out a barely audible, "Ew," and I really try to not imagine...*that*.

"Hank," Laine says, desperately trying to redirect the conversation, "your ranch is beautiful. I'm doing some freelance writing and would love to feature Silver Ridge Ranch in my articles. I could interview the ranch hands this week—maybe even you, if you have some free time."

"A rancher never has free time," Hank says, and his words slur together a bit, likely the effects of yet another long day.

"Dad," I grumble.

"Son," he replies, the deep wrinkles in his face contorting with a hard stare.

Dinner continues in awkward near-silence, punctuated by the clinking of cutlery and the occasional polite comment from Laine or Mom. Here and there, Laine attempts to draw Hank and Wells out, her determination unyielding. But it's like trying to push against a brick wall with a feather—they're impenetrable.

We finish the meal with Mom's fresh rhubarb pie. As my father passes the pan to me, it drops from his grasp, tipping upside down over the tablecloth with a loud clang before splattering a crimson stain all over the rug under the table. Mom and Frankie sit completely frozen while a wide-eyed Wells stands from his chair, laying a hand on our father's back.

"Dad, are you alright?" Wells asks, his voice more frantic than it needs to be. Maybe he's overreacting to make me feel guilty.

Hank smacks a hand against the table and kicks his chair back. He pushes Wells just enough to move him out of his way as he walks out of the room.

Instinctively, I look to Laine, embarrassment, shame, and anger roiling through my stomach all at once. Before I realize what I'm doing, I'm following my father.

"We need to talk," I call out to Hank, who is already at the front door.

"Sutton," Mom pleads, "leave it alone for tonight."

I look at her, a silent apology in my eyes. "I can't."

Hank stops, slowly turning his head toward me. As I get closer, his mouth twists, like he can't decide whether the thought of me confronting him is worth laughing or fighting over.

"You can't treat Laine like that," I say as I get closer, straightening my spine. I've been taller than my father by a couple of inches since high school, and I might have another inch on him now that his body seems to sag a bit, his spine curving down slightly at the top. "You can't pretend she doesn't exist. You're mad at me. Don't take that out on Laine."

"What do you expect, son?" Hank says.

"I expect you to be civil." Clenching my jaw, I feel my anxiety prickling in my chest. "I wouldn't be here if Laine hadn't encouraged it."

"Well then, I certainly don't want to reward her encouragement by being civil."

He leaves without another word.

13

LAINE

AS THE ECHOES of Hank and Sutton reach us, the tension in the dining room is palpable, crawling over my skin and scratching at it like rough wool. The sound of the door closing behind Hank might as well be a thunderclap in a library. Immediately, Wells follows his dad's trail, shooting a scowl at Sutton when he passes. Magnolia jumps up from her seat, her stance as stiff and straight as a flagpole. Frankie reacts in the opposite manner, sinking down in her chair and pinching the bridge of her nose. I, meanwhile, try to keep my *Mona Lisa* smile in place. Though, I feel more like a Picasso right about now.

Magnolia clears her throat, her chest rising and falling rapidly. She sends me an unconvincing smile. "Laine, darling, I'm sorry. Hank has been...going through a lot. I should go check on him," she mutters, all but sprinting out of the room with enough nervous energy to power all of West River. "He'll clean this mess up, don't worry about it." By her tone, I know she means only the literal mess, not the metaphorical one.

Frankie stands next. "I'm going to…" she says, her voice trailing.

"Yeah, I should head to bed too," I reply.

Frankie coughs out a dry laugh and pushes her wild mane of blonde curls behind her shoulders. "Oh, I'm not going to bed. I'm going to go kick Wells' ass."

I grin. "Can I watch?"

"Trust me," Frankie says over her shoulder as she walks out, "it won't be pretty."

Sutton returns to the dining room soon after, looking more disheveled than I've ever seen him. His hair stands at wild angles, presumably from raking his hands through his curls in frustration. The classic button-down he's wearing is coming untucked. His eyes are so narrowed I can hardly see any of their whites.

"Your dad is such a sweetie," I joke, trying to crack Sutton's tension. "A real softy."

He smiles, though it doesn't reach his dimples, and collapses into the chair next to me. "Oh yeah, we're like two peas in a pod."

I'm shocked that I have to hold myself back from the impulse to reach for Sutton's hand. That movement came so naturally, but it's not as if his family is here to see it now.

"Do you think we're doing a convincing job?" I whisper, eager to get Sutton's mind off his father. I lean close enough to him I can smell his cologne, ginger and a hint of musky floral. Maybe he intentionally strays from woody colognes or anything reminiscent of the ranch. "I think we need to up the ante," I continue. "We're hardly acting any different from our usual."

Sutton's lips quirk up in a half-smile. "Or maybe my family is actually vacating the premises one by one simply because they can't handle our dazzling chemistry."

"That could be it."

"Yes. Not the fact that my father told me I was never welcome back."

"And certainly not because there's anything awkward about your brother and your ex getting married."

"At least she and I didn't date long," Sutton quips, dry humor coloring his voice.

"Yeah, five years is nothing." We're quiet for a moment, and my eyes drop to the rhubarb stain across the tablecloth and floor. "I didn't really want pie, anyway."

Sutton lets out a half-bitter laugh. Then his smile fades, and I can see his thoughts spinning behind those vacant eyes.

"Hey," I nudge his knee with mine, "let's go hide out from everyone."

He nods, and I pull him to stand, wrapping an arm around his torso as we shuffle back upstairs.

"I'm sorry you wasted that dress on a night like this," Sutton says once we're back in the guest room. He eyes me up and down, and my cheeks warm. He's never looked at me like this before—so unabashedly. I tell myself his eyes are lingering because he's just too exhausted physically move them any quicker.

"I'm sorry about my family. The good news is my dad will be gone for the next two days. He apparently has some business out of town. Meaning, we only have one jerk to worry about for a bit."

"I've dealt with my fair share of difficult personalities. I think I can handle it."

Sutton gives me a sidelong glance. I can see that he's trying to act playful, even when he feels anything but that. "Is that your subtle way of saying I'm a difficult personality?"

"Oh, Sutton Davis, you're not difficult. You're...an acquired taste. Once you let someone in, you're wonderful."

He chuckles, shaking his head. "An acquired taste, huh?"

I nod, leaning against the dresser. "Definitely. But you grow on people, like...a good mold."

Sutton lays his hand over his heart mockingly. "Comparing me to mold? Laine, you really know how to flatter a guy."

"Oh, don't sell yourself short. You're the finest mold I've ever encountered. Like a nice gorgonzola."

He laughs wholeheartedly, the tension of the night fading away into the background, even if only for a moment. *Good to have you back, dimples.* I'm relieved—and proud—that even amid chaos and family drama, I can still make Sutton smile.

"Do you mind if I turn in early? Being the disappointment of the family really takes it out of me." Sutton offers a half-hearted smile.

I wave a "go ahead," but as the en suite bathroom door clicks shut behind Sutton, I'm left alone in the guest room, the remnants of our banter still hanging in the air. It's then that I remember the bed dominating the room's space. My heartbeat quickens, sending a twist of nerves through me.

When I suggested we should pretend to be a couple, I somehow forgot this detail that goes along with keeping up that charade around his family. My mind lurches between the sound of Hank's icy voice and the feeling of Sutton's leg under my palm.

I walk to the edge of the bed, tracing my fingers along the line of a pillow. Are we going to share a bed? I mean, it's not like we're strangers. Sutton is my best friend. He's even fallen asleep at my apartment before. Still, this feels...different.

My heart races, and I scold myself for letting my thoughts spiral out of control.

Friend. Friend. Friend.

I sit down on the bed for just a split second before jolting back up automatically. It's just a bed, and we're both adults. But it doesn't feel like *just* a bed right now, not with that look

83

he was giving me just minutes ago, and not with Frankie's jab about months of pining still ringing in my ears.

Pacing the room, my anxiety gets the best of me. The idea of sharing a bed with Sutton suddenly feels much more complicated than it did yesterday. This isn't just a sleepover between friends; it's a delicate masquerade that I can't get caught up in. Glancing at the bed again, a soft blush creeps over my face. What am I so worried about? It's Sutton, after all. He's practically family.

When Sutton reenters the room, I find it difficult to look directly at him, but from my peripheral vision I can see he's in simple sweats and a white tee.

I laugh nervously, unsure of what to say. A rare occurrence. Then, I mumble out something about needing to get ready myself and retreat to the bathroom without making eye contact, pressing my forehead against the door after I close it behind me.

Already overwhelmed by my errant mind, I dig my headphones out of my bag and choose the first Spotify playlist I can find. It's one Dad shared with me, the soundtrack to a musical he dragged me to three times last year. It's the perfect noise to distract myself with.

I take my time getting ready for bed, brushing my teeth with care, washing my face twice over, and wasting ten minutes deciding what to wear. Shorts are out of the question. Even my matching pajama sets suddenly seem like they're trying too hard.

I pick the best thing I can that says, "We're definitely just friends, and I definitely haven't spent the last twenty minutes wondering if you're the kind of person who spoons in his sleep." Once I'm in my striped pajama pants, the ones with the nail polish stain on the knee, and my three-times-too-big shirt with the line "Rut the Ruck" printed on it, right under a picture of Scooby-Doo, I pop my retainer in.

There. I'm like the walking antithesis of sex appeal. With a strange comfort in that realization, I reenter the bedroom. But right as I do, I trip over something and fall to my knees.

Sutton.

He looks up at me from his pillow on the floor. "Hi," he murmurs.

"What are you doing on the ground?"

Sutton blinks slowly, his eyes half-lidded. "Is this not the bed?" he asks sarcastically.

"You don't have to do that, you know," I say. "It's not like we're strangers."

"Yeah, well, it's not like we're *actually* dating either."

My face heats, and I cross my arms defensively. "I just meant...you know...for appearances. In case your mom or someone comes in."

"So, you're *not* wanting to try method acting?" He smiles, giving up on trying to keep his eyes open.

"Don't flatter yourself. Come on." I shove Sutton's shoulder, but he hardly moves. Has he always been so *solid?*

Sutton chuckles and rolls to his side, almost knocking me over in the process. He grunts as he stands, shuffling to the bed with heavy feet.

"How are you already half-asleep?" I ask.

"I haven't been sleeping well since I found out about the engagement," he says, practically gagging on the last word. "My counselor suggested I try to take a sleeping pill at night until I can get my anxiety under control."

I guess that's one way for us to avoid the pre-sleep awkwardness.

Sutton climbs onto the bed and settles onto his side, turned away from the center of the bed, his eyes drooping. After turning the lights off, I tiptoe to my side of the bed. I stay as far on my edge of the mattress as I can, keeping a respectable distance between us.

For a few moments, we lie there in a tense quiet. The rustling of the sheets is the only sound as we shift to find comfortable positions. Eventually, Sutton ends up on his side, his body angled toward me.

His breathing evens out, showing that he's finally drifting off to a full sleep. I, however, am anything but tired. My thoughts rage in my mind like a storm. I turn onto my side to study Sutton. In this space of vulnerability, he looks peaceful, his features relaxed. Curls hang down on his forehead now that they're no longer styled away from his face. His lips pout out a bit, and there's no crease between his eyebrows. It's a pleasant change from his usual stoic, guarded expression.

As the minutes tick by, it feels like a weight presses against my chest.

Why do I feel so unsettled?

The heat builds under the covers, creeping all over my body and up my neck. I kick my feet out of the quilt, then my legs, then my whole body. I pull the bottom of my pants up to my knees. But it's no use.

I imagine it would take a full brass band marching through the room to wake Sutton right now. Regardless, I slowly slip out from the sheets and tiptoe across the floor as quietly as I can, wincing at every creak of the floorboards.

Once I have the hallway door open, I stand in the open frame for a minute, listening for any sounds, particularly an argument between Hank and Magnolia or an ass-kicking from Frankie to Wells. But it's silent.

I pad across the old wood floors, marveling again at the rustic grandeur of the house as I descend the stairs. I avoid looking at the elk mounts on the wall, half afraid the animals will come alive like they're in some cheesy horror movie. Their massive antlers cast creeping moonlit shadows across the floor. Still paranoid I'll wake someone up, I keep the lights off and rummage through the kitchen cabinets, looking for a cup, settling for a Mason jar.

"You couldn't sleep either?"

I nearly drop the jar at the sound of Frankie's voice. I turn around to find her leaning against the kitchen doorway, a playful grin on her face.

"Nice shirt," she snorts. "Are you wanting water? Or something stronger?"

I laugh shakily, still on edge. "I've made enough of a fool of myself tonight without the help of alcohol."

Frankie smiles gently and takes the jar from me, filling it at the sink. "You didn't make a fool of yourself. That pie—that *stupid* pie...my dad's attitude. It wasn't about you."

"Really?" I laugh, unconvinced.

"Well, it wasn't entirely about you, at least," Frankie jokes. She holds my water back out for me, and I stare at it, unblinking.

"Is that...safe?" I ask, taking the jar as if it's filled with some kind of chemical warfare. I don't think I've ever seen someone drink from the tap in the city.

She rolls her eyes lightheartedly. "Fresh water from the well. Try it."

I do as I'm told, but nearly spit it back out. "It's so *flavorful*."

"Don't be so dramatic," she laughs. "That's what real water tastes like."

"I apparently don't have a refined palate. I'm used to the water that's gone through a dozen rounds of sanitizing and refinement."

"Brave enough to face Hank Davis, but not brave enough to drink tap water?"

"To be fair, I had a week to prepare to meet your father. I only had about three seconds to prepare to drink well water."

Frankie's smile softens. "I'm glad you're here," she

murmurs after a silent beat. "When Sutton first talked about you, I dreamed about it—about you—becoming something more."

Guilt punches me in the gut, leaving me breathless.

"After all," she continues, "you were the first girl Sutton talked about. I'm sure he went on dates in the city, but never long enough to warrant true feelings. Even though he swore he couldn't date you—being your TA, and all—and then swore that you had a no-dating rule, I still dreamed that somehow you two would make it work in the end. I can't tell you how amazing it was to see him happy tonight."

"I don't know if a dinner complete with a father-son yelling match constitutes a 'happy' moment," I say, trying to move the conversation away from me.

Frankie scoffs. "Family drama aside, I've never seen him look at someone the way he looks at you. You're perfect."

I laugh and shoot her a *yeah, right* look.

Frankie rolls her eyes. "According to Sutton, at least."

"Thanks," I whisper. As much as I'm drawn to Frankie, my instincts are begging me to leave before I give our farce away. Our lie doesn't seem so harmless now. "I should—I should go get some rest."

I turn to head back upstairs, but Frankie stops me with a hand on my elbow. "Can you do something for me, Laine?" She squeezes her eyes shut for a moment. "Will you... Will you promise you won't break Sutton's heart? Even if things don't work out between you two, just be gentle with him. I don't think I can bear to see him go through another harsh breakup." Frankie pauses, exhaling sharply. "Cassidy tore him apart. And I can't watch that happen again."

At least I can be honest with this, seeing as how I can't break something I don't truly hold.

"I promise."

14

SUTTON

MY SLEEPING PILL wears off right as the morning sun is peeking over the mountains outside the window. I squint in the dawn light, trying to make sense of everything.

And then I see her.

Even in that ridiculous shirt, with her limbs wildly strewn out, and her bangs sticking up at all angles, Laine looks beautiful. Somehow, a subtle wash of red still stains her lips, turning them a shade that perfectly matching my mother's peonies out in the garden.

Realization hits me all at once like a punch to the face. I actually slept with—rather, near—Laine. The girl I've been—as Frankie so embarrassingly put it—pining after. Pining ever since the night of the date auction. Maybe even since she came into class late in her bright patterns, demanding to be seen.

It's a good thing I took that Ambien, otherwise I would've been up all night, acutely aware of her every movement, terrified I would do something embarrassing in my sleep. I almost close my eyes again to bask in Laine's nearness, but it doesn't feel right. Sleeping alongside her when I was knocked out was one thing. Lying here conscious, as my feelings are becoming harder to ignore, is a whole other thing.

I sit up as quietly as I can manage, my eyes still on her. She stirs a bit, covers her face with her arm, and tucks the corner of the patchwork quilt under her ankle. Her breaths even out once again, and her body relaxes completely.

I take twice as long as usual to get dressed, even though I'm just getting ready for a day on the ranch. It's not my dream itinerary, working with Wells today, but Laine needs to make headway on her articles, and I don't want to distract her. Knowing my father would be gone for a couple of days for his unspecified appointments, I encouraged Laine to take advantage of that and get as much interviewing done around the ranch as possible.

I've had little of an appetite since arriving back in Montana, so even though the cook has a solid start on the breakfast spread he's prepping for all of the ranch hands, I grab only an apple on my way outside.

Staying away from the barns yesterday was intentional. Laine would have loved a tour of them, I'm sure, but I couldn't bring myself to get too close right away. The farthest building, the bunkhouse, is already alive with raucous laughter and teasing. I nearly get to the open door before doubling back and heading for the stables, not yet ready to face the others I'll be working with today.

If I stop overthinking, it can almost feel as though no time has passed. The sound of dirt under my old boots, the morning chill, that distinct smell of hay and sun-warmed wood mingling with the sharp tang of leather and faint traces of horses—it's a scent that lives somewhere deep in my memory, tangled up with summers spent working under skies of endless blue.

Did I even move to New York?

Did I spend six years in school?

Or am I still eighteen years old, living every day on this stretch of practically untouched land?

Hank sold my paint horse the same day I moved away, but the others I was familiar with are still here, with the addition of a couple of new adults and three foals. Even Duke's horse is here, in the last stall. He's a gorgeous quarter horse with a russet coat, a blaze of white down the center of his face, and matching white socks on each leg. When Duke was here, he was on his horse daily and pampered it to death—constantly training, brushing, and bonding with it. His horse, in turn, took on Duke's same personality—gentle yet powerful. However, it's been six years since Duke was here. And if Wells took over the care of his horse, maybe *his* personality rubbed off on it, meaning I need to approach cautiously.

"Hey, bud," I whisper as I close the final distance between the horse and me. I hold a hand out high, pausing midair to study the horse's reaction. It blinks and tips its nose down, almost bowing. My hand falls to its forehead and down its muzzle. "Come on," I murmur. "You're mine today."

The ranch hands come in as I'm bridling Duke's horse. I look at the group of twelve, doing my best to not appear as sheepish as I feel. There are a handful of unfamiliar faces, but some of them have been around since I was a kid.

"Mornin'," I say, shocking myself by subconsciously dropping the "g." I pull the horse along with me as I walk to the group. Some smile. Some glare. All seem to know exactly who I am, but I introduce myself anyway. "I'm Sutton Davis. I'm Hank's..." Am I technically the oldest now? No, that doesn't feel right. "I'm his...other son."

"The writer," one of the younger in the group says, crossing his thin arms. Just by his wiry build, I know he's new to the ranch.

"Editor." Assistant editor, technically. And *technically*, not even that for a few more weeks. They don't need to know that, though.

Bill, who has been working at Silver Ridge since it was my grandpa's, nods at me, the closest thing I'll get to a welcome. "You're here for Wells' wedding?" Bill's silver mustache hangs so low it nearly touches his chin. He was always friendly to me when I was young and even kept a pocket full of Werther's Original caramels to give to me and my siblings whenever we walked by. But now, there's no hint of kindness in his eyes. And of course, no candy offering.

I know my father and brother feel I abandoned the ranch and, by extension, they feel I abandoned them. I suppose the others here must think the same. Beyond that, Wells surely hasn't had the best things to say about me to them over the past years.

"Yeah, I'm here for the wedding," I confirm.

A few of the familiar employees lean over to the ones I don't recognize, hushed conversations slipping between them. I can't actually hear what they're saying, but it's no mystery. *That's the brother who dated the bride-to-be.* The fresh faces light up with amused delight.

Then, one of them barks out a laugh. "She must be a hell of a lay," he says, loud enough for us all to hear.

A voice so strong it's unfamiliar in that moment booms out. "*Who?*"

Wells strides in, his scowl accentuating the dark shadows under his eyes. He's only twenty-three, but his voice was enough to flatten any humored smiles. To me, he's still the sixteen-year-old kid getting in trouble for sneaking into bars and getting into fights. As such, his bravado makes me cringe, but for a moment, I can see him as the others do. Strong-willed. Commanding. Powerful.

I can see him trying to be our father.

Wells scratches his beard, looking even taller with his

cowboy hat on. "*Who's* a good lay?" he asks again, his fiery gaze flitting to me for a second.

Everyone is tight-lipped.

Wells walks directly to the guy who made the comment, his stare unyielding. "You're on shit-shoveling duty today. I want the stalls mucked and washed out. Every horse is coming home tonight to fresh bedding. It better smell like a damn field of roses when we get back." Wells grabs a nearby pitchfork and shoves the handle toward the guy's chest—hard enough to push him back a step. "Got it?"

"Y'sir," he mumbles back.

Wells continues staring at him, even when giving directions to the others. He tasks a few with fence repairs, half with moving cattle, and the final few with miscellaneous work near the home base.

"What are you doing?" Wells asks me, finally looking away from the shit-shoveler.

"Whatever you need me to." I look at the faces of the crew again. "Laine, my...girlfriend..."—I wince, *still weird to say*—"will be around today," I tell them. "She's a journalist and is doing a few articles about West River and Silver Ridge Ranch. She might ask some of you questions, if that's okay."

Wells nods, his jaw flexing, and turns back to his crew. "I'm not going to *make* any of you do an interview, you *all* will be kind. And gracious. You'll tip your hat and say things like 'ma'am' and 'excuse me' and 'pardon.' And you won't embarrass me." The group gives an audible agreement.

It takes effort for me to keep my mouth from popping open in surprise. After all, Wells embarrassed himself plenty yesterday, by his own attitude. The last thing I expected was for him to stand up for Laine. Frankie really must have let him have it last night.

"Get to it, then," Wells instructs his men, heading for his horse.

"Is it alright if I take Duke's today?" I ask Wells as he passes me.

"Whatever."

"And thank you," I say. Wells keeps his back to me as he gets to work on his own horse, but I continue anyway. "Thank you for asking them to be nice to Laine. So far, she thinks this place is a little slice of heaven, and I'd like for that to continue."

Wells says nothing.

"Is there anything specific you want me to help with today?" I ask.

He turns to me, his body as tight as a drawn bowstring. "I don't care what you do, so long as you don't get in the way. We don't need you here."

I lead Duke's horse out of the barn without another word.

Everything comes back naturally. Mounting Duke's horse. Kicking my heels against his sides. Feeling that brisk morning breeze as we trot through the fields, working our way along the emerald grass, wandering deep into the trees. The mountains progress in levels, and once I get to the lowest ridge, I pull the horse up to the edge, studying the views below.

The morning sun casts a golden glow over the panoramic landscape, illuminating the vast expanse of rolling hills and steep mountains that circle the ranch. The fields stretch out in waves, like a lush green blanket peppered with vibrant wildflowers. Here and there, cattle graze lazily, their forms mere specks against their backdrop. The river at the base of the mountain roars over rapids, winding swiftly through the small, private valley. But it's the mountains that command the most attention. Their peaks reach for the sky with dignified pride, standing like guardians over my family's home.

I close my eyes, drinking in the smell of wet dirt and the songs of nearby birds. Everything feels so raw, so real, so *quiet*. It grounds me in a way that the city never can. And for the first time in years, I feel like I can take in my first true breath.

I can claim that I don't regret my decision to move away. I can tell Laine about how my father made life here a challenge. I can truly and honestly love so much about my life in New York. But I can't deny that I've also missed some aspects of life at Silver Ridge. There is no calm like that found in the mountains.

If not for the thought of missing out on time with Laine, I could stay here in this spot all day. When I start back down toward the barns, I prod Duke's horse into a full gallop, my body bouncing in time with the beat of the horse's run.

And there she is. Red cowboy boots and all.

Laine sits on the top of the corral, watching Bill and Wells work on breaking one of the foals. She waves her arms high in the air when she sees me, calling my attention as if my eyes weren't immediately drawn to her. Even in the city, in crowds of people, I could spot Laine in a second.

In addition to her boots, she's in a patterned tank top that flares out at her waist and cutoff jean shorts that show off the curves of her thighs. And yes, she has her red lipstick on, though it looks more sheer than usual.

When I dismount Duke's horse and tie him up, I waste no time getting close to Laine. Her beaming smile is enough to almost forget about dinner last night.

"I didn't enjoy waking alone this morning," Laine says with a wink, loud enough for Wells and Bill to hear. She slides herself backward toward me, and I reach up, grabbing her by the waist and lowering her to the ground. Almost without thinking, I hug her from behind. "Nice touch," she giggles in my ear. "Very convincing."

Laine spins around to face me. My hands linger on her, now resting on her hips. She looks up questioningly. "Can I kiss you?" she whispers under her breath, tilting her head ever so slightly back toward the corral, where Bill and Wells are watching our exchange.

My heart drops to my stomach, and my mouth goes dry, but I give her a minuscule nod. Before I have time to overthink it, Laine brings her hands to my neck, pulling me down as she tilts up. My heart is beating so fast she can probably feel it as our chests press together. I can barely see the corners of her lips twitch up before our mouths connect.

This isn't real, I remind myself in a last-ditch effort to maintain clarity.

Fake dating or not, Laine's kiss sets me on fire. Her lips are as soft and warm as I imagined, and they mold to mine perfectly. She draws back for just a moment before reconnecting again, longer and deeper this time. Her smile breaks the kiss, and she laughs breathlessly against my chest as she lowers back down on her heels.

Without a word, she grabs my hand and turns back to the corral, with her back to my chest. She pulls my arm across her so it drapes over her collarbone.

Wells stares at us, his mouth tipping into something almost resembling a sideways grin, and I finally see more of the kid I used to know.

15

LAINE

FINE. I'll admit it.

Sutton looks good as Mr. Cowboy.

There's something undeniably attractive about the way he fits into the rugged ranch atmosphere, as if he'd never lived the life of a city boy. His sturdy frame seems tailor-made for this landscape. I'm not sure how back in the city I didn't realize just how broad and toned he is. The worn jeans, the simple white shirt that hugs his biceps, and the cowboy hat perched on his head—it all comes together to create an image of classic handsomeness. Despite how much I've seen of him in his New York attire, this version of Sutton still feels more authentic.

All day, I try to be Professional Laine. I *try*. I interview every person I see at the ranch, asking interesting questions and recording everything. Even so, I find myself constantly distracted.

Focus. Focus. Focus.

It's no use. Whenever I try to think about my articles, I catch sight of Sutton. He works on the foals with care and attention. He lifts bales of hay like they're no heavier than a briefcase. He has this silent strength about him, more potent now than ever, and everyone around seems to notice it too. But best of all, whenever he sees me, he smiles, dimples and all.

I was certain that, no matter what my parents said, I wouldn't blur any lines. No emotions would get tangled. Sutton and I are friends, nothing more. There can't be more. Because no matter how well we get along, we're too different. Not just mismatched puzzle pieces, but a puzzle piece and a Scrabble letter mistakenly tossed in the same box.

Sutton is so *together*. He knows what he wants, and he works hard for it.

Sure, I have my good qualities. I can make people laugh and feel loved. But I also self-destruct. I get distracted and discouraged and indecisive. I abandon every hobby I pick up. I barely graduated from college. The opportunity with *Wonderings* practically fell into my lap. I don't have much of an idea of what I want, aside from a vague dream of happiness. I have no true vision for myself or for my life, and I can't drag Sutton into my mess in any capacity deeper than as a friend.

It wouldn't be fair to him.

But still, that kiss.

That damn kiss.

I can't keep my mind off it, and whenever I *do* allow myself to dwell on it for more than two seconds, my pulse races. The kiss was for show—for Wells—but I hadn't anticipated the way it would make my body feel like nothing but a pile of firing nerves.

Then again, maybe it's the thin mountain air making me all dizzy and lightheaded.

Or maybe it's the excitement of being lovesick, even if it's a farce.

As the day winds down and the sun dips behind the

mountains, turning the clouds in the sky into orange and pink ribbons, I gravitate to the corral once again. Sutton is inside the fence with a foal, petting it reassuringly and feeding it hay pellets from a tin bucket.

With a deep breath, I remind myself why I'm here, to write some articles and help my friend. Not to let myself get distracted by dimples and stolen kisses.

"You really like him, huh?" Wells asks me as he walks over from the barn, leaning on the corral gate beside me.

Wells is handsome, like Sutton, but still has a hint of boyishness to him. His hair is longer, the waves at the back encroaching on mullet territory. And while Sutton's beard is close-trimmed, practically stubble, Wells' beard is thicker, just short enough to show the strong cut of his jaw. Maybe his physical similarities to Sutton made it easier for Cassidy to jump between the two.

That thought makes me want to gag.

Wells scoffs, and I realize I was staring at him. "Is that a no?" he asks, smirking.

"Huh?" I blink, nearly forgetting his initial question. I hope my flustered state can pass as a believable, deep-in-love response. "Oh, yeah. What's not to like about Sutton?"

"I can think of a few things," Wells grumbles to himself.

Footsteps sound behind us, and we turn to find Frankie approaching. She was working at the radio station all day, so she's the only one of us without a layer of dust and grime. Her golden curls are like a halo framing her face. "How was your first day at the ranch?" she asks, hugging me on the side opposite Wells.

"It's been amazing," I tell her. "You know, I'd love to interview you one of these days, too. See the world of a small-town radio station owner."

"Name the day," Frankie says. Her gaze softens as she watches Sutton, and a small grin spreads across her cheeks.

"Don't distract Laine," Wells says to Frankie. "I was trying to hear what she really thinks about our brother."

"I came at a perfect time, then," Frankie says, her eyes still on Sutton. When he sees her, she waves him over. "But first! Tell us about how you first met."

Wells groans at the cheesy question, but he stays at my side, obviously curious despite himself.

"Go ahead," I say, waving a hand at Sutton as he approaches.

He's quiet for a moment, and I imagine he's trying to fabricate some grand, romantic story. When he finally starts talking, he keeps his burning gaze trained on me. "I first saw Laine Rodriguez when she barged into class late. She was wearing a Barbie-pink turtleneck, a matching hat, and this rainbow plaid scarf. Whenever I looked at her, she was twisting her rings around or mindlessly fiddling with the frayed edges of her scarf or pants."

My mouth opens into a shocked, wide-mouthed smile. *How does he remember all this?*

"I was annoyed at first," he continues, a glint in his eyes, "because I hate when people are late to class. She wanted me to tutor her, but I said I didn't have time. The next night, Laine showed up at a date-auction fundraiser I was volunteering at. She paid three hundred dollars for a date with me—"

"*Almost* three hundred dollars," I correct.

"You can imagine my utter heartbreak when I discovered Laine didn't actually want to go out on a date with me and insisted it was just for tutoring."

I roll my eyes, and Sutton bites down on a smile.

"We spent hours at her apartment that night. And aside from her being beautiful, which I was already more than aware of, Laine was also funny and charming and had this incredible ability to make me want to open up to her. Her presence was—*is*—intoxicating. We've spent almost every day together for three months, and each day is better than the last."

My smile fades a bit. Sutton's too. He looks at Frankie, shrugging as if to say *that's it*.

"Reading all that Shakespeare made you such a romantic," she laughs, punching his shoulder lightly through the bars of the gate.

I'm still speechless. He portrayed our first encounters so beautifully, even I could be convinced it was the start of an epic love story.

"Ready to call it a day, *honeypot?*" Sutton asks, grinning mischievously when he tacks on the ridiculous pet name at the end of his question.

I nod, still unsure of what to say.

"I'll meet you inside. I'm just going to put the foal away."

"I'll do it," Wells offers. He gives me a near-smile, and it transforms his entire face. I was determined to hate Wells after what happened last night, but it's difficult to hate someone who resembles his older brother so much—a brother I'm pretty fond of.

Sutton climbs over the gate, and I really try not to ogle at the flex of his arms or the way Levi's fit him even better than the chinos he wore in the city. When he's on the ground, he reaches for my hand. I can feel the calluses already rising on his palms just from one day back at Silver Ridge. Frankie's and Wells keep their eyes on us, even as Sutton places a finger under my chin and lifts it up, brushing his lips against mine in a sweet, simple kiss.

There's that thin mountain air again, making me feel lightheaded.

"Come on, you two," Frankie says, grabbing my other hand.

We walk, a chain of three links, back to the house.

"Wells sure seemed happier back there," I say once we reach the back porch.

Frankie giggles. "I think it might have something to do with seeing you two together."

"Right, because Wells has always been a real Cupid," Sutton quips.

"I'm sure it's more about him feeling a bit more confident that you aren't going to steal his bride within the next two weeks," Frankie says, holding the back door open for us.

"Speaking of," I say, "when will I finally get to meet…" My words trail off as I lay my eyes on the woman in the kitchen.

Cassidy.

I assumed she would be the opposite of me, likely because I'm the last person in the world I can imagine Sutton truly liking. Turns out, I wasn't far off. She's not blonde like I pictured her. Instead, Cassidy has copper hair that hangs almost to her butt. It's not vibrant or full-force—no Hayley Williams circa 2008. Rather, it's so light it's almost peach. While I'm short and curvy, Cassidy is tall and thin. Her complexion is like printer paper compared to my tawny amber skin, and freckles dot across every inch of her face. Even in our features, we're stark contrasts: she's a gentle doe with her wide, expansive eyes and button-like nose, while I bear more resemblance to a fox with my slightly upturned and narrower eyes.

It's hard not to feel self-conscious standing ten feet away from her. Not only because she's gorgeous, but also because she was Sutton's first, longest, and possibly only love.

I can't force myself to look away from Cassidy, but I don't think she's even noticed me yet. The second we came through the door, her eyes landed on Sutton and haven't yet moved. His palm has gone limp in mine, and when I release my grip on it, his arm falls lifelessly at his side. Meanwhile, Frankie tightens her grip around my hand.

"Sutton," Cassidy exhales, her round lips tilting into a sideways smile. She has the voice of a Disney princess. All at the same time, she approaches Sutton, he approaches her, and Frankie and I step back until we're in the doorframe.

I'm not sure how long Sutton and Cassidy stand there staring at each other, but eventually, she reaches out for him and draws herself against his chest, wrapping her arms up around him. Sutton stands motionless for a moment, but then he follows her lead, his broad frame towering over her. My mouth goes dry.

Suddenly feeling like I'm intruding, I walk backward off the porch, nearly tripping on the steps, and briskly make my way across the lawn. Frankie is close behind, rambling on about how the hug is surely harmless.

"It's fine," I say through a plastered-on smile.

Yeah, it is fine, I remind myself.

"What's going on?" Wells asks, his grin fading as he reads our expressions.

"Nothing!" Frankie and I say in unison, a bit too quickly.

Wells' face drops, and his eyes dart over to the cherry-red truck in front of the house. Without another word, he takes off toward the house. I can practically see the steam coming from his ears, *Tom and Jerry* style.

Frankie and I watch Wells, our feet planted in the grass, too nervous to be right in the action, too engrossed to walk away. Wells gets to the open door, stands in the frame for one short second, and retreats the way he came, slamming the door so hard the glass windowpanes in it shake.

Not long after, Sutton is running out the back door behind him. Our eyes lock for a moment, and he gives me this torn look. He continues forward, catching up to Wells at the far fence. Frankie and I watch, motionless. Even from a distance, the tension sparks, like a lightning storm we're watching on the horizon.

We can't hear what Sutton says, but everyone in the bunkhouse can probably hear Wells' response. "You can't explain your way out of this one. I saw you with her!"

"It was a *hug*," Sutton insists, now almost as loud as his brother, his flaring his fingers at his sides.

"Is that what you call it?" Wells spits back. His words come faster, rambling together. "You know, you can claim that you aren't hung up on my fiancée, you can bring a new girl to the ranch and parade around like you're Prince Charming, but that wasn't a 'friend' hug. You've had six years to move on, Sutton. It's over. She. Chose. Me."

"Yeah, she chose you because I wasn't around anymore. She *settled* for you." As soon as he says it, Sutton's mouth stays open, surprised at his own words.

Frankie audibly gasps.

"I—I didn't mean that…" Sutton stammers. His words hang in the air like a heavy cloud. I'm stunned, never before hearing Sutton be harsh. I didn't think he had an ounce of his father in him.

Wells shakes his head in disbelief, his hands balling into fists. "No. She chose me because she was tired of being with a depressed wet blanket." Wells stomps toward Sutton, and for a moment, I worry that he'll take a swing. But then, he marches right by, his shoulder crashing against Sutton's so hard he stumbles back.

For a moment, Sutton does nothing. He just stands, one hand covering his face. Then, he takes off in the opposite direction, around the house. I take a few minutes to collect my thoughts before trailing behind him. Frankie, meanwhile, follows Wells.

As I walk around the back of the house, I hear a steady rhythm. *Crack*. Pause. *Crack*. Pause. When I get around the corner, I see Sutton, his back toward me, placing a log atop a cut-off tree trunk. He's shed his dusty white t-shirt, and as he brings an axe behind him, I can see every defined muscle in his back tighten. Lifting the axe up high, he swings it down on the log, splitting it in half. He continues this for a few minutes, splitting the wood until a small pile has formed at his feet. And I continue watching.

It's quite pathetic, really, how easy it is to forget what just happened when I'm watching Sutton chop wood. It's like I'm watching a Calvin Klein ad. A heavy feeling settles in my stomach, and I can't seem to look away.

There's a raw intensity to his movements. Each swing of the axe is a release of frustration.

My boots crunch on the ground as I take another step toward Sutton. He must hear it because he pauses, axe in mid-air, and turns to face me. His expression is broken. Vulnerable.

"Laine," Sutton says, his voice rougher than usual.

My eyes betray me, flitting down to his chest. His front is even more impressive than his back. On his ribcage, just under the muscles of his chest, he has a tattoo of the same symbol that was above the ranch's main gate, the same symbol branded on the cows. The S with the curved lines above and below it. Silver Ridge Ranch has always been a part of him, and I just didn't realize that until now.

I take a tentative step closer. "Sutton, are you okay?"

"I'm sorry you had to see that. The hug...it meant nothing."

"So I've heard," I hum.

"And when Wells was arguing, I said the first thing I could think of to put him in his place. I can't believe I said that."

"Me either," I snort, grabbing the axe from Sutton and leaning it against the tree trunk. "Can you tell me more about you and Cassidy? I'm flying blind here."

Sutton sighs, raking both hands through his hair.

Please don't look at his chest, I ask myself politely.

Too late, I think immediately after.

"You know that Cassidy and I grew up together. We knew each other from preschool and dated all throughout high school."

"Sure."

"When I first moved to New York, I thought we would work through it. I planned on moving home for the summers, and I thought she would visit the city here and there during the school year. I thought, at the time, that we were so in love that it had to work out. But Cassidy knew something I didn't."

"That flights from Montana to New York City are astronomically expensive?"

"She knew we weren't in love. Not really. Things were easy between us because it was all we knew, not because we were destined to be together. Shortly after I left, she and Wells started spending more time together. I had no idea, though, until I came home for Duke's funeral. As soon as I got to the ranch, I found them...you know. *Together*."

"No!"

"In my truck."

I let out a harsh exhale.

"Cassidy tried to patch things up with me. She apparently told Wells that she was making a mistake by being with him. To make matters worse, my father lectured me nonstop the week of the funeral, telling me it was my duty, as the newly appointed eldest son, to take over the ranch. He was scrambling to make sense of everything and make a plan. I didn't want to be a part of that plan, though. But my dad wouldn't hear it. He told me that if I was walking out on the family when they needed me most, I would never be welcome back."

"Wow," I whisper. "That's some serious *Days of Our Lives* stuff."

Sutton smiles, then laughs, then sighs. "You're not mad I didn't tell you about this before?" he asks me, his eyes looking darker than usual.

"Why would I be mad?" I ask. *Weirdly jealous? Maybe.* "It's not like we're actually a couple."

"Right," Sutton murmurs, rubbing the stubble along his jaw. "I know."

16

LAINE

"ARE you sure Cassidy wants me to come?" I ask, twisting around in the passenger seat of Magnolia's SUV to look back at Frankie.

"She specifically asked me to invite you," Frankie says, shrugging. She looks as apprehensive as I feel.

"It'll be fun," Magnolia insists, nodding as if to convince herself of her words. "What's not to love about cake testing?"

She has a point. If I'm going to be spending the morning with my best friend's ex, then there might as well be dessert involved.

"I think Cassidy wants to spend more time getting to know you before the bachelorette party," Frankie says.

An image of me with a genitalia-topped hat and pink feather boa pops into my mind, and I shudder. Further embarrassment in front of Cassidy is the last thing I need. "I doubt she wants me to go to her bachelorette party."

"Sure she will!" Magnolia says, waving a hand dismissively. Changing the subject, she asks, "Is Sutton working at the ranch today?"

"He is." I try to not sound disappointed.

After the argument yesterday, Wells and Cassidy left to go to town, probably so Wells wouldn't have to see Sutton. Though, that wouldn't have mattered much, seeing as how Sutton went upstairs at eight-thirty, took a shower, then his sleeping pill, and promptly fell asleep. It's felt like ages since we had a good chance to talk, to hang out, to just be...Sutton and Laine.

Thankfully, Frankie and Magnolia kept me company last night. We stayed up until one in the morning as they taught me all of their favorite card games: crazy eights, rummy, hearts, and some I swear they made up on the spot.

The bakery, like most of the shops in West River, is a part of one long building with half-a-dozen other businesses. But unlike the others, the front of the bakery is painted baby pink. Lace curtains hang in the windows. It looks like it could be a set from *Steel Magnolias*.

Cassidy is already sitting at one of the tables inside. The ruffled floral dress she wears matches the bakery's charming aesthetic, and she has pulled her copper hair back in a loose bun. Somehow, she looks even more beautiful than she did yesterday. Her emerald eyes are on me instantly.

As we take our seats around the table, mine directly across from Cassidy's, I notice how gracefully she moves, how at ease she seems. If she's as nervous as I am, she doesn't show it. I guess *she* shouldn't be nervous. After all, she's the one that dumped Sutton. She has the high ground.

"Thank you for coming, girls," Cassidy says, tipping her head to the side.

"We wouldn't miss it," Magnolia responds. It's hard to imagine that Magnolia could actually like the person who dated two of her sons—and broke one of their hearts—but her smile sells it.

"And I'm so sorry about yesterday, Lainey," Cassidy says.

"It was all a big misunderstanding. I think Sutton and I just got...caught up in emotions."

My stomach lurches, but I force myself to return Cassidy's grin. Before I can say anything, Magnolia interjects.

"What happened yesterday?" Her eyes dart between Cassidy, Frankie, and me, her mouth downturned. I can see her mind reeling on about the worst-case scenario.

"Nothing!" Frankie and I say simultaneously, just like we did yesterday to Wells. And just like Wells, Magnolia doesn't buy it.

Frankie's attempt at a smile looks painful. "Cassidy and Sutton were just hugging, right?" She narrows her eyes at Cassidy.

For all that Frankie and I know, more than "just a hug" could have happened. But I can't imagine that—Sutton wouldn't cross that line.

"We were just...embracing each other," Cassidy says.

Gross. Why couldn't she have just said *hug?* Sure, it wasn't the kind of hug *I* would give an ex. It was weirdly long, weirdly intense. But still, it was a hug.

I notice Cassidy's gaze flickering to me briefly, as if she's trying to gauge my reaction. It's clear that she's aware of the friction in the air between us, but we both refuse to let it show.

Cassidy leans in slightly. "I promise you, Lainey, I have absolutely no intention of coming between you and Sutton. I know things have been a little awkward, but I genuinely want us to be on good terms. After all, you're a part of Sutton's life now."

Cassidy is a little too soap opera right now to feel genuine. I nod anyway.

When an employee brings out our first round of cake slices, she stops directly in front of me. Her round cheeks ball up with a grin.

"Are you the famous Laine?" she asks, hands on her hips.

Clearing my throat, I say. "Famous? Not quite. But Laine? Yes."

"There's been quite a lot of chatter around town about you," she explains. "I was wondering when I'd get to meet Sutton's new girl."

I laugh weakly. West River is a tiny town, and it must really be desperate for gossip if *I'm* the preeminent topic. "Well, now that we've met, you can tell everyone how charming and funny I am," I joke with a wink. "And gorgeous too. And don't forget humble."

The woman laughs heartily, slapping my shoulder. Cassidy rolls her eyes to nobody in particular. We work our way through ten different combinations of cake and frostings. It's my dream, trying all flavors without having to personally commit to any of them. If not for Cassidy's occasional glare, I would be having the time of my life.

As we're polishing off the final few samples, Cassidy leans her elbows on the table and props her chin in her hands, tilting toward me. "Lainey," she says, a mischievous look on her face, "I'm sure all of this wedding talk has you thinking."

Play dumb. "It has me thinking that cake testings should really be a more common occurrence."

Cassidy smirks. She knows I'm being avoidant. "When do you think you and Sutton will get married?"

Fake relationship or not, her bluntness takes me off guard, and I inhale a mouthful of cake crumbs, coughing loudly into my fist to clear them from my throat. I try to laugh through it. "We've only been dating for a couple of months. And with him starting at Imagineer Books soon and me just starting at *Wonderings*, it's not the best time for another big life change."

"But when you know, you know, right? And I'm sure you already know if he's the one." Cassidy squints at me like she's trying to pry directly into my thoughts. When I don't respond right away, she gives me an exaggerated look of confusion. "Sutton *really* hasn't talked about it? That's so strange. When we were only *fourteen*, he started talking about spending our lives together. I guess every relationship is different. Life is funny that way."

I give her a single, abrupt laugh. "And now you're marrying his brother. Life is funny that way."

Cassidy's gaze pierces through me. I mentally kick myself for letting my words slip out with no filter. Beside us, Frankie tries to hide her laughter with a palm over her mouth.

Magnolia jumps in with an attempt at diffusing the situation. "I think we should show Laine around West River."

Yes, please. Get me out of here.

Frankie jumps up and holds a hand out to me. "Let's do it." Clearly, I'm not the only one wanting to get away from the awkwardness.

"You guys go ahead," Cassidy says flippantly. "I have some things I need to do.

Frankie and I don't object. Magnolia looks like she's about to, but Frankie pulls her by the arm, a subtle pleading behind her eyes.

As soon as we're outside and out of Cassidy's line of vision, Frankie grumbles, "Ugh. She's the worst."

"Don't say that," Magnolia chides. "She'll be your sister soon."

"Don't remind me," Frankie says.

Magnolia's mouth pops open. "Francesca!"

Frankie makes a face at her mother's use of her real name. "Ever since the engagement, Cassidy's just been so..." She makes a guttural, groaning sound. "And you should have *seen* the way she hugged Sutton yesterday, Mom. It was like watching a Venus fly trap with one of its victims."

I shake my head, laughing. "You can't just blame her. If

Sutton didn't want to hug her, he shouldn't have. He's not a helpless little fly."

"Around her, he might as well be," Frankie says.

I'm shocked to hear Frankie talking like this. Even when she was mad at Wells at dinner my first night here, she played it off with a joke.

As if reading my mind, Frankie adds, "I'm just protective of Sutton. That's all." She sighs. "Usually Cassidy isn't so bad."

"Cass is on edge from the wedding prep," Magnolia says, looping her elbow with mine. "She makes Wells happy, and that's what matters."

Magnolia shifts the conversation. She asks me about my family, my hobbies, my work. We talk about school, and I tell her my side of the story of meeting Sutton for the first time. She smiles when I tell her that he spent a lot of time not only with me but also with my parents.

Main Street in West River is only a half-mile long. There are exactly two crosswalks in town, one on either end of Main. We pass an old-fashioned candy store, a western-wear shop, two restaurants and one cafe, a jewelry store, and even the radio station. Frankie waves to the man working at the microphone on the other side of the window. He must be at least eighty years old. He waves back enthusiastically.

The longer we walk, the more I notice people's eyes on me. Though West River only has two thousand residents, there are still dozens of people walking along Main Street. And every single one stares at me. I never felt like I drew any double-takes in the city, but here, it's like I'm an animal in a zoo, being watched—sometimes with apprehension, sometimes with delight, but always unabashedly.

I whistle. "What, is there no cable in West River?"

"Not a lot happens in a town this size. I wouldn't be

surprised if you show up on the front page of the paper," Magnolia quips, giving me a very Sutton-esque half-smile.

Frankie bumps my shoulder. "Haven't you been listening to the radio? I've been giving Laine Rodriguez updates at the top of every hour."

U

SUTTON IS STILL WORKING when we get back to the ranch, and both Frankie and Magnolia have some work to do, so I take advantage of the alone time by walking along a tree-hugged trail beyond the front clearing. It's beautiful, undeniably, but it's also too quiet. There aren't any sounds of clogged traffic, construction, or overlapping conversations like there always are in the city. It's eerie.

In the silence, my mind races. First, I scan the pines and ponder the question of how close a bear would have to be to me before I would see it. Pretty dang close, I think.

Then, I think about Sutton.

I think about his hug with Cassidy, realizing I would rather run into a bear than run into the two of them together again. I think about his breathing, soft and steady as he slept beside me. Mostly, I spend my time trying to *not* dwell on the mental image of Sutton chopping wood, sans shirt. Because friends don't think about friends shirtless.

When my efforts to stop thinking about Sutton prove fruitless, I pop my headphones in and pull up a playlist on my phone. In my pre-trip prep, I spent hours listening to country and folk music. Now, it's my guilty pleasure. And John Denver's voice cranked up to max volume is just what I need to get my mind off things.

Once the sun descends in the sky, I turn back to the house. I was careful to stay close to the tree line when hiking, just to be sure I didn't get lost.

Inside the house, the living room is vacant, so I continue upstairs, throwing my bag on the bed. I almost take my headphones out, but worried more errant thoughts will cascade through the silence, I keep them in, deciding I'll wait until the last second before my shower to take them off and hope the roar of the water will be distraction enough at that point.

But when I open the door to the bathroom, I collide with a solid wall on the other side. I let out a surprised yelp as I stumble back, yanking my headphones from my ears.

Sutton stands there, his post-shower towel barely clinging to his hips, his damp curls kissing his forehead. His deep eyes widen, and there's a flash of red across his cheeks.

A jumbled, "Whoops," is the best I can croak out. My gaze involuntarily drifts over the planes of Sutton's body and the "S" tattoo on his ribs. Water droplets cling to the definition of his torso.

He stammers. "I should have knocked."

"You were the one coming out," I remind him.

"Right. I guess you should have, then," he says, one corner of his mouth twitching.

Before I can think of something witty to say, I hear a voice behind me. "Would you—Oh! Sorry." Magnolia is covering her face with one hand, but I can still see her blushing. "The door was open, so I... Sorry to intrude." Her laugh is laced with embarrassment. "I was just coming to see if you two want to play rummy with Frankie and me. But if you're busy—"

"I'm in," I interject. Magnolia's and Sutton's blushing must be contagious, because my own face warms. I follow directly behind Magnolia, not wanting to spend one more awkward second in that room.

Sutton joins us soon after, and we play card games for hours. I'm especially grateful for Magnolia and Frankie's teachings yesterday, because it means I'm able to beat Sutton more often than not. But no matter how many times I win, he is relentless with his playful trash talk. He must have had a good day at the ranch, because he's smiling more and more. He even plays up the "fake dating" card, shooting me flirty looks, tracing circles on my knee, and staring at my mouth whenever I talk.

And when Sutton finally does win, on our eighth or ninth game (I've lost count), he leans over and kisses me triumphantly. It leaves me breathless, but he sends me a wink after he draws back, reminding me this is all a farce.

I try not to feel disappointed.

17

SUTTON

"SHE'S PRETTY GREAT, HUH?" Mom asks, joining me in the barn. We look out the open sliding door to see Laine. She's been busy all day, first interviewing the cook and then taking pictures for her *Wonderings* articles.

"Yeah," I exhale, looking back at Duke's horse before Laine can distract me from the question.

Mom wipes some dirt off her overalls. Even though she's been working in the garden all afternoon, she still did her makeup and hair. Despite growing up on a ranch, she's always loved to dress up.

"Your dad's coming home tonight," Mom reminds me, trying to act nonchalant about it.

"Yeah. Too bad, though. I was just starting to feel comfortable here," I say, not entirely sarcastically.

"Your father has been going through a lot lately," Mom says, her voice as gentle as ever. "Give him some grace."

"And what exactly is he going through that could justify the way he acted our first night here? Did some cattle get out of the fence? Did a cowboy show up to work drunk? Let me guess, property taxes are rising again. You'd think by now he'd be better at handling the stress of the ranch."

The corners of Mom's mouth pinch. "Even with your father's attitude, is it good to be home?" She steps closer, eyes brimming with hope.

I smile, determined to get the smile back on her face. "It *is* good to be back. Don't get me wrong, there's so much about New York that I love. But I didn't realize how much I missed it here. I forgot all the things that make Silver Ridge special."

"And it's even more special when you have someone to share it with," Mom says, smiling mostly to herself.

"I *had* someone I shared it with before," I remind her, chuckling. "Cass practically lived here during high school."

"But that was different, don't you think? Different from you and Laine?" Mom asks, her brows furrowing. "You didn't...truly love her, did you?"

"I think I did," I murmur. Mom's shoulders droop, like she's a deflated balloon. "It was different, though. Cass and I knew each other our entire lives. We were in the same classes, the same friend group. It was easy to be with her. Like, I loved her by default. But I never felt..."—I pause, searching for the right way to express it—"*enlivened* with her. It wasn't soul deep. I loved her as a best friend, as someone who was always there with me and for me." At the sight of Mom's furrowed brows, I add, "But don't worry, I don't have any lingering feelings for her—whatsoever."

"That's good. I was a touch worried about the—Oh, how did Cassidy put it...the '*embrace*.'" Mom has to fight off a laugh.

"It was nothing. I thought it would be weird *not* to hug her. But when I did, she started crying, and I didn't want to make her feel bad. Wells just got the wrong idea."

"I see," Mom hums. "You might want to make the terms

of the 'embrace' clear to Laine, though. She seemed a little uneasy about it."

"I doubt that very much," I say, rolling my eyes. Of course, only I would know why Mom's assumption is ridiculous.

"Honest!" She laughs. "She obviously didn't want to make a big deal out of it, but I could see a touch of jealousy. It was sweet, really."

Jealous. I roll the word around in my mind, imagining, even if only for a moment, what it would be like if Mom was right.

"You know," she says, "I was going to make a run to Missoula to get some things for the wedding. Maybe you and Laine should go. You've hardly had time, just the two of you, since you got here."

I smile just thinking about it. Not only because it means I can see less of my father when he gets home tonight, but also because, though I've seen Laine every day since we arrived, I somehow still miss her.

WHEN LAINE FINISHES TAKING PICTURES, her hair is ruffled, and her lipstick is almost completely worn off. Those deep brown eyes are at half-mast. But when she sees me on the porch, she perks up, hurrying her sluggish steps, trying to hide her exhaustion.

"How did the pictures go?"

"Don't ask," she says, laughing weakly. "They're probably terrible. It's been too long since I've been behind the camera."

"I'm sure they're good. You're a jack of all trades," I assure her.

"And master of none," she mumbles. I can tell that she's

trying to be lighthearted, but there's a bitter sincerity to her words.

Out of fake-dating habit, I wrap an arm around her shoulder, even though nobody is around to see it. "Don't worry, I have the perfect distraction for you. I've been wanting to show my gratitude to you for helping me out these two weeks. Do you remember on graduation night when we went to a different restaurant for every course of the meal?"

Her entire face lights up. "How could I forget? It was paradise."

"I don't want to get your hopes up too much, because there's no way we can replicate that in West River."

Laine's face falls. "Why not?"

"Because there aren't enough restaurants for each course."

"Ah, fair point."

"*But* I have the next best thing. One word. Two syllables. *Costco.*"

"You're kidding!" Laine slides out from under my arm so she can face me head-on. She looks like I just told her we are going to Paris, not to a grocery superstore.

I couldn't fight off my smile if I tried. Laine is so radiant when she's happy. It's like the air around her actually starts to shimmer.

"My mom needs some things for the wedding, and I remember you once said that you dream of going to Costco just to visit all the sample tables. Want to join me?"

"Yes! But let me go get changed. Costco is far too romantic of a date for this outfit." She gestures at her dusty bootcut jeans and the pearl snap shirt she borrowed from Frankie.

Laine must be really looking forward to our night of sampling, because she's downstairs in less than thirty minutes. I've never known her to take less than twice that to get ready. While she still has her red cowgirl boots on, she paired them with a short dress with applique flowers all over it. She's like a garden come to life.

"Am I overdressed?" she asks as we're walking to my truck.

I didn't know that word was in Laine's dictionary. "For Costco? No such thing." It's a lie, of course. She did overdress—most people there will be in jeans like the ones she just changed out of—but she looks too damn cute to say any different.

I open the passenger door for Laine and offer her my hand, helping lift her into the car.

During the entire hour-and-a-half drive to Missoula, Laine and I can hardly get a breath in because we're in constant conversation. Frankie and Mom have fallen in love with her. As a result, they've been practically attached to Laine's hip.

It's been too long since we got to be alone together.

"How have you felt, being back at the ranch?" Laine asks, right as Costco comes into view.

"Surprisingly good. I missed the mountains. I missed my family—or, most of them. I missed the town. And even though I was sick-to-my-stomach anxious about coming home, it's gone relatively smooth."

"Aside from your dad being a jerk and your brother nearly punching you?" Laine jokes.

I scoff. "Right. And about that...you know nothing happened between me and Cass, right? It really was just a hug."

"An awkwardly long hug," Laine adds, half-smiling, half-grimacing.

I find a parking space and put the truck in park. It groans for a moment before quieting back down. "Cassidy started crying when we hugged," I explain. "And I didn't want to hurt her feelings by pulling away too fast."

"Okay," Laine says, her voice almost a whisper.

"I just—I felt like you should know that. I want to be clear that I have no feelings left for Cassidy *whatsoever*."

"Okay," she repeats, more convinced this time. She nods to herself. Then, switching gears, she says, "Come on, cowboy. We've got samples to test."

We spend almost two hours in Costco, going through each aisle and filling our carts with things from Mom's list. Laine looks around the warehouse the way tourists look around in Times Square.

A few times, when I'm not pushing the cart, I find myself reaching out for Laine's hand. It's almost scary how natural it feels.

I do my best to focus on the tasks at hand and not on how beautiful Laine looks in that dress. The easiest way to do that is to be on the constant search for the sample tables. By the end of the shopping trip, we've tried every one. Even if a sample is mediocre, if it's cold when it's supposed to be warm (or warm when it's supposed to be cold), we rave about it. The novelty doesn't wear off, and the only reason we leave the store is because they're closing.

"This has been the best fake date ever," Laine says, holding her classic Costco food court hot dog with the same loving carefulness one would hold a new baby. "That place was like another planet."

"I'm glad it lived up to your expectations."

Laine's eyes land on something on the bulletin board on the outside wall of Costco. She walks up to it, mouth agape, like she's in a trance. "Oh. My. Goodness. We have to go." I follow her gaze to a flyer for a bar where, according to the ad, there's line dancing and live music every night. "Please, can we go?" Laine asks, rocking onto her tiptoes.

I smirk. "You want to go to a place called *The Cowboy Cantina* on a Tuesday night?"

"Desperately."

While I'm not as spontaneous as Laine, I'd do anything to make her happy. "Sure. Let's try it. But I'll warn you, there's probably nothing 'cantina' about it." I load the food into the coolers in the truck bed. "The nearest place to us to get authentic Mexican food is Albuquerque."

The bar is on the outskirts of town. Its flickering neon sign, though probably once vibrant, now emits a feeble glow that barely manages to pierce through the darkness of the night. The building itself seems to sag under the weight of time, its wooden front weathered and worn. The dirt parking lot has no curbs, so cars and trucks are packed in haphazardly.

Even from outside, we hear the sound of boots on the dance floor and the twang of a country band. Once we go through the creaky front door, we're greeted by a cloud of stale air and cigarette smoke. The scent mingles with the unmistakable odor of years' worth of spilled beer.

Despite all of that, and despite it being a Tuesday night, the atmosphere is electric, alive with the energy of the crowd. Couples and friends bounce around the dance floor in amateur synchronicity. Though the band playing on the makeshift stage won't be winning a Grammy anytime soon, nobody seems to mind. Or maybe they're just too drunk to notice.

"Wow," Laine breathes, her eyes sparkling.

I grin at her reaction. "Quite the experience, right?"

"Very *Footloose*."

The song drifts to an end, and people line back up for the next one. Without a second thought, Laine pulls me into the center of the floor, radiating with excitement.

As the music starts, so do the dancers. Thankfully, the footwork is simple.

"It's a good thing I wore my cowgirl boots!" Laine shouts

over the music. Focusing on the woman in front of her, she copies her steps. It only takes a minute for Laine to get the hang of it. And then every movement of hers is fluid.

"And it's a good thing I was a dance major for a semester!" she shouts.

Laine is dressed nicer than anyone else here, but even in the classic Montanan uniform of blue jeans and a simple shirt, she would stand out—her smile, her arms, the way her head throws back with laughs of delight. The dress just adds to it, hugging her curves, accentuating her swinging hips.

At one point, I grab Laine's arm and swing her into me, and she squeals. "Okay, Kevin Bacon!"

As the music continues to pulse through the dimly lit space, I find myself caught up in the energy. Laine's laughter is infectious, and I get swept away by her excitement. She moves with a surprising grace, her steps becoming more confident with each beat of the music. I'm not surprised, though. Laine approaches everything in life with an open-hearted enthusiasm. Her confidence and authenticity are like a magnetic force, drawing me in and making me feel alive in a way I haven't in a long time.

The song reaches its peak, and the dance soon ends. Laine's laughter mixes with the cheers of the crowd. She turns toward me, her eyes bright and her cheeks flushed from the exhilaration of the dance and the stuffy heat of the room. The next song starts, one much slower, and couples turn to face each other, still out of breath as they sway.

Laine and I gravitate together, and her hand slips into mine. I pull her close, resting my other hand on the small of her back. The warmth of her body feels like it might set my skin on fire. I look down into her eyes, and for a moment, the world around us seems to fade away. Maybe the other couples can catch a breath during the slow dance, but my pulse is racing faster than ever.

As the song continues, Laine rests her head against my shoulder, her breath warm against my neck. Our bodies move as one, and I can't help but be aware of every point of contact between us—the press of her hand against my chest, the brush of her cheek against my shoulder. The curves and angles of our bodies blend together.

And I know with certainty: I'm done for.

I knew I had feelings for Laine—feelings I struggled to ignore—while I was her TA. Feelings I have since tried to forget, thanks to her "no dating" rule. But in this moment, with the world focused right here on this sticky dance floor, I know I can't hide my feelings any longer.

I open my mouth, unsure of exactly *how* I should confess what I feel, but still knowing I need to. But I'm only able to murmur Laine's name when a disruption breaks through the anxious pounding between my ears.

"Hey, gorgeous, mind if I cut in?" a voice slurs, the words dripping with insincerity.

I look over to see a guy around our age leering at Laine. Instinctively, I tighten my grip around her.

Laine smiles at him politely but shakes her head. "No, thanks."

The guy's smile falters, eyes narrowing. "Come on, sweetheart, don't be like that."

"She said no." My voice comes out harsh and rough, like a true Davis man.

His demeanor shifts from annoyance to aggression in an instant. He reaches out for Laine's wrist. I push his arm away and step in front of Laine.

"Hey, back off," I demand, trying to keep my control.

The guy's face turns red. I can tell by the smell of his breath that cheap whiskey—and lots of it—fuels his aggression. "And who the hell are *you*?"

"Her boyfriend."

He grumbles something under his breath and reaches around me to touch Laine again, this time his hand grasping at her hip.

Without fully realizing what I'm doing, I'm shoving the guy's chest so hard he trips over his boots, landing hard on his back. "Don't touch her."

He's so drunk he struggles to stand. I take the opportunity to guide Laine toward the door. "Let's go," I murmur. "Are you—"

Before I can finish my question, I'm being knocked against the wall from behind. I spin around just in time for the guy's fist to connect with my jaw. Sharp pain webs across my face like a thousand bee stings. My head strikes back against the door frame, but I barely register it. I nudge Laine to the side before balling up my fist, ready to fight back.

But before I can retaliate, Laine puts her arm on mine, and it's as if someone doused me with water, my concern for her overwhelming my anger. "He's not worth it," she urges, her eyes wide.

Laine laces her fingers with mine and pulls me out into the parking lot.

"I'm so sorry," I say once we're in the truck, the doors locked. My adrenaline is wearing off quickly. "Are you okay, Laine?"

She lets out a quick laugh. "Me? You're the one who got *Million Dollar Baby*'d in there."

"You're okay?"

Laine reaches over and holds my face between her hands. "I'm *fine*. I promise."

"I shouldn't have reacted like that. You were having fun. I should have just pushed him outside, not let him ruin the night."

Her hands move down, lingering on my neck, and she scoffs. "You're not the one who grabbed my ass." I make a face of disgust at the thought of what happened, and she adds in a playful tone, "Not that *you* grabbing my ass would ruin anything."

"Hilarious," I say, deadpan, feeling warm all over again.

Laine drops her hands into her lap, and I immediately miss the feeling of them against my skin. "A Costco trip and a bar brawl," she muses. "I'm checking off bucket list items left and right. But we should probably get out of here—getting our tires slashed is *not* on that list."

As we pull out of the parking lot, I rub the back of my head to ease the throb of pain. My palm is wet with something hot and wet. *Shit.* Not wanting to make the night any worse, I keep my hand over the blood, pressing into the cut from the doorframe in an attempt to both slow and hide the bleeding. Apparently, it doesn't work, because it takes only a few moments for Laine to notice the red seeping between my fingers.

"Sutton!"

"I'm fine," I insist, smiling at her and praying that will dismiss her worries.

It doesn't.

"Pull over!"

At the sight of the worry in her eyes, I do as I'm told, the truck rumbling against the gravel as we slow to a stop.

Laine pulls my hand away and directs my head so she can examine the cut. She rakes through my curls. "It's a pretty deep gash," she whispers. "We should go clean you up."

"Let's just get home." She's about to object, so I add, "I promise I'll let you doctor me up there. For now, there might be napkins in the jockey box."

She finds only one napkin, and my blood quickly saturates it after only a minute against my head. Fearing I'll stain the truck's headrest, I yank my shirt over my head, balling it up before handing it to Laine. She tries to protest, but I insist. "It's an old shirt. Don't worry about it."

"You're sure you're alright?" Laine asks, scooting to the middle of the bench seat so she can keep my shirt planted firmly against the back of my head. She uses just enough pressure to keep the mess contained and bleeding under control without hurting me. Her other hand presses against my bare chest, as if she's afraid I'll fall into pieces if she doesn't physically hold me together.

She spends the entire drive like that, her eyes never leaving me aside from the few times her gaze flicks down to my torso. Each time, her face looks a shade pinker.

"You look beautiful," I whisper as we near the end of our drive.

Laine scoffs. "You must have hit your head harder than I realized."

18

LAINE

"WHEN DID you first realize you liked Sutton?" Frankie asks from behind the sound desk.

"I'm supposed to be the one asking the questions, remember?" I glance at Frankie from under my eyelashes. Fake relationship or not, my skin flushes at the mention of Sutton. "Why did you want to buy the radio station?" I ask, desperate to focus on work.

Frankie drums her fingers along with the rhythm of the song playing. "I never thought I would buy it," she explains. "I don't know if I even truly *wanted* to. But you remember Clive?"

I nod, thinking back to the old, weathered man who was working at the station earlier.

"His wife's family started the radio station, and his wife took it over. After she passed, Clive tried to run it himself. He was old, though, and was having a hard time learning the ins and outs. I was working at U of M's student radio station, so when I heard what happened, I offered to work at Clive's whenever I was home. Eventually, Clive told me he was going to sell the station. It was hard to find anyone who wanted to run a station in a tiny town. He was going to settle for selling the transmitter to a bigger station, maybe one in Missoula that could use it to broaden their reach." Frankie's face twists.

"And you didn't want that to happen?"

"No," she says, nearly a gasp. "The station is for *West River*, not for the big city."

I try not to laugh at the thought of Missoula, Montana—population seventy-five thousand—being "the big city."

"We broadcast things like the school lunch menu, birthdays, community events, lost and found. It's all about the locals, *for* the locals. It ties the community together, keeps us close-knit. I couldn't stand to see us lose that."

"What did you major in at U of M?"

Frankie grins and says proudly, "I got my Bachelor of Arts in Music with an emphasis on Composition."

"You didn't want to be a rancher like your father? Or teach dance like your mom?"

"My mom had me in dance from the time I was two all the way up to my high school graduation. But we both knew I cared a lot more about mixing tracks for the recital than actually dancing in it. And while I love being on the ranch part-time—a bit more than part-time with everything going on lately…" Her voice trails. She shakes her head, her expression dropping for a split second before she repaints a wide smile across her cheeks. "Anyway, I need a bit more creativity in my life than the ranch alone can offer. So now, I live the best of both worlds and split my time between the station and the ranch."

I nod, jotting down interview notes. "Do you still compose your own songs?"

Frankie narrows her gaze. "On the record, you can say something poetic like 'songwriting will always have a piece of my heart.' But off the record, no. I haven't been able to write anything since breaking up with Caleb."

She says his name as if I'm supposed to know who that is, but I just raise my eyebrows.

"Sutton never told you about my ex?" After I shake my head, Frankie clarifies. *"Caleb Carter?"*

"I don't think so…"

"And the name doesn't sound at *all* familiar?"

I'm drawing a blank. "Should it?"

Frankie laughs, and her freckled nose crinkles. "As if I couldn't love you more. You have no idea how refreshing this is. Okay, still off the record, I dated this guy, Caleb Carter, all throughout high school and half of college. We started a band together. Well, convinced he was the one with all the 'star power,' he put our songs—which I wrote, by the way—out himself. One went viral, even hit number one on the country charts, and he took all the credit. And now, he's one of the most popular up-and-coming country artists."

"You're kidding!" It's hard to think about anyone being able to do Frankie wrong.

"And now, all anyone seems to talk about in West River is how great he is. It makes me want to poke my eyes out. And I get requests *every* day to play his music at the station." Frankie fake gags.

"I need to hear all about this loser," I insist, tilting forward.

"I'm afraid we don't have enough time for that. I could fill a book with all the drama that has come from Caleb Carter being in my life."

"Wow," I exhale, leaning back in my chair. "So, you're twenty-four, already you've graduated college, bought a radio station, and wrote number-one songs?"

"Pretty great, right?" Frankie practically glows from the praise.

"How do you stay confident in yourself?" I ask. "I can't order a sandwich without second-guessing my toppings."

"It's important to have a vision in life. To know what you want and love yourself enough to go for it, to make your life *yours*. For me, it's the station. When I see how it brings the community together, it reaffirms my purpose."

I nod, scribbling down her words. "That's inspiring, Frankie. To have that kind of clarity and conviction."

She smiles warmly, a hint of nostalgia in her eyes. "I wasn't always this way. I had to be very cautious about questioning myself, especially when Caleb's success took off. But I knew that comparing myself to him was pointless. I had my own path to walk." Frankie claps her hands. "So, any other questions?"

I glance at my phone, where the recording is ticking on. We've been at it for nearly two hours, but I still feel unsure. "Nothing else I can think of."

"Great! Then back to *my* question. When did you realize you had feelings for my brother?"

Afraid I might project my nerves, and therefore my lying, I resist the urge to fiddle with my jewelry. "You know…Over time."

Frankie's eye roll makes it clear she won't take that for an answer.

"Fine," I groan playfully. "Looking back, it's a wonder that I didn't have feelings for him right off the bat." The image of Sutton standing on stage during the date auction flashes through my mind, and it suddenly feels twice as warm in the room. "But he was my TA, and I needed him as a tutor, not as a boyfriend."

Frankie waits, semi-patiently, through a long pause. After a while, though, she prods me on. "You still haven't explained when you finally started to like him."

"I didn't want to date Sutton," I admit. *I still don't...right?* "My parents were college sweethearts, were married for almost thirty years, and then, one day, realized they didn't love each other." My breaths quicken. "I guess that, after a few failed college relationships of my own, I was afraid to settle down. I swore"—*swear*— "that I would take a long break from dating."

"But?"

I take a deep breath, steeling myself against the rush of emotions threatening to swallow me whole. How do I explain the tangled mess of feelings I have for her brother when I'm still trying to make sense of them myself?

"But," I begin, my voice trembling with uncertainty, "then I saw Sutton—*really* saw him. Not as my TA or my tutor. But as him."

Memories flood back, bringing with them a wave of warmth and confusion and a nagging deep in my core.

"It was in the quiet moments," I continue, "the stolen glances across the lecture hall, the late-night study sessions that stretched into the early hours of the morning. It was in the way he listened—truly listened—to every worry I had, every doubt I shared. Somehow, even without speaking, he made sure that I would be okay—that *everything* would be okay."

I chew on my lip. "It felt like...like I was standing on the edge of a cliff, unsure whether to step back or leap into loving him," my voice trembles. "And then one day, I realized that, somewhere along the way, I had jumped—fallen, really —without even realizing."

Frankie's face lights up with an infectious grin as she leans forward, her eyes sparkling with excitement.

"I'm so happy you jumped," she declares, her voice filled with genuine love. "From the first time Sutton told me about you—the night after your first date, or tutoring session, or whatever you want to call it—I knew he felt something for you."

I listen intently, the tangle of confusion in my mind scrambling as Frankie speaks.

"He couldn't stop talking about you," she continues, her enthusiasm bubbling over. "He had this spark in his voice whenever your name came up, this...this softness that I'd never heard before. It was like he was under some sort of spell, completely smitten by you."

She's exaggerating.

"I think he's drawn to you in a way that he doesn't even understand himself."

Neither of us speaks for a long time until I ultimately change the subject, asking to take pictures of Frankie and the station for the *Wonderings* article. Frankie obliges, thankfully dropping the topic of Sutton.

Anxious that the photos won't turn out, I take a couple hundred, praying at least a handful will work. Then, as we're about to head to the cafe for some much-needed caffeine, Frankie's phone rings.

"Hey, Mom," Frankie says, winking at me. "Of course I didn't forget." She makes a face at me that says *Oh yeah, I totally forgot.* "Are you sure?" Pause. "Like, *sure*-sure?" She snorts. "Yeah, I'll tell her."

"What did you forget?" I ask when she hangs up.

"I promised I would be at the dress shop for final fittings," Frankie says, fighting a groan. "But the good news is, Cassidy wants you to come. So now, I don't have to suffer alone."

"That can't be a good idea," I say. Not only has my every interaction with Cassidy gone sour, but I was also looking forward to spending more time with Sutton.

"Do *you* want to be the one to tell the bride no?" Frankie asks, the corner of her mouth twitching up. I sigh, and it's enough of a surrender for Frankie, because she continues, "And I hope you like pink."

I raise an eyebrow.

"Because apparently one of Cassidy's bridesmaids dropped out—broken leg—and she wants you to fill in."

"No." My answer is immediate, my voice so harsh it shocks me.

"Please," Frankie begs. "*Please*. I'll be miserable without you. I need you there, a tether to the sane world."

"You've seen how Cassidy is with me."

"I know, I know. But maybe this is a good chance for you two to make amends."

"There's no way she actually wants me to be in her wedding."

"With less than two weeks to the big day, it's either you stand in or the balance of the entire wedding party will be thrown off."

"You're telling me there isn't another girl in West River who can stand in?"

"It's a small town—slim pickings. Besides, maybe this is her waving a white flag."

My scoff communicates more than words ever could.

After fifteen minutes of groveling, I haven't worn Frankie down one bit. No matter how hard I protest, it's no use. It's practically impossible to say no to Frankie.

Of course, West River is too small for a bridal shop, so we have to go back to Missoula for the dress fittings. On the way there, Frankie hands me her aux cord.

"You choose the music," she says.

I push it back to her. "You're the driver—it's your choice."

Frankie's head tips back with a laugh. "Laine, I love you, but this is ridiculous. You say you hate making decisions, so we're going to do some exposure therapy. This isn't an important, life-altering choice. Just pick a song already."

19

SUTTON

FRANKIE KEPT Laine out all night, so I didn't see her again until waking up the next morning. I open my eyes to find her already awake, propped up on one elbow, watching me with a fond smile. Sleep tousled her hair, and delicate pieces of her bangs fell along her forehead. The soft morning light across her chocolate eyes makes them shine like moonlight on a dark lake.

"Good morning," Laine greets, her voice a gentle melody that matches the tranquility of the moment.

I stretch my arms over my head, trying to shake out the lingering drowsiness. Thankfully, the sight of Laine is a stronger energizer than any cup of coffee could be. "How long have you been awake?"

"Not long. The quiet woke me."

I raise my eyebrows.

"It's never this quiet in the city," she justifies.

Noticing my old copy of *Peter Pan* sitting at Laine's hip, I ask, "You get some good reading in?"

"I started it, knowing it was one of your childhood favorites. But I got distracted."

Laine smiles, and warmth swells in my chest. We've been sharing a bed all week, but this is the first time she's been awake before me. It's the first time we've actually talked like this.

"I don't have a lot of these moments," Laine murmurs. "I'm usually so impulsive and fidgety and talkative. It's nice to just…be still with you. It's *easier* to be still when I'm with you."

I shift onto my side, mirroring Laine's position, and prop my head up with my hand. "Well, then, let's be still." I've always known Laine to be a whirlwind of energy, constantly go-go-go. But in this quiet, stolen moment, I get to see a new side of her.

"As much as I like the everyday Laine, I like this side of you too," I confess, my eyes tracing the soft contours of her face.

Laine ducks her head and studies her hands. "Yeah, well, don't get used to it. It doesn't come around often."

I chuckle, my heart pounding. "I like all sides of you, Laine. The exuberant one, the introspective one, and everything in between."

Her eyes meet mine again, and I'm struck by the sincerity in her expression. There's a connection between us that has been growing stronger with every passing day—a connection that's as undeniable as it is unspoken. I've felt drawn to Laine since the first day I met her, and for once, it feels like she might, just *might*, feel a sliver of that.

She reaches out and touches my upper lip. "What's that scar from?"

"Horse-riding accident," I explain. "When I was twelve." I reach my own hand out, gracing my fingertip across Laine's matching scar. Her breath is warm against my palm. "And yours?"

"When I was fifteen, I had a six-week obsession with

gymnastics. I thought I would be the next Nastia Liukin."

"Naturally."

"I gave it up to try my hand at ceramics." She reaches out for my hand resting between us, tracing the ridges of my knuckles absentmindedly.

After a stretch of silence, Laine says, "Thank you for bringing me to West River."

"Have you liked it?"

"More than I even expected. It's beyond beautiful here. And I've loved spending time with your mom and Frankie."

"How have the articles been coming?"

Laine's expression drops a bit. "Okay, I think. I love interviewing everyone, seeing into their lives and living a bit of it through their stories. I just hope it all comes together in my writing. Today I'm going to be interviewing your dad. Hopefully that will give me the final few points I need for my article on modern-day cowboys."

"I'm sure your articles will be great...but are you sure you want to interview *Hank?*"

"He's the lifeblood of the ranch," Laine says, resting her hand atop mine. "This legacy has gone all the way down the Davis line, starting with his great-grandfather. Your dad is the head-honcho, the big buckaroo, the classic cowboy."

"Alright, enough alliteration. Just...just don't let him hurt your feelings."

∪

THOUGH I WAS SUPPOSED to be spending the day working with Bill and the foals again, I find myself sitting under the open window of the porch, eavesdropping on my father's interview. I've never known him to be intentionally rude to someone he doesn't know. On the other hand, I also feel like I don't know my father at all these days. If he *does* step out of line, like he had at dinner, I want to be there for Laine.

She spends nearly an hour at the start of it asking him softball questions. But slowly, she digs deeper.

"Did you always want to take over the ranch?"

Hank is quiet for a few long seconds. "No."

Laine stays silent, allowing for him to expound, which he does after a gruff sigh.

My father's voice is slower than I remember it. Some words blur together, like he has a mouthful of pudding. "I always knew I *would* take it over, but I didn't want to."

I feel a pinch in my chest.

"Why is that?" Laine asks.

"I knew I would take over Silver Ridge because it's what every eldest son in the Davis family does. And for a long time, I was eager to follow suit."

"Until?"

"Until I met my Maggie." My father's earnest tone takes me off guard. "She grew up on a ranch in Texas. I went to work there the winter I turned nineteen. Even though she swore to herself she wouldn't end up with a cowboy, we were inevitable. But Magnolia had big dreams of being a dancer. She even had plans to move to New York City. And before long, I had plans to join her. I told her I would give up anything to be with her. Even though I knew deep down, as a Davis, that might not be possible."

My face contorts. How did I live with my parents for eighteen years, yet they never told me these details? And how is Laine so good at making people feel comfortable enough to share things like this? I try to picture my father in the city, but I come up blank. It's like trying to imagine a new color.

"What happened?" Laine asks after a pause long enough

that it's clear Hank wouldn't keep talking without being prodded.

"My father passed away from a heart attack. It was my duty to return home and continue his work." Hank's voice is harsher now, and I know the next words that are coming before he says them. "I only wish Sutton had that same loyalty to the family."

Bitterness coats my mouth. I try to swallow it down.

For a while, neither one speaks, but Laine eventually breaks the silence. "Sutton dreams of being an editor."

"Crazy dreams are for children," Hank says gruffly. "It's time for him to grow up."

"I know you don't believe that," Laine says, and I can perfectly imagine the smile on her face. "Sutton has worked hard to be an editor, and he's nearly there."

"He's not living in New York to chase dreams. He's in New York to run away from his real life."

Laine sighs. "He's been happy being back, you know. It's like he's whole, able to be Montana-Sutton *and* New York-Sutton. Editor *and* rancher. And I think if you give him the space to do a little of both, you might see more of him around here."

"And what makes you think I want him here now?"

Laine ignores him, pivoting the conversation. "You said you've been running Silver Ridge since you were nineteen. What's that? Fifteen years now?"

My father laughs. *Really* laughs. I can't remember the last time I heard it. Not since Duke passed away, surely. "Just about that, yeah," he says.

"Nineteen years old? You were still a kid. That's a lot of stress for someone that age."

"It wasn't easy."

"And you always expected to take it over. Imagine Sutton,

never thinking he would have that responsibility, thinking it would be Duke's to run. And then, as he's still mourning the loss of his brother, Sutton is asked to uproot the life he had been working toward. At nineteen years old. Just a kid."

My father doesn't speak for a long time, and I wonder if he's glaring Laine down. He's not someone who is used to being contradicted. But then he says, his voice softened with a strange amusement, "Is this why you wanted to interview me? So you could defend Sutton?"

"That wasn't the plan," Laine says, chuckling. "He's pretty amazing, though. And I'd hate for you to miss out on enjoying that firsthand."

"Do you love him?"

Laine lets out a sharp breath. "Sutton?" After a long pause, she relents. "Your son is hard not to love."

Laine's words, though obviously embellished for the sake of upholding our fake-dating story, are like a soothing balm to the knot in my chest. From my vantage point under the window, I hang on every word exchanged between my father and Laine. Their conversation shed light on hidden corners of my family's story that I never had the chance to explore.

There's another silence, and I can imagine my father studying Laine, his brows likely furrowed in contemplation. "You're not like most city folk I've met," he finally says.

"Oh?"

"You've got a way of understanding without judgment, of getting people to open up. And you do it without being nosy. At this point, you might know me better than my own children do."

"Maybe you should change that," Laine says.

He harrumphs.

"Maybe you're like me," she continues. Hank must make a face, because Laine laughs. "I know, I know, that's a weird thought. But sometimes I feel like I'm a pointillism painting, those ones made up of thousands of tiny dots. I think those I keep at a safe distance will like me, because they're seeing a big, overarching picture of who I am. But anyone close to me will see that I'm just a mess when it comes to the details."

"You're saying I'm a mess?"

"Not any more of a mess than me, if that's any consolation."

My dad's laughter rumbles again.

♕

TWO HOURS LATER, I walk into the guest room to find Laine applying makeup. Her dress fits snugly at her chest, then flares out in layers at her waist. It's complete with puffy, see-through sleeves. She looks beautiful.

"Is it too much?" Laine asks, eyeing me in the mirror's reflection.

I grin. "That depends on what our plans are for tonight."

Laine turns around to face me, grimacing. "I forgot to tell you? Apparently, being a bridesmaid for Cassidy means going to her bachelorette party tonight in Missoula." She bites her red bottom lip. "Is that...weird for you, though?"

"My fake girlfriend going to my ex-slash-soon-to-be-sister-in-law's bachelorette party? What could be weird about that?" My voice is drenched in sarcasm. "Trust me, in a town this small, everyone gets all entangled in each other's lives. It's not the first time something like this has happened in West River."

"I'd rather just stay here and be with you," Laine murmurs, twisting the rings on her fingers.

"I happen to be going to a bachelor party tonight, so we're even."

"Who do you think will have the hotter strippers?" Laine teases.

I laugh, already thinking about the awkward night ahead. If Wells is any bit as much of a wild partier that he was in high school, this could be interesting.

Not wanting to think any more about the things that await me tonight, I ask, "How did the interview with my dad go?"

Laine snorts. "Should I be worried that your thoughts jumped from strippers to your father within two seconds?"

"Har-har," I deadpan. "Was he nice to you?"

"Surprisingly so. He seemed tired—exhausted, really—but I think it went well."

"Yeah," I hum. "Growing up, he would be pretty beat after coming home from work in the evenings. But it seems like it's worse now."

"I compared him to a pointillism painting, and he seemed to appreciate it." Laine says, telling me her analogy. "If you get too close to him, it's easy to miss the big picture."

"I think he's more like the sun," I say, pushing a stray hair out of Laine's face. "Warm from afar, but stand too close, and you get burnt."

Laine thinks on that for a moment before saying with a sideways grin, "Yeah, I think he'd prefer my analogy."

"You're probably right."

"Have you talked to Wells lately?" Laine asks out of the blue.

"No. No, not really," I mutter.

"Well, I think we need to get better at selling this thing between us when he's around," Laine says. "He seemed happiest with you when he thought you were too busy with your new girlfriend to worry about Cassidy."

"We'll sell it," I say, trying to keep from smiling too wide.

A knock sounds at the door, and Frankie peeks her head in. "Time to go, Lainey!"

"Have fun tonight," Laine says to me. She tiptoes up, dips her head back just enough for me to understand she's subtly motioning to Frankie, and I meet her in a kiss. "Don't make out with any strippers," I murmur, quiet enough so only she can hear.

20

LAINE

THE ONLY THING worse than wearing a pink cowboy hat topped with male genitalia on it is wearing it around your fake-boyfriend's sister and ex. It's even worse than I imagined. All the bridesmaids have one. Cassidy's hat is glittery white and has a veil attached to the back.

"Thanks for coming," Cassidy says, pulling me into a hug. "And thank you for filling the last-minute bridesmaid spot." Judging by her eager affection, she must already be on her way to getting drunk.

"Grab your shirts too!" Cassidy's sister says, shoving hot-pink tank tops toward me and Frankie. As the maid of honor, she's hosting the party at her apartment.

Frankie and I unfurl our shirts at the same time. Mine says *Save a Horse, Ride a Cowboy*, and hers says *Saddlin' Up Forever*.

"Oh, sorry, I wore a dress," I say, sending a mental thank-you to myself for making that choice.

"It's mandatory!" Cassidy's sister insists. "You can borrow some shorts from me."

"Nice try," Frankie whispers to me, stifling a laugh.

Within a few minutes, all six bridesmaids are in matching shirts and hats. The shorts I'm borrowing are a bit too tight and too short, but I try to ignore it. I swig my drink back, hoping it'll dull the inevitable onslaught of continued embarrassment that will be on its way. Normally, a goofy party isn't something I'd protest. But every girl here, aside from Frankie, gives me the same suspicious look. Meanwhile, Frankie stares back at them all, her narrowed eyes a *just try it* warning.

"You're Laine, right?" one bridesmaids asks me finally. Aside from Shania Twain's "I Feel Like a Woman" playing on the speaker, the room goes silent. Everyone's dagger gaze is on me.

"Well, I'm certainly not the stripper," I joke.

The party starts off about as I expected—naughty Pictionary and gift-giving at varying degrees of spice. I'm sure Frankie can't feel much more comfortable than me, especially with all the talk about how Wells will "really *love*" Cassidy's new outfits, but Frankie somehow keeps her bubbly demeanor at the forefront—at least until one of the bridesmaids starts a game of Never Have I Ever.

At first, it's fine. Never have I ever sent a dirty text, or gone skinny dipping, or been with a friend's ex. But quickly, things take a turn.

"Never have I ever...kissed two brothers," one bridesmaid says, grinning mischievously at Cassidy, then at me. The look she gives me gnaws at my stomach.

"So gross," Frankie whispers, her face twisting as she watches Cassidy take a long, almost victorious swig of her beer.

"Who was better, Wells or Sutton?" someone asks.

Frankie and I swap horrified looks.

"That's *so* not fair!" Cassidy giggles.

Everyone, aside from Frankie and me, groan in protest of Cassidy's discretion, and she quickly gives in.

"Well, there's always something special about your first. Sutton and I had plenty of practice over the years, but we were always sort of…vanilla," Cassidy says, eyes flicking to me for a split second. Her words slur, and I wonder if she would offer all this up if she wasn't two beers and three shots deep. "But Wells really knows how to take charge. And you know how he hates being shown up by his big brother."

The girls fall into a fit of loud laughter. The pit in my stomach deepens, and I look down, half expecting there to be a hole clear through the middle of it.

"Is Sutton still vanilla, Laine?" Cassidy's sister asks.

"I plead the fifth," I mutter, heat prickling over my skin.

"I think I'm going to be sick," Frankie says under her breath. Louder, she announces, "I'm going to top off my drink."

Leaping from my seat, I follow a step behind her.

As soon as we're up and retreating to the kitchen, the front door opens, and a man with a snap-button shirt, baggy, lumpy sweats, and (no surprise) a cowboy hat comes in, a Bluetooth speaker in his hand. He smirks at Frankie and me.

Is he really a—

Before I can finish that thought, he strips his sweats off in one smooth motion to reveal a pair of briefs under ass-less chaps. Frankie ducks her head and steps into the kitchen with me right behind.

From the living room, we hear, "Howdy, ladies," and a chorus of excited squeals. Soon after, some song starts about shaking it for the birds and bees.

I look down at my bedazzled innuendo shirt and too-tight cutoffs and sigh. "Tonight is an all-time low."

As if on cue, the stripper's voice booms from the living room. "Who's ready for the ride of their life?" We sip our drinks and listen to the excited chaos unfolding in the living room, unable to hold our laughter in when we hear a girl shriek. From my sanctuary in the kitchen, and with Frankie at my side, it all feels a little less mortifying.

U

EVENTUALLY, Cassidy's sister calls us a couple of Ubers to take us to a bar. Somehow, I end up in the middle seat of a dinged-up Honda Civic, wedged between Cassidy and Frankie.

"Did Sutton ever tell you about us?" Cassidy asks, hiccupping in the middle of her question.

"Yeah, I know you dated," I say. "And even if I hadn't, I'm pretty sure I could have figured it out tonight."

Through giggles, she says, "But did he tell you about how in *love* we were?"

"Cass," Frankie warns, squeezing her eyes shut, "let's leave all that in the past."

Cassidy holds up her hands in a small surrender. "Whatever. I'm just saying, if *I* were Laine, I would want to know, especially because Sutton and I shared all our firsts. First kiss, first dance, first engagement."

My throat tightens.

"That's enough," Frankie says, practically begging now.

"Well, *almost* engagement," Cassidy clarifies. By the look on my face, she must understand that I, in fact, knew nothing about the engagement. I have no right to be jealous, but I feel that little green-eyed monster crawling up my back anyway. And he's heavy.

"Sutton and I were in that young kind of love. But when he moved to New York for school, I knew it wouldn't last much longer. We tried to make it work for a while. But when

Duke...you know...Sutton came home, and he was all wild and erratic."

"Cassidy, please," Frankie urges, eyes sharp with panic.

Ignoring Frankie, Cassidy continues. "Sutton got into this *ha-uge* fight with his dad in front of everyone and stormed off. When I found him, he asked me to marry him."

My throat cinches tighter yet, as if being coiled by a snake. I rub it, coaxing oxygen to flow through again.

"I said no," Cassidy says, looking proud. The Uber pulls to a stop outside of the bar.

I throw the car door open. After taking a few steps toward the bar, I backtrack. Unable to hold back, I duck my head down into the backseat just as Cassidy is shimmying out. "Was that before or after he found you messing around with his brother in his truck?"

Okay, now I can go. My hands tremble at my sides while I leave the other girls behind. Frankie hurries to catch up with me, looping her elbow around mine so we can walk in together.

"It's fine," I mutter before Frankie has to think of something to say.

It *should* be fine, considering the fact that Sutton and I aren't even an actual couple.

The music is loud, the patrons are wild, and the lights are colorful. It's exactly the kind of place I could see myself going on impulse, just to see what it's about, and making the most of it no matter what. But now, this bar is just reminding me of dancing with Sutton at The Cowboy Cantina, which reminds me of the feeling of his arms tightening around me and that happy, almost hungry, look in his eyes.

Thankfully, there is a silver lining in the center of the room. And it's mechanical.

Cassidy runs over to it immediately, and everyone steps aside to let her cut the line once they see her veil-topped cowboy hat. She hops onto the mechanical bull with the confidence of someone who's had one—or four—too many drinks. The crowd cheers and hollers as the bull jolts alive. She keeps one hand on her hat and the other on the bull's handle, laughing heartily through the spins.

I pull my phone out. All night, I've been resisting the urge to text Sutton, but I'm losing willpower with every drink that enters my system. And as much as I'd love to see Cassidy get thrown off the bull, talking to Sutton is even more tempting.

> Did your stripper have ass-less chaps too?

Within seconds, three dots appear.

> Couldn't say. As soon as I heard the opening notes of "Boot Scootin' Boogie" outside the door, I hid in the bathroom.

> That could have been your soulmate.

> Missed opportunity. But I do see this gorgeous girl at the bar we're at. I think I'm going to make a move. Wish me luck.

My stomach sinks. Sutton is out charming some beautiful stranger while I'm here trying to keep up appearances at a bachelorette party I sincerely don't want to be at.

I try to push the feeling aside, reminding myself that we're not truly together, and he's free to do whatever he wants.

Within seconds, though, I feel a pair of strong arms wrap around me from behind, pulling me into a warm embrace.

"Miss me?" Sutton's voice murmurs in my ear, sending shivers down my spine.

I'm too drunk to worry about reining my grin in when I turn around to see him. "What are you doing here?"

"Wells wanted to show us all how good he is at riding a bull. And though he insisted he wanted the real thing, I convinced him that this would be a suitable—and safer—alternative."

Sutton steps closer, his fingers brushing a strand of hair behind my ear. His touch sends a shiver through my entire body. "Wells is watching us," he says, nodding toward the bar as his lips tilt into a half-smile. "Still think we need to ramp things up?"

You're in too deep, I tell myself. But then Sutton steps closer, and I'm drawing in before I realize it. The music seems to muffle, replaced by the sound of my pulse thrumming unevenly in my ears. My chin tilts up, almost involuntarily, and I brush my lips against his.

Slowly, my hands gravitate to Sutton's hair, grabbing fistfuls of his perfect curls, and I hold him closer to me. I *need* him closer to me. Sutton, apparently, is thinking something along the same lines. He holds my face between his hands. They're big enough that his thumbs graze along my jawline while his other fingers press against my neck.

My mind usually feels as though it's constantly racing, bouncing between one thought and the next before I can get oriented. Now, it's on overdrive.

It's all for show.

He's your best friend.

It's not real.

His lips part, his breath warm against me, and my thoughts become far more focused.

Sutton. Sutton. Sutton.

We've kissed a few times since arriving in Montana. But this kiss is different. More urgent, more *real*. A warm buzzing washes over me, settling deep in my stomach.

When we finally break apart, we're both breathless, our foreheads resting against each other. My heart is pounding, and I almost convince myself I can see the desire in Sutton's eyes, probably mirroring my own.

Sutton stoops down again, this time bringing his mouth to the side of my jaw. His voice is a mere whisper as he speaks, his lips tickling against my ear. "I think that should do it." He rests his head against mine for a moment before adding, "I like your hat."

The warmth climbs back up my body, spreading across my cheeks. I'm not usually someone to get overly embarrassed, but something about sharing a kiss like *that* while wearing a hat like *this* does the trick.

I laugh off my blushing and gesture to my *Save a Horse, Ride a Cowboy* shirt. "It completes the look. You like?"

Sutton's eyes narrow, and he smirks to one side, a single dimple flashing. "I might like it more if I was still a cowboy."

Wow. Maybe it's the booze, but I can tell Sutton is feeling as dangerous as me tonight. It takes every ounce of willpower in me to turn back to the mechanical bull.

Suddenly, I'm incredibly grateful Cassidy asked me to come to her bachelorette party.

Somewhere in the immeasurable time between the start and end of...whatever that was—*kiss* feels too plain a word— Cassidy got bucked off. Unsurprising, seeing as how she can barely walk in a straight line tonight. Frankie is on the bull now. Her curvy, athletic build seems like it was made for this. She grips onto the bull tightly, giggling with her head back. Even in the dimmed colored lights, Frankie's eyes shine. Her long blonde curls spring around her head, an uncanny resemblance to Taylor Swift's *Fearless* cover. As always, Frankie is full of life. As always, it's contagious. Apparently, a ride on a mechanical bull was just what she needed to get her mind off hearing way too intimate details about her brothers.

Frankie stays on for such a long stretch, she eventually jumps off willingly. "It's someone else's turn!" she yells to the operator, flashing a bright smile. Leave it to Frankie to be selfless even when it comes to mechanical bulls. Immediately, she beelines for Sutton and me. Something about the way Frankie smiles at me makes me feel like I have another best friend.

"You need to try that, Laine!" she insists, a laugh lingering in her voice.

I shrug and return her expression. "Say no more." I catch Wells' eye from across the bar. He's still studying us, one eyebrow raised. Maybe the kiss between Sutton and me didn't look as convincing as it felt. Wells is suspicious, and whether that's suspicious about the validity of our relationship or suspicious that Sutton might still have feelings for Cassidy, I need to fix it. I grab Sutton's hand, and he tightens his fingers around mine immediately. "I'll only ride if Sutton joins me."

The bull operator must know what we're about to ask, because he's already shaking his head as we approach. "No, sorry. One at a time."

"But it's my first time on one. And this guy is a real-deal cowboy," I say, using my free hand to squeeze Sutton's bicep.

The operator and I go back and forth for a few minutes until I eventually crack him with, "I'll Venmo you twenty dollars."

Sutton and I climb into the foam-padded pen, my heart racing, not just from the prospect of riding the mechanical bull, but from the charged atmosphere between Sutton and me. The neon lights cast vibrant hues across our faces, and the pulsating music seems to synchronize with my heartbeat.

He lifts me onto the bull with ease, his hands grasping tight to my hips as he does so. Then he climbs on behind me. Grabbing my hands, Sutton places them on the rope handle in front of me. One of his stays on mine, and the other holds around my waist. My stomach flips.

The bull moves slowly at first, and my skin crawls as it sweeps across Sutton's body. Before long, however, I can't overthink that much. The bull swings harder and faster, thrusting us around, forward, and back and stopping here and there just to throw us forward even harder. For a moment, we aren't Sutton and Laine. We're just crashing limbs and pressing skin. Because Sutton is so close to me, I can't see his face, but I can feel his laugh rumbling against my back.

The world outside the pen blurs into vibrant colors and distorted hollering, and it feels like time stretches for us until the bull lurches to the side so harshly we're thrown off, landing in a tangled heap, breathless and laughing.

"You okay?" Sutton asks after we catch our breath. He helps me stand and pulls me into a hug, squeezing his arms around me.

"That was amazing," I exhale. My hat flew off at some point, and Sutton brushes loose tendrils of hair from my face.

The bachelor and bachelorette groups gathered during our ride, and we make our way to them, knees wobbly.

When Wells grins, he actually looks his age of twenty-three. "Quite the show," he says, tightening his arm's grip around Cassidy's shoulders.

Sutton hugs me from behind again, planting a kiss atop my head. The adrenaline of the bull ride is replaced by the now familiar hum of electricity in me that accompanies Sutton.

Wells is still smiling at us approvingly.

"As if he could doubt us now," Sutton murmurs, almost to himself.

The night carries on with a few more drinks, plenty of laughter, and of course, the occasional awkward comment from a bridesmaid. We eventually leave the bar and pile into Sutton's truck, exhaustion settling over us. Sutton has apparently sobered up enough to take the driver's seat. Cassidy is in the backseat with Wells. Within minutes, she is half-asleep against his shoulder. In similar fashion, Frankie, seated on my right, settles against the door. Even with everyone else's eyes closed, Sutton reaches over and holds my hand the entire drive home.

When we finally get back to our room at the ranch, Sutton and I exchange tired grins, both of us too tired to do much more than kick off our shoes and collapse onto the bed. My adrenaline is beyond expended, and the energy from earlier in the night has dissipated, leaving behind a comfortable stillness.

Sutton reaches to the bedside table and grabs his prescription bottle. I snatch it from him. "You can't take a sleeping pill if you've been drinking."

He grabs it back, popping it open. "I didn't have a drink all night," he says, grinning enough for his dimples to carve into his cheeks. "And if I don't take this, there's not a chance in hell I'd get a blink of sleep tonight."

Sure enough, soon Sutton is sound asleep, and I'm doing enough overthinking for the both of us.

21

LAINE

MY BOOTS CRUNCH against the rocks along the worn dirt trail. It's nearly midday, and the sun is warm against my face. I've been walking for at least ten minutes by now, so I pull Sutton's note from the pocket of my coveralls, to be sure I read it right.

> We're going to work on prepping the wedding location today. You are welcome to join if you like and if you aren't too busy with work. Take the trail directly west of the house and you'll find us.

At the bottom of the paper, Sutton continued,

> I hope you sleep well.

That last bit is in pencil while the rest is in pen, so he must have added it later—probably when he realized I was sleeping in late for the first time since arriving in West River. He didn't sign the paper. He didn't need to. I spent months studying Sutton's Shakespeare notes and reading his feedback on essay drafts. I trace my fingers across the handwriting, smiling down at it. It's only been a couple weeks since our last tutoring session, four months since we first met, yet it feels like I've known him for a lifetime.

Wrestling with my thoughts last night, I forgot to plug my phone in to charge. When Sutton got up, presumably *much* earlier than me, he closed the curtains and even left a glass of water on my bedside table, along with the note. I slept in hours later than expected because, thanks to my overthinking, I didn't fall asleep until the early hours of the morning. After I eventually woke up, I returned my parents' calls, leaving out some details from my recap, like the tandem mechanical bull riding and the night we went line dancing.

Those evenings probably sounded harmless.

But they definitely didn't feel that way.

After a few more minutes of walking on the trail, I hear the whirring of a lawnmower. As I reach the top of the next hill, another small pocket of the valley opens up. I slow to a stop and let out a small gasp, awestruck.

At the front edge of the clearing, emerald grass flutters in the breeze. Halfway through the small valley, a vast stretch of lavender fans out, a canvas of vibrant purple that extends all the way to the next hill. The lavender sways, a slow sea of waving color. And the *smell*. It's nothing like the artificial version I've experienced in detergent and cheap candles. Like most everything at Silver Ridge Ranch, it's pure and raw and real.

The entire family works together. Frankie and Sutton unload long benches from a flatbed trailer under Magnolia's direction. Wells trims the white-blossomed trees on the outskirts of the grassy area. And Hank tuts along the back edge of the grass on the lawnmower.

There's something incredibly serene about this moment, about the way the family works together. It's as if the ranch itself is alive, its heart beating with the labor of those who care for it. Had I not already known about the strife between Sutton, Hank, and Wells, I never would guess it looking out at them now.

I gravitate to the lavender field, drawn by an irresistible curiosity. With each step, the sweet scent of lavender becomes more pronounced, wrapping around me. Bees flit from flower to flower. The clouds above are so perfectly white and fluffy they look like they belong in a Pixar movie. I'm not sure how long I stand there, entranced, before I hear a voice behind me.

"What d'ya think?" Wells comes to my side, hands on his sides as he watches the lavender shift in the breeze. His pale eyes take on their purple tone, turning periwinkle. Seeing his content smile, it's hard to remember the harsh, tense Wells I've come to know.

"I think it's the most beautiful thing I've laid my eyes on." My voice is as soft as the rustling leaves in the tree over-head. "Are there a lot of fields like this on the ranch?"

"This is the only one. I planted it five years ago."

"I didn't imagine you as a big floral kind of guy," I say.

A layer of dirt constantly covers Wells. He's loud and tough and, considering what Sutton told me, was quite the rebel for a while. He's the last person in the family I can imagine planting flowers.

"Do cows like lavender or something?" I ask.

One corner of Wells' mouth twitches. "Yes, actually. Apparently it can be good for their digestion when added into their feed. That's what I told my dad when I asked him if I could plant lavender here. But that's not really why I did it."

"I guess even tough cowboys have a soft spot for flowers," I remark with a playful grin.

"Well, don't go spreading that around too much. I've got a reputation to uphold," he replies, his voice shaded by mock seriousness. Then he sighs contently. "Lavender is Cassidy's favorite flower."

"And you planted an entire field of it for her? That's quite the gesture, Romeo."

Wells hesitates for a moment, his gaze shifting back to the lavender. "Five years ago, I realized that I loved Cass. It wasn't a crush. It wasn't to mess with Sutton. It was just... love. Not only that, but I knew I wanted to marry her. I planted this lavender hoping someday she would want to marry me too, and then we would have the perfect place to seal the deal. Plus, no matter how much we might butt heads or how hard it gets, I wanted to have something beautiful to offer her."

His words sink in, and for a moment, the last bits of Wells' tough exterior crumble away, revealing a vulnerability that surprises me. He's more like Sutton than I could have dreamed.

"Five years ago? But you just got engaged last month, didn't you?" I ask.

Wells chuckles softly, a rueful smile touching his lips. "Yeah. But sometimes it takes a while for things to fall into place. The ranch has had...its challenges. Especially the past few months."

I raise my eyebrows, but Wells just answers my unspoken curiosity with a shrug.

"And besides that, even after I knew I loved Cass, I didn't really *want* to love her. I mean, she's my older brother's ex, after all. No matter what Sutton might think, it wasn't intentional. But it was no use. I was hers before I realized it."

We stand there silent for a few minutes, and a feeling of

completeness settles in. Wells was the last one in the Davis family I've connected to. The puzzle pieces have fallen into place.

U

WELLS AND HANK leave after a couple of hours, running to town for some kind of appointment. Later, as the sultry afternoon is just beginning to cool, Magnolia shouts my name. Even from halfway across the clearing, I can see her brilliant smile. Sutton is at her side, and it takes everything in me to not jog the distance between us just to get there a few seconds faster.

As soon as I'm close enough, Magnolia reaches out and holds one of my hands. Then, she uses her free hand to grab Sutton's. Her blonde hair looks even lighter in the sun. She's practically glowing. "I have a little surprise for you two," she says, her eyes crinkling with a grin. "Frankie helped too."

"What occasion?" Sutton asks, his tone tinged with light-hearted suspicion.

Magnolia shrugs. "Graduation, welcome home, late or early birthday, whatever. Frankie and I set up your surprise at the lake. I know you're probably starving, but don't eat before you go. Head home, get cleaned up, and have *fun*."

My stomach turns with anticipation 0f an evening alone with Sutton.

His eyes meet mine, and I can tell he's just as anxious about the surprise. "Thanks, Mom," he says, plastering on a smile.

Once we're back at the house, I do an *everything* shower—exfoliating, shaving, the works. I take my time brushing my teeth and flossing. I'm not sure why, though. I remind myself that we won't be romantic when his family isn't around to see it.

Because Sutton told me that we'll have to go on horse-back, I dress in my best "cowgirl" outfit: Wrangler jeans, a thin, white button-up, a bandana tied around my neck, and of course, my boots to top it off.

"Look at you, Annie Oakley," Sutton says when I meet him at the fence outside, as if he's one to talk in his own cowboy hat and boots. Already, he has our two horses ready to go. "You remember what I taught you about riding?"

I nod and swallow the dryness in my throat away. *Have the horses always been so big?*

Sutton, as always, interprets my expression. "Don't worry," he says. "I'll be right here with you. And Darla here is a sweetheart."

"Hey, Darla," I croak out as I climb over the fence. As soon as I'm over, Sutton straps a helmet on me. I almost protest because I haven't seen anyone on the ranch wear a helmet while riding. But I look back up at Darla's height and tighten my lips.

"Put your foot in the stirrup here, hands up on the saddle horn, and step down hard, like you're trying to push it down. I'll help." Keeping his promise, Sutton stands directly behind me, his hands already on my hips. The nervous drumming in my chest beats harder.

"You realize I'm five-foot-six, don't you?" I say, clumsily poking the toe of my boot into the stirrup.

"We average out to five-eleven, so it's fine," Sutton says, his fingers tightening on me.

After three slow, steadying breaths, I put all of my power into pressing down on the stirrup. Sutton's hands move ever so slightly lower, cupping under my hips so he can help hoist me up as smoothly as possible. Miraculously, it works, and before I know it, I'm on Darla's back, the ground looking impossibly far away.

"You alright?" Sutton asks, one hand still on my leg. It

feels like sparks travel out from his fingertips, as if he's harnessing lightning.

Trying to think of anything to say to distract myself from my anxiousness, I say, "I think this was all an elaborate ruse so you could touch me like that."

The corners of his mouth twitch. "Yes, Laine. My mother created an elaborate plan for us to go on this date solely so I could touch your ass. You caught us."

After some more instructions from Sutton, we're on our way along the trail. The steady sound of hooves striking the ground creates a soothing backdrop for the rustling leaves and occasional birdsong. With Sutton right at my side, and behind me when the trail narrows, I feel more at ease atop Darla. Sutton has always been a comforting reassurance, whether it was convincing me I would ace an exam or checking over my resume as many times as I asked, or now, simply being here for me as I tackle my nerves.

Remembering the story of Duke's passing, I spend most of the ride with my eyes on the ground, looking for any snakes or small animals that could spook Darla or any big rocks she might stumble on. As we venture deeper into the woods, the surroundings make subtle changes, and I look up occasionally to bask in the beauty. The trees grow taller and denser, casting dappled shadows on the trail.

Cool air carries the smell of pine and, after about forty minutes, the sound of lapping water. The throb of anxiety in my chest is back full force. Darla was an unexpectedly welcome diversion, but soon I'll be on solid ground again with nothing to distract me from the fact that—lately—my entire body feels more alive when Sutton comes near.

We break through the trees and there, surrounded by vibrant wildflowers, is a mountain lake. As we near it, I see that its surface is so clear I can look past the reflected foliage of the trees and the impossibly blue sky and see all the way to the bottom of the lake. There, colorful rocks and pebbles create a mosaic of blues, greens, and reds, distorted by the soft ripples in the water.

I'm speechless. I love the city, but *this?* How did Sutton ever leave?

Sutton dismounts his horse and reaches up to help me down from Darla's saddle. The thought of coming down is somehow even scarier than the climb up, though, so he practically pulls me to him in a big bear hug, my body held tight to his. My legs wobble slightly as they touch the ground, re-acclimatizing to the stable ground.

Sutton's hand lingers on my arm for a moment, supporting me. "Welcome to our little paradise," he says with a grin.

"It's incredible," I whisper as if I'm in a church.

"We—mostly I—would come here sometimes to get away from everything."

The tranquility of this place is overwhelming. The gentle flow of the water against the rocky shore, the hum of insects, and the swaying of the trees. It's almost too beautiful to bear.

"What's on our docket for the night?" I ask, my mind reeling from the possibilities here, things I could never do in the city. A quiet swim, stargazing—I don't know—feeding chipmunks? I wonder if they're as ravenous as the pigeons I'm familiar with.

"I'm sure my mom and sister gave us options," Sutton says. He nods to the far corner of the lake, to our surprise.

22

___

SUTTON

I STICK my hands in my pockets just so I won't reach out for Laine's hand while we walk to our campsite. Lately, fighting the urge to touch her feels like I'm fighting to keep magnets apart.

Mom and Frankie really went all out. Our campsite is complete with a prepped fire pit, an overflowing picnic basket, a red cooler, battery-powered string lights, a deck of cards, a mound of pillows and blankets, and two sets of folded flannel pajamas.

Laine stares at the campsite and a wide, open-mouthed smile spread across her balled-up cheeks. "This is the most romantic thing I've ever seen." Her expression falters. "I'm starting to feel guilty about this whole fake-dating thing."

My heart sinks. It's impossible not to feel guilty about lying to my family, but that was the last thing on my mind when I saw the surprise that was left for us. Selfishly, all I could think about was spending an evening with Laine, away from the lies.

"Don't feel bad," I urge, planting my feet in the dirt so I don't gravitate toward her subconsciously. "You only did it to help me. Besides, I'm sure my mom and Frankie loved organizing this for us."

"Only because they love seeing you happy and in love," Laine says, laughing humorlessly.

"I *am* happy," I insist. "Your friend is the greatest thing I've had the privilege of being."

Laine rolls her eyes but that smile—that irresistible smile —is back.

"Trust me," I say, "dating or not, there's not any other way I'd want to spend my evening."

I open my mouth to say more—what I might say, however, I'm not sure—but Laine's cheeks redden to the color of unripe chokecherries, and she dips down to inspect the picnic basket. "I'm starving," she says, clearly trying to reroute the conversation.

We graze on the cheese board and roast hot dogs over the fire pit. We talk about our childhoods, somehow able to conjure up new stories we haven't yet shared with each other after all this time. We stare at the flames flickering between us. But no matter how hard I try to keep a safe distance, no matter how hard I try to avoid staring at her, no matter how many times I remind myself that we aren't a "we" at all, my feelings are fighting under the surface. They've been bubbling there all week. Really, they've been there for months.

"Sutton?" Laine asks, her voice thick. She stares up at me with those deep brown eyes, and every other color fades away. I must take too long to answer, because she continues after a quick clearing of her throat. "Is that safe to ride in?"

I follow her gaze. My old red canoe is sitting near the edge of the water. Immediately, I'm on my feet, eager to give Laine anything she wants. I hold my hand out to help her up from her stump. She takes it, but even after she's standing, we keep our hands intertwined. We pause for a few slow moments, staring silently at one another, each of us daring the other to pull their hand away.

Neither of us does.

I lead Laine by the hand, my fingers tightening around hers. Not for the sake of keeping up appearances. Just for the sake of loving the feeling of her hand in mine. I steal a glance at her, catching the way her eyes catch the light of the setting sun, glowing like molten amber.

After a minute of quick instructions at the water's edge, Laine kicks off her boots and steps gingerly into the canoe, her laugh echoing softly as the boat sways beneath her. She sits on the front bench, looking back at me with a playful glint in her eyes, a dare hidden in her smile. I grin and roll up my jeans so I can push the canoe into the water, the coolness of the lake licking at my calves before I leap in behind her. The canoe cuts through the mirrored colors of the sunset, turning the lake into a canvas of pinks, purples, and deepening blues. When we get to the middle of the lake, Laine rests her oar against her lap and stares up, watching the sky darken. She looks back at me, a content smile tipping her full lips.

"This is nice," she murmurs, her voice accompanied only by the chirping of crickets and the sound of water waving against the canoe. She looks back up at the sky, and I watch her study the stars that spot the violet backdrop, now reflecting in her eyes. I've never seen her so at ease.

A breeze flows between us, whipping a piece of Laine's hair into her face. Instinctively, I reach out, tucking it behind her ear. She turns to me, her eyes searching mine, and for a moment, the seconds slow.

A crease forms between Laine's eyebrows. I rub at it with my thumb until it fades before tracing my fingers down along the delicate line of her jaw. Laine's skin is velvet under my touch. Her breath catches, just for a second, and her lips part slightly, as if she wants to say something but isn't quite sure how.

"Laine," I whisper, unsure of the right words to follow with.

She looks down, spinning her rings around her fingers restlessly.

This is it.

I lean forward, giving in to that magnetic pull, heart hammering in my chest. For months I've tried to keep myself away from Laine. But everything in me begs for her. I search for something in her eyes that might mirror what I'm feeling. Instead, Laine's eyes, still on the bottom of the canoe, widen. Her mouth opens centimeter by centimeter as genuine fear flashes across her face.

Oh no. Too far.

Immediately, I pull myself back, a wave of ice flashing over my body. "I'm so sorry. I thought maybe you felt—"

"What is that?" Laine interrupts, her voice high. I follow her gaze to the back of the canoe, directly behind me, where a pile of rope sits. "I... I think I saw something move."

I narrow my eyes at her, then at the rope, wondering if this is some kind of deflection. Then I see it. Just a hint of movement, something small, slithering out from beneath the pile of rope, moving a few inches toward Laine. Thankfully, I see its familiar dark-green body and unmistakable yellow stripes running vertically along its body. It flicks its forked tongue out, and Laine recoils.

I chuckle, trying to reassure her. "It's just a garter snake. Completely harmless. We used to catch them all the time growing up."

But Laine remains unconvinced. She scoots back until she's at the edge of her seat and pulls her knees up to her chest, getting as far away from the snake as possible in the canoe. Her face pales. "Harmless? Sutton, it's still a snake," she protests, her voice pitched with nervous laughter.

"It can't hurt you."

"It has teeth, doesn't it?" Laine asks, frozen in place.

"Okay, okay," I say, smiling, "I'll grab it. Just…stay calm."

I lean forward, inching out my hand toward the snake, trying to grab it by the back of its head like I've done hundreds of times before. But just as my fingers near, the snake makes a break for it. In one swift, sinuous motion, it slithers away from me—and straight toward Laine.

Laine's eyes widen even more, and she lets out a shriek that would wake the dead. "Oh no, no, no, no!"

"It's fine!" I try to say, but she's not listening. She scrambles around in her seat, her eyes locked on the snake like it's about to grow wings as the boat rocks beneath us.

I lurch forward, attempting to grab the snake again, but it slithers out of my grasp. Laine jumps onto her seat, trying to get as far from the snake as possible. The canoe rocks with the movement, and she loses her balance.

With a yelp, she pitches backward, flailing her arms in a desperate attempt to stay upright. Her hand reaches out and grabs the side of the canoe for support. My dive toward her is fruitless. She tumbles into the lake, her hand catching the canoe in a last-ditch effort to save herself. Instead, with me already halfway out of the canoe, she tips it over with her. I barely have time to register what's happening before I'm plunging into the frigid water.

I come up sputtering, gasping for air, and immediately search for Laine. Soon, she bobs up beside me, hair plastered to her face. For a second, she just stares at me, her expression utter shock.

"Laine," I pant, swimming toward her, "are you okay?"

And then she laughs—a belly-deep sound that bounces across the lake, pure and infectious. That continues on until my leg grazes against hers, and she screams again, following it up with another fit of laughter once she realizes it was just me.

"Garter snakes can't swim anyway, right?" she asks, breathless.

"Right," I lie, knowing fully well that the snake could be swimming right under our feet. She doesn't need to know that.

Laine watches as I flip the canoe right-side up, her breaths still quick with adrenaline.

"You want me to help you back in?" I ask.

She says nothing. Instead, she shakes her head to the side just once. Her open-mouth smile is wide and a bit dazed. Slowly, as she stares at me, it fades.

"You okay?" I ask again, my voice barely above a whisper.

Laine nods, her eyes locked onto mine. "Yeah," she breathes, and there's a vulnerability in her voice that I've never heard before. "I'm better than okay."

We tread water, face to face, close enough for our limbs to collide as we move. The coolness of the water is invigorating, but it's nothing compared to the thrill of her presence. Laine's eyes hold mine, my chest tightens. Almost involuntarily, I drift toward her. And it seems as though she's doing the same, because soon we're nothing but a tangle of limbs.

I thought I knew what I wanted.

I wanted to be an editor. I wanted to be in the city.

But now, it's hard to imagine a world outside of this moment.

Now, all I know is that I want *her*.

We linger for a time, both of us knowing the inevitable is coming. Both of us too scared to accept it just yet. I'm not sure how long we stay in that motion, dangerously close as we tread water. It could be seconds or minutes. Eventually, one of my arms finds its way around her torso. I have to kick my legs fiercely to stay afloat. It's worth it when Laine pulls against me so close that even the icy water can't slip between us. She tips her forehead closer, and I take the invitation, furthering it as I drag my mouth against the spot where her jaw and neck meet. She shudders.

Her hands press against my back, holding me against her, and my mouth melts against hers. The heat behind her kiss courses through my body. We almost dip under the surface of the lake, both of us more interested in each other than we are in staying afloat. In a final moment of clarity, I tilt back, holding Laine against my chest, and kick us toward the shore.

"What about the canoe?" she murmurs, breathless.

"Later." That one word is all I can think to say.

I always imagined that kissing Laine—*really* kissing her— would be like a fire hose to flames, dampening my ever-growing want for her.

I was wrong. It's like gasoline to a fire.

As soon as my feet touch the rocks along the bottom of the lake, I turn my attention fully back to Laine. She's still unable to get a good footing, so I hold her up around me, looking to somehow get closer to her. Gone is caution and subtlety, the worries and anxiety.

My smile interrupts our fervent kisses.

Laine pulls back just enough to mirror my expression. Our chests rise and fall rapidly against each other. My brain is static.

"Laine," I whisper, my voice raspy. "I can't pretend anymore."

"What do you mean?" she asks, voice as bubbly as ever.

"I want to be with you. Really, wholly...*truly* be with you."

Laine's eyes widen in the moonlight's glow. Her lips part, but no words escape. Her grip on me tightens, and through our wet shirts, I can feel her heart pounding as wildly as mine.

"I mean it, Laine," I continue, my voice heavy with the raw words I've held back for too long. "I want to be with you," I repeat, my voice set. "I can't keep pretending like what I feel for you is just an act."

Laine's eyes glisten. "Sutton," she finally says, her voice filled with emotion. "You don't want to be with me." She looks up at the sky, as if the right words to say were written in the stars. "I don't even know what I want in life. I'm a mess."

With my thumb, I tip Laine's chin down, studying her, appreciating her. "What a beautiful mess."

With all the feelings I've harbored for Laine surging through me, I lean in and kiss her again. Laine's arms tighten around me, pulling me even closer, as if she's afraid that I'll disappear. I strengthen my hold, savoring the taste of her, the feel of her, the sheer perfection of her.

The crickets and owls continue their song, and the lake laps gently at our legs, as if nature itself is celebrating with us.

23

LAINE

I'VE NEVER SLEPT SO POORLY.

I swear Montanan crickets are louder than New York City traffic. Not to mention the constant rustling in the grass outside our tent, probably that garter snake back for revenge. And there's the owls hooting their never-ending hoots. Of course, there's also Sutton, dead to the world even as the clear sky lightens and the stars fade against their backdrop.

Instead of sleeping last night, my mind bounced between two very distinct tracks, like a wild game of ping-pong.

The first track—the one I much prefer—was reliving the evening we had. The contrast between the freezing, pure water and Sutton's warm skin, fighting for territory. The way Sutton murmured my name endlessly, as if he couldn't believe it was really *me* he was holding. The way he would periodically lean away from me or lift me up in the moonlight, just to look at me again before diving back into a kiss.

My mind seemed to shut off between the moment Sutton kissed me and the moment he fell asleep. It felt like both a single breath and a lifetime, and it was utterly perfect.

And then he was asleep.

And it was just me, alone with my thoughts.

Which brings me to the second track. The *What in the actual hell are you doing?* track.

The longer the mental ping-pong goes on, the faster and more erratic it gets.

He's my best friend.

I can't deny my feelings.

But I should *deny them.*

I've never felt so at peace as I did last night.

You're ridiculous.

He's perfect.

You'll lose him.

Restless, I shift under the wool blanket draped over Sutton and me. I'm turned away from him, and he instinctively pulls me closer until my back meets his chest. His hand rests on my stomach. I freeze, listening for his breaths. They're even and shallow, burning hot against the skin of my shoulder.

He's still asleep.

Enjoy this.

Escape this.

I wiggle free of Sutton's touch. His hand drops to the ground with a thud. And then, I can actually *hear* Sutton's smile. He lets out a sigh, then almost laughs before drawing closer again, kissing the skin of my shoulder gently. It sends electricity through me, and I jolt up, propping myself onto my elbows.

Sutton's chest is somehow even more impressive in the dawn light. On the night of the date auction—a night that feels a lifetime away—I was shocked to learn that Sutton was a cowboy, at least, had been one. But seeing him like this, it leaves no question. His broad shoulders, the definition in his arms and chest, down to his tapering torso—it all screams manual labor. Even years in the city didn't strip that

173

from him.

It's hard to look at Sutton like this—happy, gorgeous, and carefree—and not pick up where we left off last night. Sleep tousled his brown curls into irresistible waves. Not to mention that lazy half smile, those eyes peeking out from heavy lids.

He looks drunk, though I know that can't be possible. After all, I'm the one who drank half our bottle of wine last night after he fell asleep. And I might have had more had I not spilled the rest all over the dirt.

"Morning," Sutton says, voice scratchy. He sits up, combing through his hair with his fingers, and groans play-fully. "I hate to ask this. Because I already know the answer. But should we head back?"

Still unsure of how I'm feeling, let alone what I should say, I squeeze my mouth shut and offer a single nod.

Sutton leans in, cradling my face as his mouth presses against mine. His hands are massive, but they're soft against my cheeks, careful with me as if I'll break. My mouth parts, apparently not quite ready to resist temptation.

I've never felt so at peace.

He's perfect.

Enjoy this.

Sutton pulls back to look at me again, shaking his head in disbelief. He brushes his thumb against my lips, his smile spreading wide.

"What?" I ask, wondering if he's laughing at something stuck to my teeth or a bit of smeared dirt on my face.

Instead of answering right away, Sutton reaches for his phone, still in the pocket of his folded jeans. He aims it at me, and I cover my face. I'm sure my sporadic ten-minute stretches of sleep didn't qualify as "beauty rest." But Sutton guides my hands away. I again find myself copying his expression, which right now, I can only describe as content.

Sutton takes a picture and hands the phone over to show me.

I look completely undone. My hair is a nest. I have smudged mascara rubbed below my lashes, yet I can still see the under-eye bags below it.

"Are you making fun of me right now?" I ask, shooting him a playful glare.

Sutton pulls me to his bare chest, his laugh bouncing against me. "Of course not. I just don't think I've ever seen you without some red on your lips." He looks down at me, staring at my mouth. "I've never seen such a pretty color," he whispers, reaching around me to trace a finger across my cupid's bow.

Ʊ

"SO, what do you...like about music?" I ask, pausing to rub my eyes halfway through my question.

Clive, who works at the radio station with Laine, stares at me. The wrinkles webbing across his face deepen as he furrows his brows. "What's not to like?" he responds, his voice weary.

It's a fair response to a mediocre question. Frankie told me about Clive. I know she did. His family—or was it his wife's family—started the station forever ago. She passed away...a while ago?

Ugh.

I did the research beforehand. I brainstormed questions to ask. But the only thing I can think about now is the broad planes of Sutton's chest and the way he would twist my hair around his fingers.

"Are you okay, darlin'?" Clive asks, a polite smile distorting his wrinkles.

I take another *long* drink of coffee and nod. *Aside from the exhaustion and mental lapse.* My notebook has only a few words scribbled in it from the interview. *Clive. Likes country music. Seventy-eight years old.*

I toss my notebook onto the desk between us. I can't talk to my parents about this without getting a big "We told you so." And I can't talk to Frankie about Sutton without exposing my lies. So, Clive it is. "Have you ever been in love?" I ask, leaning my elbows on the desk.

For the first time all morning, Clive looks awake. "Course I have," he hums, almost to himself. "Beth." He says her name with reverence, like that one syllable is a prayer.

"What was she like?" I ask, partially because Clive looks eager to share, partially because I'm utterly desperate to hear about a love story gone right.

Clive leans back in his squeaky office chair and closes his eyes, reliving her. "We both grew up in West River. I don't remember a time before her. Beth had brilliant golden hair, just the color of a quaky's leaves in October. *She* was the music lover, really. Her parents started the station when we were in high school, and Beth practically ran the place from day one. And as soon as she let me, I got a job here too, just to be close. Beth would organize the music, and I would do her bidding. If they didn't need me on the boards, I would wash windows, rake leaves, *anything*. Eventually, Beth put me on the air, but not without supervision. And thus began the Beth and Clive Show, every weekday."

"And that was it?" I ask, mesmerized.

Clive snorts. "Just a little show to say 'good morning' to West River. During our first one, Beth poked fun at me for never working up the nerve to ask her out. So, she asked *me*, live on the air. I guess I didn't get much more courageous over time, though, because four years after that, she proposed during another show. Said I was taking too long."

"And you said *yes*? Right then and there?" My mind stalls

at the thought of being put on the spot for a decision like that.

"Oh, *hell*, of course I said yes," Clive says, slapping a hand on the desk. "I'd be about as sharp as a marble if I gave up the opportunity to spend my life with Beth."

I lean forward, looking at Clive like he's some kind of ancient oracle dressed in a pearl snap. "But how did you *know* she was the one?"

"Why would you think Sutton isn't the one?" Clive harrumphs. Then, seeing me open and close my mouth repeatedly as I seek a response, he adds, "You're looking like a trout outta water, dear."

It's hard not to laugh when an old man calls you out.

"Frankie told me she's never seen Sutton act the way he does with you," Clive says.

I roll my eyes. "Oh yeah, you two like to gossip?"

"All the time," he affirms, his voice serious. "Not much else to do in a town like West River. Now, don't change the subject. "Why don't you think Sutton is the one?"

Closing my eyes, untangle the webs of worry and excitement that tangled together. "I didn't want to see Sutton that way. My parents fell in love—or supposedly did—when they were my age. Then, one day, they weren't anymore. I don't...I don't want to fall in love, because I don't want to fall back out of it."

A voice behind us startles us both. "Did I just hear the word *love*?" I turn to see Frankie striding through the back door, her long blonde hair somehow curlier than usual. She gives me a mischievous grin. "How was last night?"

"You're just in time for gossip hour," Clive says, saving me from coming up with an appropriate response.

Frankie pulls up a chair next to me. "What's the dish?" she asks Clive with a wink.

Clive sucks his teeth. "I'm trying to figure out why Miss Rodriguez here doesn't think your brother is *the one*."

Frankie whips her head around to me, brows crinkled with concern, and I scramble for an explanation.

"I—I just have a hard time believing that two people can really love each other their entire lives, especially if they're so different. Sutton is all schedules and plans and goals, and I'm...living day by day."

Clive chimes in. "Love ain't about being the same. It's about complementing each other. Like a good country song, it's all about harmony." He hums a short melody I'm unfamiliar with. "Laine, differences aren't roadblocks; they're the chorus of your love story."

My phone vibrates in my pocket with a text. I pull it out, somehow both hoping it'll be Sutton while also praying it won't be. Instead, Ophelia Brooks' name pops up.

> How are things going? Can I call you tonight to discuss your drafts?

Any warm, fuzzy feelings I had while talking to Clive and Frankie get sucked out of me like air from a vacuum chamber.

24

SUTTON

I CAN'T GET the image of Laine out of my mind all morning. Her surprisingly pink lips, her untamed hair, the twin freckles that dot her shoulder. If we both didn't have plans for the day, I would have wanted to stay at our dreamlike refuge at the lake, maybe over another night, or a week. I think I'd live and die there with Laine in my arms if she'd let me.

Ever since I first laid eyes on Laine the first day of class, I felt drawn to her. When we actually spoke, actually spent time together, that feeling only strengthened.

Laine is a person who smiles at anything and everything: a pigeon stealing a fry, old people playing chess at the park, blue skies, rain. And every time I've seen her smile, I've wished my love could be the reason for it.

Last night, finally, I got my wish.

I wasn't her teacher's assistant, her tutor, her best friend, her fake boyfriend. No. I was just Sutton.

And she was Laine.

And we were perfect.

"Something funny?" Wells asks, throwing a coiled rope at me.

I fix my face, hiding my sappy grin I've been wearing all day. Wells stares at me for a moment, his eyes darkening. Whatever camaraderie I felt building between us the past couple of days crumbles. The three other ranch hands in the barn stare for a moment before Wells' glare has them back to their tasks. Still, they keep their ears tipped to us.

"What's wrong with you?" I laugh through my words, still amped up on adrenaline from last night. "Did Cassidy finally come to her senses and call the wedding off?"

The barn, even the horses, goes completely still and quiet for five tense heartbeats.

I meant it as a joke, but Wells sends a dagger look my way. He opens his mouth to say something—something that probably includes a four-letter word or two—but he snaps it shut and busies himself with his horse's saddle.

"Dad's not feeling well today," he grumbles, the conversation dying there.

Sluggish footsteps sound behind us. I turn to see Hank walking directly toward me, his weathered face looking wearier than usual. Just like when I was a kid, I straighten at the sight of him. Today, his steps are slower than usual, and only a few feet from me, he stumbles, seemingly over nothing.

All at once, I hear the cowboys behind me suck sharp inhales, and Wells rushes to our dad's side, both of them letting out a curse. He catches Hank just inches before his torso would have slammed into the ground. Our father leans against Wells, straightening. The dirty look he gives Wells could wilt a wildflower.

"I don't need your help," he mutters, nudging Wells' chest away before looking back at me, his expression soured. "You're coming with me and Wells. Saddle up."

"How long will we be?" I say it without thinking. Or, I say it while only thinking of one thing—Laine. She should be back from her interview any minute, and I was already planning on how I could steal her away from helping Mom and Frankie with wedding prep.

My father's jaw twitches. "It will take...as long as it takes." His words are slow, almost slurred.

Something about his voice carves at my stomach.

"I want to let Laine know when she can expect me back," I explain, trying to decipher why my father speaks as if he's in slow motion. Unsettlement churns in me.

Wells whispers under his breath, "For the love..."

"You'll be back tonight."

I clench my jaw, on the defense from Wells' and Hank's unexplained bristly attitudes. When I lug a saddle over to Darla, the gentle mare, Hank clicks his tongue. "Duke's horse," he instructs.

U

I FOLLOW behind Hank's horse. Wells follows behind mine. And because it's just the three of us, it's a silent ride aside from the nearby stream rushing over smoothed rocks and the sound of hooves digging into the steep path under us. Beneath me, my older brother's horse seems restless, whipping his head around every few minutes, as if trying to shake his bridle off.

Three hours into the ride, the sky shadows with dark, rolling clouds. The wind, usually calm in our little valley, picks up enough that I have to push my hat down farther on my head so it won't go flying off.

After a particularly rocky patch of trail, Wells' voice pierces through the wind, unsteady. "How are you feeling up there, Dad?"

Hank says nothing.

"What exactly are we doing today?" I ask finally. I hadn't bothered to inquire before we left, my mind already at full capacity, thinking about one thing and one thing only. By the time I wondered what the three of us could be doing without the other cowboys, the tense silence had already settled. I didn't dare break it.

I look back at Wells, but all he offers is an icy stare.

The higher our horses climb, the rougher the trail gets. Along the way, I study the rocks along our path, keeping an eye out for rattlers or uneven rock. Above us, rain patters, striking the pines' branches overhead and flicking the brim of my hat. I shift in my saddle, repositioning my denim jacket. The forecast didn't call for rain.

Hank stops his horse at the crest of the mountain. Beyond us, the range continues into sharp peaks, their tips hidden by storm clouds. I pull up alongside him.

Wells does the same on Hank's other side, again asking him how he's feeling. Hank, again, ignores the question, keeping his eyes trained on the land below us—Silver Ridge's green valley, dotted by barns and our family home. It all looks so small from way up here through the misty showers.

The muscles in Hank's face twitch.

Wells doesn't look at the ranch. Instead, he looks down at his hands, bowing his head as if in prayer. I can barely see his low-set brows from under the brim of his hat.

A roll of thunder echoes to us, and Duke's horse steps in place quickly, again rearing his head back, those black, glossy eyes wide. He knows a storm is coming.

25

LAINE

MY CHEST THUMPS ALONG in time with the roar of thunder outside the guest room window. With shaking hands, I hit the green answer button. In the call's background, I hear overlapping conversations and distorted music.

"Heyyy, Ophelia," I say, shaking my head at my singsong tone.

"Laine Rodriguez!" Thankfully, she sounds happy enough. "Can you hear me alright?" she asks.

"It's a little loud, but I can hear you."

"Sorry about that. Adam and I are at the Cannes Film Festival. But I wanted to check in while it's a decent hour for you. Working with time changes can be so complicated. Anyway, I read the notes and draft you've been working on, and I think you have a solid foundation here."

All at once, the tension I was holding unwinds like a string from a yo-yo. "That's amazing to hear. Thank you," I say through a relieved exhale.

"But—"

That one word winds that yo-yo right back up.

"I think you're losing your voice," Ophelia says. "While

none of the drafts are *bad*, per se, they aren't reading like the articles I read from your college days. These are coming off a bit...distracted."

Despite my best efforts at stringing some semblance of a sentence together, I come up short. I'm *undoubtedly* distracted, seeing as how I've been harboring very real—scarily real—feelings for my best friend. I was just hoping that wouldn't show in my writing.

"You said you had another interview lined up for today, right? How was that?"

There is hope in Ophelia's voice, and it makes my chest tighten. I think back to my empty notebook, not a single quote or anecdote from Clive written. Maybe Ophelia won't be able to hear the lying in my voice over the phone. "It went greaaaat," I say, drawing the word out. What I hoped would sound like enthusiasm only comes across as desperation.

"You also said you would have three articles by the end of the week. How's that looking?"

"You've already seen the article about what it's like to work on the ranch, with the interviews with the owner and some cowboys. I'm almost done turning the interview with the cook into a fully fleshed story. Oh! And I have a handful of recipes he gave us the green light to publish. Plus, I have a good idea on where I'm headed with the story about the radio station." *Good idea* isn't exactly the truth, and it probably doesn't sound like it either, with the way my words tumble from my mouth, just as erratic as I feel.

After a too-long pause, Ophelia says, "I take it you won't be done with the three articles tonight?"

My lungs feel tight. "No. But I think by the end of the week—"

"Laine," Ophelia says gently, "today is Saturday. It *is* the end of the week."

Impossible.

I pull up my phone's calendar. Sure enough. My deadline is tonight. This week jerked me around, moving too fast for me to get my footing. Another round of thunder reverberates through the window, and I rush to it, stricken by the endless raindrops warping my view.

Sutton is out there.

On a horse, apparently.

And his phone must be dead—maybe out of service— because my texts stopped delivering hours ago.

Lightning brightens the entire sky, illuminating the treacherous clouds.

"Laine?" Ophelia says. "Did I lose you?"

I forgot I was even on the call for a minute there. "Hi, no, you didn't. But—" Another streak of light stops me. "Sorry, Ophelia," I say, trying to piece the right words together but coming up short. "Is there any chance I can have an extension?"

"Is everything okay?" Ophelia asks. "You even *sound* distracted."

I let out a joyless laugh, trying to play her words off. "I'm great!"

Ophelia isn't convinced. "Alright...Tell you what, Adam and I are getting back to New York on Monday. Can you get the articles done by that night? You'll still be in Montana, right? Let's plan for a Zoom call next week. I'll email you the information."

"Thank you, Ophelia. I owe you."

"You do. You owe me three polished articles. And I trust you'll follow through."

Immediately after Ophelia hangs up, I call my mom's phone. It only rings once before she answers.

"Hello, favorite daughter," she says, the sounds of cooking behind her voice.

"Hey, kid!" an unexpected voice yells at her side.

"Huh? Dad?"

I try to picture them, just the two of them, together, but the image is lacking. To my knowledge, the only time they've seen each other since the divorce was at my graduation.

"What's going on?" I ask. "Did someone die or something?"

"Your father invited me over so we could talk about you—the one subject we have in common," Mom says. "It's called being *friends*, something we think we should attempt. How's our girl?"

My uncharacteristic silence is answer enough.

"What happened, Laine?"

"I think everything caught up to me," I force out, retreating to the en suite bathroom and locking the door behind me. Still worried someone might overhear my conversation, I crawl into the empty tub, as far away from the door as possible.

Mom's voice goes tight. "Did something happen with Sutton?"

"I'm in way over my head."

"Speakerphone," Dad begs.

"In over your head with Sutton?" Mom asks. It's no surprise that she wants clarification. During our last semester at NYU, Sutton practically became a part of our family. She doesn't want to lose him any more than I do.

"Yes, with Sutton. With him and all the Davises. With this trip and this wedding. And with work."

"Work's not going well?" Mom says. Defeat is clear in her tone, and it doesn't carry any touch of shock with it. She saw this coming, I guess. I never had much follow-through. "You texted me a few days ago saying you were loving writing for *Wonderings*."

Lean my head back against the cool ceramic lip of the tub, I breathe in slowly through my nose. "I *was*. I was loving it, and I thought I was doing a good job. But according to my boss, my writing came off as distracted as I feel. I have two days to write two articles. Not to mention the first one I need to rework completely."

"You can do it, Lainey," Dad urges.

His words do little to quell the worried knot in my stomach. Ophelia was right to start me off on a trial run. It's like she *knew* I wasn't actually cut out for this job.

After a beat of silence, Dad's voice is back, colder than I'm used to—colder, even, than Mom's tends to be. "Don't do this," he insists.

My mouth pops open. "Don't do what?"

"Don't quit your *Wonderings* gig," he explains. "Don't run away from it."

With my free hand, I tap my fingers anxiously. "I can't freelance. I don't know what I was thinking. My mind is always on the run. I'm not organized or focused or—"

"Laine!" Mom cuts in with a sharp exhale. "You *can* do it. In fact, more than that, you *need* to do it. I know it's hard. But I also know you're fully capable."

"Enough of the self-doubt," Dad adds. "Enough indecisiveness."

"Stick this out," Mom says, a pleading edge to her tone. "At least this one gig. You owe it to *Wonderings*. And more than that, you owe it to yourself."

For a while, we don't speak. I stare at the flashes of lightning out my window, juggling my parents' words and my worry for Sutton out there in the rain. When I speak, my voice is barely audible. "You're right."

"And the sky is blue," Dad adds.

"Tell us about Sutton," Mom says, already excited about a topic of conversation she's always keen on. "How is operation 'fake-date'?"

Through gritted teeth, I confess, "Not...as fake as we

intended it to be."

"Ha!" Dad barks so loud the microphone clips. "You owe me twenty dollars, Althea."

"Whoa now," she says, giggling—*giggling!* "That wasn't the bet. Laine, what exactly do you mean about it not being fake?"

Caught up in reliving our date last night, I must be silent too long, because Dad's voice interrupts my thoughts. "Told you! That silence is all the answer I need. Pay up."

After letting out a playful curse at Dad, Mom turns her attention back to me. "Did you—did you think this would happen?"

"You're kidding right? We're so different." I look out at the storm hammering against the window. "We're like thunder and a soft, summer breeze. And I bet you can guess which one I am. Even if I thought about Sutton in a romantic way before—which I didn't let myself do—I wouldn't have imagined he would ever feel the same way."

"Then you're blind, kid," Dad says.

I scoff. "Are you saying I'm *not* a chaotic, unpredictable storm?"

"Oh, you are," Mom laughs. "But Sutton has always loved that about you. When you're in the same room as him, it's like you're that strike of lightning he needs. You liven him up. And maybe *you* hadn't considered what it would be like to be with Sutton. But trust me, I've seen the way he can't stop smiling when you're around. *He's* been thinking about what it would be like for a long time."

"Where's Sutton now?" Dad asks.

I crawl out of my tub-turned-hideout and walk over to the window, opening it a few inches. Within seconds, the bathroom counter is soaked by angled rain. "You hear that?" I ask, nearly having to shout over the roaring wind. "He's somewhere out there."

26

SUTTON

WELLS and I sit on either side of our father, hiding from the incessant rain as best as we can under the sharp green pines. Hank twitches every once in a while, probably from the cold. Each time, Wells asks him the same thing, "Are you feeling okay?"

Our father just glares on.

Hank looks older than I expected him to in his early fifties, especially as he huddles down, his shoulders hunched to keep rain from dripping down the neck of his coat. He is still as lean as ever, maybe more so now, and weaker than when I moved away. The skin around his face hangs, the worry lines deep and unforgiving. Beyond looking older, he looks *exhausted*. His eyes droop a bit, like at any second he could fall asleep sitting up.

He's a shadow of the man I knew.

After an especially loud clap of thunder, my father's eyes slide to mine, their pale blue looking almost as silver as the thin hair that peeks out from his cowboy hat. "Do you even know where we are?" he asks, his slurring voice cutting the wind like a rusty blade.

Wells scoffs at my look of confusion, his eyes matching our father's, not only in color, but also in intensity. He flexes his jaw, choking back whatever it is he's desperate to say.

When my father speaks again, there is no gentleness in his tone. "This is where Duke died."

Across from me, Wells straightens, digging his nails into his palms as he balls his hands up.

Unsure of what to say, I study Hank. He doesn't look sad. Far from it. Instead of welling tears in his eyes, there is only a fiery flicker, clear even under his drooping lids. Hank points a trembling hand to the cluster of rocks at the edge of the mountainside. One juts out from the others, sharp and menacing. "That was the rock that broke his neck." He points across the trail, where we tied our horses up. "And that was the horse that bucked him off."

Everything in my body turns to lead.

I knew some details of how Duke died. But I heard nothing about it from my father. After I told him I wasn't going to quit college and move back home, he quit talking to me about Duke entirely, as if I didn't even deserve to remember my brother if I wasn't willing to take over his role, his life.

"Duke was devoted to the ranch. To our family," Hank continues, his eyes sending me a clear message: *unlike you.* "Duke was out all day, every day. Moving cattle, fixing fences, managing employees. He wanted to see Silver Ridge thrive, and he was making it happen. When a pack of wolves attacked one of our smaller herds, Duke wanted to solve the problem."

Wells hangs his head, his face covered by the brim of his hat. Something forms in my throat, too heavy for me to swallow away. Sweat gathers on the back of my neck, mingling with the dripping rain.

"We had a storm that day, worse than this one," Hank

says. "The lightning already had the horses on edge. And when a rattler came up on the trail, surprising Duke's horse, he reared back. The snake attacked. The horse went wild. Threw Duke off."

The lump in my throat swells bigger, enough for my breaths to tighten. Icy blood races through my pounding heart.

Hank looks out into the storm. "He died protecting our ranch. He gave his *life* for it. And I don't want that to be in vain."

My stomach rolls in synchronicity with the thunder. I look at Wells, but his hat still obstructs his face. I can see his knuckles, though, stark white over clenched fists.

"You've had your time to play around in New York," Hank says with unwavering intensity. "It's time to come back to your real life."

After a few steadying breaths, I can only come up with the same words I said to my father six years ago. "I can't be Duke."

Wells' hat lifts slightly as he tilts his head up just enough to look at me, his eyes narrow and piercing.

Hank's voice is as frigid and unforgiving as the rain that lashes against the trees overhead. "We don't need you to be your brother. We just need you to be *here*. You left when we needed you most, Sutton. You chose college and a life of *reading* over your family and this land."

The scent of rain-soaked earth mixing with the acrid bite of unresolved anger. "I didn't abandon anyone," I say. "I followed my own path. I'm going to be an editor soon. *That's* my life."

A flash of lightning casts an eerie glow on our strained faces, and I see a glimmer of something in my father's eyes—recognition, perhaps, or a hint of realization. But he quickly hardens his gaze.

"Duke is gone," he says, his voice softening just a fraction. "He's gone, and the ranch—the family—needs someone to fill his shoes."

"I can't replace Duke. No one can."

Wells' hat lifts higher, his eyes boring into mine. Our father's expectations and his fixation on my return has worn away at Wells. I can sense his frustration building.

"You're pathetic," Wells mutters through gritted teeth. "You think the city and your new, fancy assistant-to-the-editor job in a big high-rise make you better than us? Think you're too good for this place?"

It takes effort to not back down from his glare. "This isn't about being better, Wells. It's about finding where I belong. This ranch was never my dream."

Another bolt of lightning illuminates the forest, emphasizing Wells' knit brows. "Well, it's my dream! I've been working this land as hard as anyone. But all anyone can think about is how it should be you. *You*, even when you're the weak one. The one who ran."

Wells' anger is palpable. Understandable, considering the fact that he's the one who stayed. Who learned the ins and outs of the ranch. Who, at only sixteen, took on Duke's responsibilities. And yet, our father's attention remains firmly on me. Even now, his gaze has not moved from my face.

Hank interjects, his voice stern and unforgiving, "Sutton, you may have left, but Silver Ridge is a part of the Davis family. Our legacy—*Duke's* legacy—is in your blood. You can't just walk away from your God-given responsibilities." It's as if he didn't hear a word that Wells said.

Hank's words are heavy with the weight of tradition and duty. But I can't carry that weight. "Duke gave his life to this ranch. And I would give mine up if I followed in his footsteps." I gesture to my little brother, attempting a smile. "But Wells…Wells *wants* this. He's your prodigy. Not me."

Without wasting a second, Hank snaps, "Wells can't do it. Not alone."

"Wells has you," I remind him. "From what I've heard around the ranch, Wells has practically been running it on his own, anyway. I heard he's been doing better than you. Is that the real reason you want me here? Are you just ashamed that you aren't enough for the ranch anymore?"

My words hang in the air like another thick cloud. A flash of emotions dances across Wells' face. He clenches his jaw so tightly that I can see the muscles in his neck strain. When he speaks, his voice is a low, simmering growl, "You don't know anything, Sutton. You don't know what we've been through— what I've been through—while you were living it up in New York, pursuing your *dreams*." He practically spits the last word. "Don't speak to Dad that way. Don't you dare say he isn't enough."

Wells' anger boils over, and without warning, he lunges at me. He tackles me back against the ground, coating my back in thick, wet mud. From the corner of my eye, I see Hank try to get up, but he fails, stumbling back against the tree.

Wells has me pinned to the ground, my shirt in his tight fists. He's no longer the teenager I would effortlessly triumph over in our playful wrestling matches. In place of his once gangly limbs, he has cords of bulking muscle, the result of endless days of physical labor.

Thunder, lightning, and torrential rain have reduced the world to a violent chaos, soaking me to the bone. Wells straddles me, his chest heaving with anger and exertion, face contorted in a mix of pain and fury. He's a different Wells than the one I left behind six years ago. This is a Wells shaped by the unforgiving demands of the ranch. My back sinks deeper into the earth below me.

I hold back from retaliating, waiting to see how far Wells will take this. Pelting raindrops sting like needles against my skin. I struggle to break free, but Wells' grip on my shirt is unyielding.

"Your dreams," he hisses, "left me here to pick all the pieces up on my own. But my years of work and dedication mean nothing. No, it's still *you* everyone wants."

I should reason with him, to make him see my point of view, but it's like reasoning with the storm itself. "Wells, I'm not trying to take anything away from you. I just want to live my own life, make my own choices."

A flash of lightning and a crash of thunder fuel his anger. "Your choices...they've always been about you. You walked away, leaving us to deal with everything. You don't know what it's like, what it's been like for us here."

Wells tightens his grip on my shirt with one hand, releasing his other, and I can see the frustration etched into every line of his face. I reach out, trying to push him away, but he's too powerful. He's taken on the strength and resolve of this ranch.

"Just do it," I grumble. "Do what you've been wanting to do for years. Hit me."

Wells takes a deep, shuddering breath, and squinting my eyes in the downpour, I see his mouth curl into a smirk. He releases his grip on my shirt, and for a moment, I think the fight might be over. Then, with a defiant snarl, he aims a fist at my cheek.

The impact sends a shockwave of pain through my face, and my vision blurs for a moment. I can barely see Wells pull his arm back, ready for another hit. With all my strength, I push him in the chest, throwing my weight over and flipping us around until I'm on top.

"Feel better?" I ask through heavy, panting breaths.

"I don't care that you abandoned the ranch," he growls. "I

just care that you abandoned our family." He pulls me down into another grapple.

Hank yells something, but I can't hear it, not over the sound of my raging pulse in my ears.

Rain and mud turned the ground treacherously slippery, making the fight a chaotic, uneven struggle. At some point, I have Wells on the ground again, but he pulls a foot back, kicking me square in the chest with his boot and sending me back against the trunk of a tree, knocking the breath out of me. When he lunges forward to hit me again, I dodge it, landing my own blow. It connects with Wells' jaw with a sickening thud, and my hand immediately aches.

Wells' frustration and resentment find an outlet in our physical struggle. The fight is as much about emotions as it is about dominance. It's a battle between my chosen path and Wells' desired role, the heir to a legacy he was never intended for.

He bear-hugs me, pushing me out onto the trail. I land with my back on the rocks along the mountain's edge. I twist around, my elbow connecting with his chest. He chokes a breath out, but in no time, he has me on the ground yet again, this time landing a punch right along my lip. The hot, metallic taste of blood seeps into my mouth, mixing with the mud coating my teeth. I sputter, unable to see, thanks to the rain and dirt veiling my eyes. In one last push, I rock him over, forcing his back against a rock.

The rock.

Its jagged, sharp edge cutting into the misty rain like a serrated blade. A clap of thunder sounds, the loudest yet, and the earth seems to shake under us. For a moment, our struggle pauses, and we lock eyes, both of us panting, soaked to the bone and shaking, more from anger and adrenaline than from the cold.

Wells' voice is a strained growl. "You should've never left,

Sutton." He shakes his head. "You should've never come back."

With a deep sigh, I stumble back, my chest heaving. The rain continues to pour, streaking with my tears through the mud and blood on my face.

"I'm sorry, Wells," I mutter, my voice strangled with sorrow. "I never wanted it to be like this."

He doesn't respond, his unforgiving gaze still locked onto mine.

I extend a hand to help him up. He stares at it for a moment before accepting it. The two of us stand there, drenched, bruised, and emotionally drained, on the very ground that claimed Duke. I stare at Wells, searching for any glimmer of understanding, of relent. But his eyes remain stern, forged by the years of hardship he's endured without me.

"I'll go, okay?" I say, my entire body aching from the inside out. "I can tell you don't want me here for the wedding. I'll go."

After a pause so long I wonder if Wells is working up the energy to fight again, he sighs, the weight on his shoulders looking unbearably heavy. "You can't."

I blink, taken aback by the unexpected plea in his words. It's not the anger or resentment I've grown used to hearing from him, but something different, something that hints at a deeper pain.

"What do you mean?" I ask, my voice shaky.

Wells takes a step closer, his shoulders slumping under an unbearable burden. His voice is barely above a whisper. "This isn't just about the ranch. Or Duke." He looks away, locking his pleading eyes with our father's. "You need to tell Sutton the truth."

27

LAINE

I FIND FRANKIE, Cassidy, and Magnolia sitting criss-crossed in front of the living room fireplace. Frankie is wrapping homemade lavender soap bars in customized labels to give out as wedding favors. Cassidy is filling paper cones with dried flowers—their "confetti" for the first walk up the aisle as a married couple. Magnolia, meanwhile, is staring out of the windows, watching the storm rage outside.

"We've missed you!" Frankie says, her entire face brightening when she sees me.

"Yeah, I was just trying to get some work done. I'm behind schedule."

Magnolia nods her head, as if reading straight through my jumbled thoughts. Cassidy attempts a smile.

At my request, Cassidy sets me to work on wrapping the soaps with Frankie.

"Thanks for all your help with the wedding," Cassidy says, a seemingly genuine smile gracing her lips. Her red hair is piled into a high bun, but a few tendrils are free, framing her larger-than-life features.

"It's no problem," I murmur, my mind somewhere else entirely.

"Well, thanks. And thanks for coming to the bachelorette party, too. I hope we didn't get too wild for you," Cassidy continues. "It sounds like I said...some things I shouldn't have. I don't even remember much of anything, but whatever I said, I am sorry." She pauses, unable to meet my gaze.

I smile weakly, only having the energy to half-listen.

When Cassidy speaks again, her voice is gentler than I've ever heard it. "And thank you..." She pauses, and we all let her think out her words in the quiet. "Thank you for getting Sutton here. I'm sure it wasn't an easy sell."

Frankie nods. Then, almost to herself, she says, "I missed him."

Magnolia holds both hands up to her chest, knotting them together. "Yes, thank you, Laine. I—we—needed him here."

The three of them try to keep the conversation going for a while, but I don't have much to say—an entirely new predicament for me. Soon, the others lapse into the same silence, until the thunder and crackling firewood are the only sound.

Eventually, there is a strike of lightning so bright we all pause our work to stare up at it. Soon after, it's accompanied by a low, villainous rumble in the clouds. Without thinking, I jump to my feet and hurry to the window, staring out at the strobing light. I look for anything outside, beyond the streaks of rain, that could resemble Sutton.

"Do you think they're alright out there?" I ask, my voice thick.

In seconds, Magnolia is at my side. "Want to watch for them from the porch?"

I give her a wordless nod.

Before leading me outside, Magnolia picks up a thick wool blanket from the couch, cradling it in her arm. I follow her to the porch swing where we both curl up, knees to our chests, and she drapes the blanket over us.

The air is cold and clear. And that *smell*. It's like every tree, every blade of grass opened up to the rain, letting their freshness flow out. If Sutton wasn't out in those mountains, facing that storm, I might see the light show as mesmerizing rather than petrifying.

"Should we have let them go out there in this weather?" my voice trembles as I scan the rain-soaked scenery, hoping that at any second I'll see Sutton emerge from the tree line.

Magnolia wraps an arm around my shoulders and pulls me in tight. "The storm wasn't supposed to hit until later this evening. But they'll be fine. All three of those boys know how to handle this weather. They're probably taking shelter somewhere up there, waiting for the worst of it to pass."

Magnolia could say anything and I would find some solace in it, thanks to that melodic voice of hers. I wanted to cling to her soothing words. But with every lightning strike, my pulse hitches. And even though I'm warm, curled up at Magnolia's side under our blanket, I can't stop shivering.

Magnolia tries to shift the conversation toward lighter matters. "You know, Laine, I've never seen Sutton so happy. You do wonders for him."

My stomach roils like the dark clouds above us, guilt seeping through me. After the last twenty-four hours I've had, the last thing I have energy for is digging myself deeper into our farce.

Magnolia's watercolor eyes shine. "He really loves you."

I try to laugh her words off, but the sound is strangled. After another thunderclap, I ask, "Did he say that to you?"

"No. He didn't need to. But I see it. I see it in the way he's constantly staring at you—and somehow thinking he's being discreet about it." Magnolia chuckles, tipping her head to the side so our foreheads touch. "And even before I saw it, I suspected it."

I keep my eyes trained on the trees when I ask, "What do you mean?"

"Oh, Sutton thought he was being really subtle when he told me about you. But I saw right through it."

"After the date auction?"

"No, after your first day in his class."

I snort. "What could he even have said? A girl showed up late. She was very annoying and kept begging me to tutor her."

"Sutton did mention the late thing," Magnolia chuckles. "But you can't blame a guy with a color-coded planner for that. That's not what stood out to me, though. No. Instead, it was how, even when he tried to keep it brief, the way he spoke about you made it clear that you intrigued him. Excited him. And it takes a lot to get Sutton excited, as you probably know. You were special from the beginning."

I chew on her words, wanting so badly to believe them.

"Sutton doesn't enjoy depending on others. But he needs you. It puts my mind at ease knowing that he's loved, even when he's away from home." Magnolia nudges my shoulder, a playful lift at her mouth. "Maybe before too long it'll be your wedding we're preparing for."

When I try to smile, my cheeks resist, like I'm trying to push the corners of my mouth through stone. A gnawing pull in my chest begs me to come clean, to face the stupid lie I dreamt up. But when I open my mouth to do so, I see Sutton's face, the shame that would cross his features if the truth came out.

We stay on that porch swing for what feels like a lifetime. Magnolia continues on with her dreaming. She talks about how, maybe someday, me and Sutton might return—or even move just a bit closer. She asks about the possibility of coming for holidays. She dreams that, if we have children, we will bring them here for visits, show them the ranch. Eventually, the guilt becomes too much, and I excuse myself to go to sleep.

Attempt to sleep, at least.

In the guest room, I pull all the curtains closed. But even without seeing it, I can still hear the hammering rain, the relentless thunder. A chill runs through me, and I grab the nearest thing to bundle in—Sutton's well-loved cable-knit sweater. I can still smell his cologne, its musky ginger and hints of floral, and I breathe it in heavily.

Before long, it's clear my mind won't be slowing anytime soon. Though I should rest, especially after my restless sleep at the lake last night, I already know I won't be able to relax enough to do so. Not with the shame, worry, and uncertainty raging through me, just as violent as the storm. I reach for the closest entertainment in sight, Sutton's childhood copy of *Peter Pan*, starting back at the first line: *All children, except one, grow up.*

28

SUTTON

WELLS' words hang in the air, laden with unspoken pain. I stare at him, my mind racing to grasp the weight of what he just said.

"I don't understand," I finally utter, my voice barely more than a whisper. "What truth?"

Waiting for Hank to be the one to confess, Wells stays quiet. All he does is place a hand behind my back, nudging me toward our father, still huddled under the canopy of pines.

Hank takes a shaky breath, and I see a vulnerability in his eyes that I've never witnessed before. "I have ALS."

He says the words so simply it takes a moment for their true meaning to register. My mind whirls with disbelief and denial, but my father's blank gaze tells me that this is no cruel joke.

I take a step closer, saying the first stupid question that comes to mind. "Dad... Are you sure?"

Wells finally speaks, his voice filled with the grief he's been shouldering. "He was diagnosed six weeks ago, but he's been showing signs for a long time now."

My mind races, trying to make sense of the reality crashing down around us. My father, a pillar of strength and resilience, is now faced with something that will tear down that core center of his being. Within seconds, the ranch, the legacy, everything I thought I knew shifts. Things click into place.

The rushed wedding.

My mother's and sister's insistence that I come.

Wells' unpredictable emotions.

My father gone so often for "appointments."

His shakiness.

The dropped pie.

His exhaustion.

His anger.

My throat constricts as I look between Hank and Wells. My father's words reverberate through my mind. *Our legacy is in your blood.* I suddenly realize the true meaning of that. He wasn't just talking about the ranch. He was talking about our family, about the burden he can't bear alone.

My voice breaks as I promise, "There has to be something you can do. Maybe a clinical trial or—"

"Sutton," my father says, cutting me off, "I'm not going to spend the last of my time on this earth in a hospital. I won't do it. I'll go to my checkups. I'll do my physical therapy. If it gets bad enough, I'll pay a nurse to help me around the house. But I'm spending as much time as I can on this ranch. With my family." The resolute stubbornness in Hank's gaze is as solid as ever.

Adrenaline, still slick and hot in my veins, surges through me. They kept this from me. My family has been suffering in silence while they kept me in the dark, outrageously oblivious, outrageously self-absorbed.

A bitter taste fills my mouth, tasting far worse than the blood, and I feel the pounding of anger—no, defeat—rising within me. I step away, raking a hand through my soaked hair. "How could you not tell me?" I continue, my voice shaking with frustration. "I could have been here. I could have helped."

Wells, still as amped up as I am, laughs sharply. "Right. Like how you were so helpful after Duke died."

His words hit me in my gut, more painful than any of his punches.

"Wells," our father says, his monosyllabic warning enough.

The anger inside me flares again, and I grumble back at Wells, "Don't bring Duke into this. I was already a year into NYU when he died. You think I should have just abandoned that to come back?" I flex my hands as if I can force my frustration out through my fingertips. "I've spent years trying to build a life for myself, to find my true place."

Wells' gaze is harsh and unforgiving. "I changed *my* plans. I was going to go to college too, you know. But I knew I had to be here for Frankie, for Mom and Dad. I was only sixteen, and I knew I would stay for them. Taking on Duke's responsibilities, working hard, I never once considered leaving this family."

"How was I supposed to come back? I came home to find you sleeping with *my* girlfriend in my truck," I snap, scrambling for anything that can even out the argument I know I'm losing.

"You left because I bruised your ego?" Wells' loud, biting words bounce off the mountains.

"You know that wasn't the only reason I left. I was never meant to stay at Silver Ridge."

Wells paces in tight circles. "Don't give me that *bullshit*. You were raised on this ranch same as me. You learned to rope, to ride, to rodeo. From the time you were born—from the time we all were born—we knew this place would be a part of us. You just chose to shut that part of yourself out."

"Fine!" I throw my arms into the air, spiraling further out of control. "Maybe I did. But I couldn't be here, couldn't bear to look at this place. And it wasn't just about school, or Cassidy, or my dreams. Really, it was about how all I could think about when I was here was *Duke*. Everywhere I looked, there was another reminder that he was gone. His room, his boots still at the door, his stupid horse! It was like losing him over and over, day after day."

"Coward," Wells hisses.

Hank tries to mediate, his voice anything but gentle. "Enough, both of you. What's done is done."

It feels like someone has hollowed me out. I sag to the ground, guilt dampening the fire that was roaring within me. For a few minutes, we sit in silence while I grapple with all this new information. No matter how I look at it, though, there's only one way forward.

"Wells is right," I eventually say. "I was being a coward. I couldn't face the loss of Duke. Maybe I still haven't." I pause, trying to fight my way through the mental static in my ears. "I should have been here. But this time, it'll be different. I'll stay. I'll be here for the family."

Hank's expression doesn't soften. "I don't want you to resent the ranch. I don't want you to come back and be miserable and angry."

"I was miserable knowing that I missed out on the last year of Duke's life," I say. "I'm not making that mistake again with you. *That* would be misery."

Wells' ever-furrowed brows lift with a mixture of tentative relief and surprise. Hank nods, just once, in approval.

"What about Laine?" Wells asks, still unconvinced that I'll actually stay this time.

I try to set my jaw the same way Hank does. "What about her?"

U

IT TAKES hours for the lightning to let up and the rain to slow enough for us to make the trek back to the house. Below me, Duke's horse is still skittish from the weather, and his hooves slide around a bit in the thick mud. I'll have to work more with him from now on.

From now on.

Even though the storm has subsided, there is still one stirring within me. In my mind, the life I thought I was working toward has shattered. I cling to the pieces, trying to make a new, complete picture. But it's no use. I know what I have to do. Beyond that, I know what that means I can no longer have.

No New York.

No becoming an editor.

No *her*.

I can't bear to think of her name, even though it whispers in the back of my mind, boring into my skull. That perfect, vibrant color of her lipstick clouds my vision, painting my world in a beautiful, terrible wash of red.

Before her, my life in the city was all work. Long hours. Internships. Letters of recommendation. LinkedIn updating. Ambition and goals and drive.

After her, it felt like I could live again. Her presence eased my guilt about leaving my family, and I could laugh and breathe again.

No matter how hard I try to stop it, mental snapshots of the last four months shuffle by, as clear as if I were seeing printed photos. Her pink hat on the first day of class. Her smile at the date auction. Morning coffee runs. Late-night study sessions. Literature discussions with Cyrus and art lectures from Althea. Thrifted red cowgirl boots.

Hank, Sutton, and I ride in silence all the way back to the barn. After putting Duke's horse away, I shuffle back to the house, each step taking mindful effort. The stairs inside look as long and steep as Everest, so I take them one by one, dreading the inevitable.

I stand for a long time outside the guest room door. Then, unable to go another second without seeing her, even if it kills me, I open the door a crack.

Laine left one of the bedside lamps on, allowing me to see her splayed out on the bed, on top of the messy covers. She still has makeup on, and it's a bit smudged. Her short black hair and bangs are just as wild, and her brows are knit, even while asleep. Beside her on the bed, my worn copy of *Peter Pan* sits face down, only a few pages left.

I wince at the sight of her in my sweater, already knowing I won't be able to stand wearing it again.

After a mere look at Laine, I feel my will crumbling. Everything in me wants to join her, to tuck her under the covers with me. I could kiss along her neck and draw lazy circles on her arm as she drifts deeper into sleep. Maybe she would stir enough to smile up at me, and everything else could fade away, even if just for a moment.

But if I go to her, I won't be able to tear myself away.

Even unzipping my bag to find a pair of sweats and a fresh shirt would risk waking Laine. So, after retreating to the hallway and closing the door behind me, I walk to Wells' room and knock at his door. When he opens it, I see Cassidy on his bed behind him, under the covers, her cheeks pink. Her smile fades when she sees me, sees the layer of blood and mud across my clothes.

"Uh, sorry," I stammer, shaking my head and averting my

eyes to the floor. "I was just going to see if I can borrow some clothes to sleep in."

"Yeah, of course," Wells says, ducking back into his room before reemerging a moment later with a small stack for me. He doesn't hand them over right off, though. Instead, he holds them under his arm, raising an eyebrow. "What happened to the clothes you brought?"

"They're in the guest room."

Wells' silence tells me that wasn't enough of an answer.

"I can't go in there tonight," I mutter.

Coward. I hear Wells' voice echo back through my mind. *Coward. Coward. Coward.*

"Wells?" Cassidy calls from the bed. We both look at her. Those familiar emerald eyes are wide, questioning. "Does he..."

"Yeah," Wells says, "he knows."

She looks at me then, years of friendship and love clear across her face. "I'm sorry," she says, barely loud enough for me to hear.

No response feels right, so I just give them a weak nod and shuffle to the bathroom. After peeling my muddy, wet clothes off, they fall to the ground with a heavy thump.

In the shower, my body tingles, thawing from the rigid, cold hours we spent on the mountain. The water runs dark for five minutes, cutting slowly through the blanket of dirt and blood. I scrub my entire body, wash my hair three times, and finally, when the water comes off clear, I dress in Wells' clothes. All the while, I think about my father.

With Laine in the guest room and my old bedroom still full of storage boxes, I'm left with no choice but to lie out across the living room couch and pull the wool blanket over me. I rear back at the smell of Laine's perfume, all too familiar, laced into the fibers. I throw the blanket to the ground. Before setting my phone down for the night, I pull up a new email, typing and sending it to Imagineer Books without bothering to mull over the right wording or even check it for errors.

I regret to inform you I must turn down the offer to work at Imagineer Books, effective immediately, due to unforeseen family matters. I am grateful for the offer. If the situation was different, I would be eager to join the team.

Sutton Davis

29

LAINE

I FALL in and out of sleep all night. Each time, I search the sheets beside me. And each time, there's nothing to find.

When I wake to a hint of pale sunrise seeping through the curtains, the absence of Sutton guts me. Mind racing, I throw myself from the bed and jog downstairs and through the house. There's no one. No sign of Frankie or Magnolia. No Wells or Hank. And certainly, no Sutton.

My heart pounds in my ears, and I rake through my hair, grabbing fistfuls of it.

He's probably fine, I tell myself. A much louder thought overtakes it almost immediately. *And what if he isn't?*

A singular, soft beat sounds from outside. I rush to the window but see no one. Then again, *thud*. A long pause. *Thud.*

Barefoot, I run out the front door, too frantic to close it behind me. My feet pad against the bouncy grass, still wet from morning dew.

Thud. Louder this time.

The day's early chill bleeds through the weave of Sutton's sweater hanging around me. Fog hangs around the house, thick and suffocating.

I near the sound, gaining clarity. It's a ragged crack. A noise I've heard only once before.

Sure enough, I round the back corner of the house to find Sutton, axe raised, splitting logs with his back to me. Already, a heap of firewood stands at his feet. Despite the chill, he has no coat on, just a black tee I don't recognize. It's too small for him, tight enough to show the ropes of muscle stretching and pulsing as he hammers the axe down, the wood splintering and flying to either side of him.

I watch for a moment, as if the image of him might dissipate right into the fog. Every rhythmic thud of the axe hitting wood eases some of my anxiety until, finally, I can smile.

Laughing from relief, I call his name. He pauses. The axe drops to his side, lifeless. But he doesn't turn. Unable to stop myself, I approach him from behind and wrap my arms around his torso, burying my face against his solid back. Under my arms, I feel his breaths quicken, and he tenses, creating an invisible wall between us.

Stumbling back a step, I watch Sutton's shoulders slump. He pushes his hands through his curls and stares up at the sky for a moment.

"Sutton?" I say, like it might break a curse holding him still and quiet. "Are you okay?"

He doesn't turn, so I grab onto his arm, yanking it back so I can swing him around to face me. What I'm met with makes it feel like the morning chill has plummeted straight through my chest. His eyes are flat, somehow grayer than their usual brown. And one of those eyes I can hardly see, thanks to the swelling puffed up around it, marbled blue and purple. The bruise spreads across most of the neighboring cheek. His other eye, though not swollen, is marred by a dark shadow beneath it, the testament to a long, sleepless night. His bottom lip also swells on one side, a red split cutting through it.

I say his name for a third time, whispering in a voice I hardly recognize. *Is it even him?* I scan his face and body slowly. Cuts and bruises scatter across his tan skin. He looks terrible, battered. Even worse than his black eye is that dead look behind it.

"What happened to you?" I ask through a gasp.

He tightens his mouth, and it exaggerates the swollen side.

"Did you get into an accident?" Reaching up, I gently nudge the unbruised side of his face, tilting it so I can inspect him for more damage. My eyes burn with welling tears, and Sutton's eyes soften, just for a moment, before he steps back, away from my touch. "What happened?" I repeat, my tone practically begging him for an answer.

Still, nothing.

"Did...did Wells do this to you?"

Sutton looks back at me, his eyes darkening. "I'm fine," he says, his hoarse voice telling me otherwise.

Desperate to give Sutton any ounce of the comfort and reassurance he constantly gives me, I wrap my arms around him, breathing him in. I hate the way his shirt doesn't smell like him. It's yet another thing dividing *this* Sutton from the one I know. My fingers press into his back, as if I can push life back into him. After too long, he returns the hug. But it's timid, awkward. Like he's trying to keep his distance even while I'm nestled right up to his chest.

When I speak, I keep my cheek against him, unwilling to look back up at those strange eyes. "You have to tell me what happened."

"Laine," Sutton says, voice catching. "I'm not going back to New York."

30

SUTTON

LAINE'S ARMS go limp around me. She takes a few shaky steps back, staring up at me. Her eyes are set over shadowed bags similar to the ones I saw in the mirror this morning. Her black pupils dilate under knit brows. Those full lips downturn. I scan her face over and over again, trying to take in every detail of her while I still can, committing her to memory.

"I don't understand," she whispers, wrapping her arms around herself.

My exhale is sharp through my nose, my jaw locked too tight for air to escape. "My dad is sick," I finally reply, hoping Laine won't ask for details.

But of course, she does. "You got a black eye because your dad is sick?"

My fists ball up at my sides. I do my best to separate the words from their meaning, to make them simple, just like my father did when he told me. "He has ALS."

Laine's nose wrinkles as she fights off the tears glistening in her eyes. "What... What's his outlook?"

It's an easy enough question to answer, considering the

fact that I stayed up all night researching my father's disease. "Over time, it'll rob him of his ability to move, to speak, to breathe." I pause for a moment to swallow the lump in my throat. "There's no cure, Laine. He's—He's going to deteriorate. He's already well on his way."

"That's horrible," she mutters, spinning her rings with trembling fingers.

I take a deep breath, trying to steady myself. "Yeah, it's... not great." The understatement is painfully clear to us both.

Laine takes a half-step forward, reaching out for me. Her fingers graze my elbow. I flinch, and her arm drops back down, dead weight. "It's awful. But you can't just give up your dreams because of it," she says after a painfully long pause.

I squeeze my eyes shut, clinging to any whisper of duty and guilt.

She continues on, her cadence even faster than her usual. "You worked so hard to get that job at Imagineer Books. It's your chance to make a real impact on young readers, just like you wanted."

Meeting her gaze, I see the turmoil within me reflected back. "This is my family. My father. I can't leave them when they need me the most. Not again. Not like when Duke died."

She takes another step closer, her voice gentle now, but no less determined. "You don't have to leave your family. You can travel back and forth between New York and Montana. Maybe you can do your job remotely, or you could at least try to negotiate a flexible arrangement. I'm sure you have options."

I shake my head. "It's not that simple, Laine. This isn't something I can do halfway. My dad's illness will require my time and energy. I need to be there for him. It's time for me to grow up."

Frustration and desperation tinge Laine's voice. "You're giving up a part of yourself, a dream you've had for years. I don't want to see you just throw that away."

Gritting my teeth, I feel my will to stay in West River shred to pieces with every word Laine says. "I can't be in two places at once. My family needs me, free of distractions."

Recognition flashes across Laine's face. She, just as I already have, realizes that our paths are diverging. Her eyes flutter, and I can see her thoughts whirring, searching for a solution. "Well, I can help too. I'll fly to Montana every month, every couple of weeks. I can help drive Hank to appointments and help around the ranch."

My chest burns at her offer. I shouldn't be surprised, given how spontaneous Laine is, that she would want to drop everything, change everything, for me and my family at the drop of a hat.

I can't—I won't—ask Laine to leave her life in the city to suffer alongside us. The next years with Hank, however many there will be, will be miserable for him—and for my family as we sit by, helpless. So, I think of anything I can to get her to leave, to continue on with her exciting, colorful life and leave me behind in my world of gray.

"It's not like what we had was real," I mutter. The lie is acrid against my tongue.

Laine's mouth opens just enough for a shocked gasp to slip past her bare lips. "But at the lake," she stammers, "you said you wanted to be with me. That you wanted it—*us*—to be real."

Swallowing the dryness in my throat, I double-down. "I just got caught up in the charade."

"We don't have to date," Laine says, an edge of panic and frustration to her voice. "I can come visit whenever you need an extra hand. Just as a friend."

Don't sentence her to that, I beg of myself, squeezing my eyes shut. I can't even look at her. "I don't need impulsiveness or indecisiveness right now. What I need is stability."

"So...you don't need me," she says through clenched teeth.

I open my eyes to see a tear spill over the edge of her lashes, streaking down one cheek. It takes everything in me to not wipe it away, to resist the urge to grab Laine, hold her, tell her the truth. Tell her that if I was being selfish, I would ask her to stay with me. That in the dark days ahead, she could be my light, as she always has been. I would tell her she's *exactly* what I need.

But I can't ask her to face my darkness. I can't risk dimming her light.

Laine has always been an open book, so easy to read. And now, I study the shock and hurt written across her face.

"You're my best friend, Sutton," Laine uttered.

I lock my jaw the way I've seen Hank and Wells do time and time again. "I'm sorry." Finally, at least one morsel of truth.

With effort, Laine straightens, lifting her chin higher. The corners of her mouth pinch. "I guess I should go back to New York."

Though it pains me, I say, "That's probably for the best." After all, I can only deny the pull to be with Laine for so long. If she asked me to go back with her, how long could I resist that selfish, hungry part of me that aches to be hers?

As Laine walks away, I cover my mouth with my hand, physically restraining myself from stopping her.

31

LAINE

MY BARE FEET are numb from the cold, but I force them toward the house. I can't stand to look at Sutton for one more second. Hurt and sympathy collide in my chest, raging a war against each other. I try to wipe the mental image of Sutton, bruised and broken, from my mind.

I go through the back door so I can avoid any other Davises and tiptoe silently across the floor and upstairs. My chest burns at the sound of Frankie and Magnolia in the kitchen. Part of me wants to join them, offer my condolences, and soak in the warmth of their company. A bigger part of me wants to get the hell away from Silver Ridge Ranch before I have to face further devastation.

In the guest room, the first thing I do is tear Sutton's sweater off, throwing it into a ball at the foot of the unmade bed. After redressing in the first things I grab, my too-big Scooby Doo shirt and the Wranglers I thrifted specifically for this trip, I pile everything else into my bags, not bothering to fold or organize anything. When I get to the bathroom, I can only make myself brush my teeth and comb through my mangled hair before giving up on the rest of my appearance.

With one sweeping motion, I slide everything from the bathroom counter into my toiletry bag and shove it down into my suitcase.

I'm too frazzled to double-check that I left nothing behind. At the last second, I scrawl a note for Sutton on a receipt I find deep in my overstuffed purse. I slide it into *Peter Pan* and replace the book on the shelf. If he goes looking for the book, maybe my message will be one he needs to hear.

I pause at the top of the stairs, peering out over the landing. Frankie and Magnolia seemingly left, and there's no sign of anyone else in the house. In fact, all I hear is the ongoing crack of Sutton's axe outside, muffled through the walls.

There's no sign of anyone else in the Davis family outside either, at least not within my line of sight. Thankful that I might be spared the embarrassment of an awkward farewell, I sneak to the barn, checking for any sign of Wells before entering it.

Each of the ranch hands smiles at me, their rough exteriors cracked after my week spent here. Bill, the oldest in the group, is the first to greet me.

"You look as well-rested as a tumbleweed in a dust storm," he chuckles, tipping his hat at me.

Too anxious to bother beating around the bush, I ask, "Any chance you're going to town this morning?"

Bill's smile drops. "Boys," he announces to his crew, "go on and get back to work. I'll be back." They do as instructed, but I notice over half of them sneaking looks at me and whispering to one another. The pieces won't be hard to put together, especially once they learn that I'm going back to the city just six days before the wedding.

"Do you want to tell me what's going on?" Bill asks under his breath, gruff as ever.

"Not really," I whisper, tightening my grip on my bags. "I

need a ride to Missoula. To the airport. I would ask Frankie, but…"

Bill sucks his teeth. "I can't be gone that long—unless you're okay to wait until the workday is done." He takes one look at my expression and nods. "Didn't think so. I can take you to town, though. There's a bus that leaves in an hour from the Gas 'n' Go."

"Yes, please," I say. "The sooner, the better." Bill turns to lead me out to his truck, and I grab his arm. "Can we… Can you not tell anyone about this until I'm gone?"

Bill's silver mustache twitches. "Does Sutton know?"

Just hearing his name makes my breath catch. "He thinks it's best if I go," I say.

Shaking his head in disbelief, Bill grabs my bags from me. Once we're at his truck, he throws them into the dirty bed. And then we're off down the long dirt road back to town. Not wanting to watch the landscape go by one last time, I try to keep my eyes on my phone, frantically searching for the next flight out of Montana. I book it immediately, flinching at the price and typing my credit card number in. I wonder how long it will take me to pay the flight off, especially if I don't get hired on full-time with *Wonderings*.

"You know, don't you?" Bill asks as the bus stop comes into view. One look in his watery eyes, and I know exactly what he's referring to.

"Sutton found out last night. I found out this morning."

Bill puts the truck into park. "I'm sorry Sutton pushed you away. He's been like that ever since he was little. He never liked facing conflict. Never liked admitting when he was sad. He'd just shove his feelings to the side and pretend they didn't exist. Guess he's still doing that."

I try to clear the lump—the boulder—in my throat. "I guess."

Bill's hands tighten on the wheel. "This past week, seeing

him again, it's been like seeing a new person. I've never seen that kid smile so much. And most of the time, those smiles were aimed right at you."

It was all for show, I want to scream. *It was all fake.* Instead, I mumble out, "Thank you for the ride," and hurry from the car. Bill helps with the bags, and then he's off to Silver Ridge, leaving me alone with nothing but my nonsensical thoughts.

Losing Sutton—even if I never had him at all—is indescribable. Worse, knowing that my flaws I've tried to hide from my whole life are to blame. He said it himself. *Impulsive. Indecisive. Distracting.*

I play the words again and again in my mind until their syllables lose all meaning.

32

SUTTON

EVERYTHING HURTS.

My jaw. My eye. My chest.

It takes me nearly an hour to work up the nerve to face Laine again. Chopping wood did little in the way of releasing the tension I was harboring. Instead, it just left me sore and sweaty. Walking inside, I catch a glimpse of my reflection. I almost look as bad as I feel.

"What the hell happened to you?" Frankie almost shouts when she sees me, scrambling up from her seat on the couch. "Is that a black eye?"

"He knows, Frank," Wells says, coming in from the kitchen. His words are so quick I'm sure he's been waiting to say them all morning. "Sutton knows."

Frankie's brilliant smile drops, and it's like she sheds a mask. Immediately, her brown eyes—*my* brown eyes—shine with tears, and her nose wrinkles, wiggling her freckles. She squeezes her eyes shut. "You know about..." She can't get the words out.

I nod, willing my lungs to fill as normal, despite the pressing weight against them. "Dad told me."

Frankie catapults toward me, crashing against my chest in a bear hug. Her ragged sob heaves against me, tears soaking into my shirt. She's nearly six feet tall, with a strong, built frame, but with her head tucked under my chin, she feels like the young little sister I remember.

"I wanted to tell you. But Dad—Dad didn't want anyone to."

"I know," I hum, rubbing her shoulder.

After a few minutes of crying, Frankie lifts her head just enough to look at Wells. He watches us from the corner of the room. "Get over here, idiot," she says, trying to laugh as she holds an arm out for him. Wells falters but eventually gives in. As soon as he's close enough, Frankie grabs him by the torso, sandwiching herself between us.

All our breaths come out uneven, and each of us sheds some tears. Wells tries to hide his by wiping his cheek against Frankie's blonde curls, but some catch in his beard, glistening. It could be minutes or hours that we stand, clinging to each other. The three remaining Davis siblings.

And it hits me—we never had this when Duke passed. Mom cried constantly that entire week I was home, and probably well beyond that, I'd bet. Frankie cried during the funeral. Wells' stone-cold demeanor broke only during the burial. Meanwhile, I felt too ashamed to let them see my tears and only let them loose in the sanctuary of my room. It felt like I wasn't worthy of mourning a brother that I, by my father's measure, abandoned. And while our crying today may have started as pre-grieving for our father, it is equally our long-overdue grieving for our brother.

"We're going to get through it," Wells promises. And that look, that strong determination, makes me almost believe it.

Eventually, we gain some semblance of composure, painting our masks on. Wells squares his shoulders and sets his jaw. Frankie gives a wide smile. And I grow quiet.

"Have you guys seen Laine around?" I ask. "I need to talk to her." Really, I need to apologize.

"I thought she was with you," Frankie says.

"You didn't see her come inside, maybe an hour ago?"

Frankie shakes her head, her mouth straining as she tries to keep from frowning.

"Wells? Anything?"

"No, but I was about to go check on the guys. I can ask if they've seen her."

"I'll join you outside. Just...just let me check upstairs." It takes all my will to not sprint to the guest room. The door to it is wide open. Inside, I find the bed hastily made, the sheets untucked and the pillows askew. But what's more important is what I *don't* see.

There's no sign of Laine. No suitcase. No clothes.

Though I know what I'll find—or won't find—I go to the bathroom. The counter is empty, aside from my toiletries all in an organized line on one side. I push my hands through my hair. My eyes fall to the ground where, just barely peeking out from under the vanity, a tube of lipstick must have fallen. I pick it up gingerly.

With Laine's lipstick gripped in my palm, I follow Wells outside and to the barn. He assigned tasks early this morning, so most of the cowboys are already out. A few, though, are working at the barn and corral today. Each of them looks at me from the corner of their eye before averting their gaze in the opposite direction.

"I'm going to check..." I say, already walking away from Wells and through the barn without finishing my sentence.

No sign of her.

I walk through the bunkhouse. Around the outbuildings. By the sheds.

Nothing.

My knuckles are white around the lipstick tube. With my

free hand, I pull my phone out, clicking on Laine's name from my favorites list. The call rings once. Twice. Voicemail. I try again.

Once. Twice. Voicemail.

My pulse races, and I let a quick breath out, striding to Wells and Bill. The latter frowns at me from under his long, horseshoe-shaped mustache.

"Still nothing?" Wells asks, already knowing the answer.

I move my head in a tight, small shake. "Bill, have you seen Laine around today?"

He clears his throat and rubs at the back of his neck uncomfortably. "I—I thought you knew. She said it was your idea."

A curse slips from my mouth. Then another. And another as I kick a bucket sitting nearby. When I speak again, my voice sounds more like my father's than my own. "I need you to tell me where she went."

Bill looks at his feet, his hat obscuring half his face. "She said you wanted her to leave. I didn't want her to try hitching a ride from some stranger, and she said she was too embarrassed to ask anyone in the family for a ride, so I drove her to the gas station. She took the bus to Missoula."

"And you didn't think to *tell* me that my girlfriend was leaving?" My tone comes out harsher than I would like.

"Explain," Wells prods Bill, an icy edge to his narrowed gaze.

Bill coughs awkwardly. "Laine made it sound like you two...well, like you ended things."

"That's not..." My voice fades, and I feel a sharp tingling at my fingertips.

Wells looks at me, dropping his usual bravado as his mouth pops open. "Tell me that isn't true."

My sigh cuts through the cool air. "It's complicated."

Frankie's shout sounds from the porch. "Any luck?" she

calls, her hands cupped in a makeshift megaphone around her mouth. My parents and Cassidy stand at Frankie's sides.

A weight drops in my stomach. I walk over to the porch to face my family, wincing at their expressions, a mix of curiosity and concern. Wells is right behind me, and I can feel his eyes on the back of my head, silently demanding an explanation.

"So?" Frankie says, drumming her fingertips on the porch railing.

"I have something to tell you—all of you."

My parents exchange glances, and Cassidy shoots a questioning look to Wells. I hear his jacket rustle with a shrug.

"We should sit," I say, mostly to buy myself more time. I reenter the house with methodical steps, planting myself on the bench of the fireplace's hearth. My family, timid and suspicious, takes their seats on the couches opposite me.

"Is Laine okay?" Mom asks, deep eyes even darker with a shadow of worry. She sweeps her eyes over my ragged face. "Are *you* okay?"

My father's expression isn't much different. "What's this about, son?"

"I haven't been honest with you all," I say.

Frankie scoffs, clinging to any shred of positivity left in her. "Dishonesty must be genetic," she jokes.

I look down at my hands, at the lipstick tube still in my palm, taking in a slow exhale. "Laine and I weren't actually dating," I finally confess. "She was—is—my best friend. And when I told her about the wedding, about how embarrassed I was feeling about not having a date, she offered to act like we were dating."

My mother's face contorts, and my father's brows furrow. Wells and Cassidy look at me with incredulous stares. Frankie simply blinks, as if she doesn't speak my language.

Mom, as usual, is the first to break the silence. "Sutton Davis, you did *what*?"

I push my hair away from my face, avoiding their gazes. "Laine and I weren't really dating. I'm sorry. I shouldn't have lied to you. It got out of hand."

"You're kidding, right?" Wells says, each word tight.

My family's disappointment is palpable.

Hank, looking wearied from our terrible evening, shakes his head an inch to the side. "You shoulda been honest with us. Lying to us, bringing Laine here under that pretense...it's now how we raised you."

There's nothing I can say that can excuse what I've done. But as bad as it is to come clean, it would have been worse to continue the lies. I can't stand having one more ounce of guilt in a vise around my throat.

Frankie is visibly shaken. "Couldn't you have picked someone less *perfect?* Like, someone with an annoying laugh or someone who talks during movies or who smacks her lips when they talk?" Her attempt at a laugh is feeble. "I thought...I thought I might get a sister. Another sister," she adds, looking over at Cassidy. "I thought Laine was the one."

My family nods in agreement.

"So, where is Laine?" Mom asks.

I clear my throat. "We thought it would be best for her to go."

Cassidy still hasn't spoken, so I turn my attention to her. To my surprise, her eyes are red, tears threatening to fall over the edges of her lashes.

"I'm sorry, Cass. It was pathetic. I know you were planning on having her in the wedding, and I know this will probably mess things up. But I want to make it right—or as right as I can. I'll pay you back for Laine's bridesmaid dress, flowers, everything." Cassidy opens her mouth, probably to object, so I quickly add, "It's the least I can do. Please."

Cassidy purses her lips, mulling over my words. After a painfully long pause, she says, "I really believed you loved her."

33

LAINE

BY THE TIME I get to my apartment building, I'm seconds from collapsing. It's just past midnight, and the city is as loud as ever. Have there always been so many cars? This many people? Before going inside, I look up at the sky, just to be sure. Of course, there are hardly any stars. And even the darkness isn't as rich as it was in Montana.

After nearly falling asleep in the elevator, I finally make it to my familiar door. Exhaustion even affects my fingers, and I fumble with my keys. The door opens before I can even unlock it myself.

"Laine!" Dad says, pulling me to him.

Mom is with us in an instant, piling in on the hug.

My bed calls to me. Nervous that my legs might give out in mere seconds, I push away from my parents' grasp to lie belly-down on the cheap mattress.

I feel Mom sit beside me, but I can't even work up the energy to open my eyes.

"Laine, baby," she hums, shaking my shoulder. "Laine, are you okay?"

"I'm fine," I mumble out, voice muffled by the cushion. "What are you doing here?"

"Sutton told us you were coming back early," Dad explains, stooping down close to me. "Can we talk about what happened?"

I mumble out something resembling, "Not now."

"Okay," my parents whisper in unison.

Within seconds, one of them is draping a throw blanket over me, and I hear the other roll my suitcase into my room. I'm already half-asleep when I pick up on their quiet conversation.

"Do you think she's sick?" Dad whispers from the farthest spot in my apartment, which means he's only ten feet from me.

"No. She wouldn't fly home if she was sick. You know Sutton wouldn't let her leave before he nursed her back to health."

"You think it was about him, then?"

Mom sighs. "Why did they think that lie would end well?"

"We should call Sutton again, don't you think? Whatever happened, I can't imagine he's in good shape either."

No, I want to shout out. *Don't call.* But my body is completely depleted. My eyelids weigh fifty pounds each.

"Sutton?" Dad asks, his voice sounding far away as I slip deeper and deeper into sleep. "Yes, she's safe."

∪

WHEN I WAKE LATE in the morning, it feels like there are a hundred needles drilling into my temples. After finally mustering the courage to open my eyes, I see a glass of water and two aspirin pills on the side table.

A dozen missed calls and texts wait for me, but I scroll

past any from the Davises until one from Ophelia jumps out at me.

> Just emailed you the information for our Zoom meeting.

I sigh, devouring the single crumb of relief I feel. As anxious as I am about my subpar work for *Wonderings Magazine*, it's a welcome distraction.

> Hey, Ophelia! My trip got cut short. Thankfully, I got all my interviews done. But if you'd like to meet in person in the city, I'm available.

Her response comes quick.

> Great! Let's meet over brunch tomorrow.

Twenty-four hours. Twenty-four hours that will be so busy with writing and editing I won't have a chance to worry about anything—or anyone—else.

Though I would love to dive right into work, I can actually smell the stress and post-travel woes on me. First things first.

Even the guest bathroom at the Davis ranch house had a full tub, double sink, and an enormous window overlooking green fields. I try to ignore that as I shower in my bathroom, which is roughly the size of a coat closet. The narrow medicine cabinet's mirror fogs up from steam, but I don't wipe it away, unwilling to see who will stare back at me.

Once back in the main room, I almost double-back at the sight of it. Has my apartment always looked this wild? It's as if I'm seeing it with fresh eyes. Posters, art, and pictures hang along the walls, no rhyme or reason to any of them. Junk piles on every surface—books, clothes, shoes, remnants of my short-lived hobbies, unidentified charging cords from one thing or another. Before I realize it, I'm ripping the clutter away from the walls, revealing more of the white paint than I've seen in years. Once I've cleared the walls, I get to work on everything else, tossing anything that could possibly be distracting into a terrifying heap. When I'm done, I'm left with a space that looks more like a cubicle than an apartment.

With a clean slate, I type furiously for hours, forcing myself to stay on task. Write, read, edit, repeat. On and on until the daylight fades from my tiny window, and a knock pulls me from my focus.

I almost don't answer it, but two familiar voices call my name on the other side. When I work up the will to answer the door, I'm greeted by unconvincing smiles.

Dad whistles, slow and low. "What happened in here, kid?"

"What?" I ask, only half-listening.

"You tore everything down," Mom mutters.

I look up at them then and am met with wide eyes and tense shoulders. I exhale sharply through my nose. "It's time for me to be responsible. You've both been telling me that for, what, my entire life now?"

"Tearing your room apart isn't exactly what we had in mind," Dad says, walking in and sitting on the edge of my bed with a bag of takeout in one hand.

Mom gives me a sideways hug. "We want you to have goals and work toward them, sure." She pauses to gesture around my room. "That doesn't mean you have to change who you are. You're colorful and...full of life. And if that means your room gets a bit cluttered, so be it."

I don't respond.

My parents exchange glances, and Dad is the first to break

the silence, his words cautious, a long pause between each. "We talked to Sutton."

My stomach lurches, but I force my face to stay neutral.

"He didn't say much," Mom says. "Mostly, he talked about being worried about you. He wanted to be sure you made it home safe, that you were doing okay. He also said that he messed up. And whatever he did, he feels terrible about it."

When it's obvious I won't be responding to that, Dad asks directly, "What exactly *did* happen?"

I try to fight my word-vomit, but as soon as I open my mouth, it all comes out. I tell them about meeting Sutton's family, and the wedding prep, and the bachelorette party. The interviews, and the town, and the ranch. I even tell them about the night at the lake, leaving the details out, obviously. And finally, my voice faltering, I tell my parents about Hank's diagnosis and Sutton's decision that he no longer wants to be with me, not as a charade. And certainly not for real.

"I thought he really…" I pause, unable to say the true word on my mind. "I thought he really cared for me. I thought what we had was genuine." I roll my eyes at myself. "But he doesn't want me around. I'm a distraction. Too unpredictable to depend on. I—I lost my best friend," I choke out.

"Lainey," Mom begins, her voice softer than I've ever heard it, "you've been through so much in the past week. Going from friends to…more, to ending things."

Dad chimes in, his tone equally gentle, "We know how much you care about Sutton and how much he cares about you. But when people make decisions when they're under pressure, they rarely make the right ones."

"We've been hoping for a long time that you two would finally figure out what we already knew," Mom adds with a small smile.

I straighten, wiping away a tear that managed to escape. "Didn't you hear what I just said? He said he didn't want me in his life anymore."

My parents share another glance, and Mom says, "We saw the connection between you and Sutton over the past few months. We've watched you two grow together. You were always having fun, laughing, helping each other. What you had…well, it seemed real to me."

34

SUTTON

AFTER A MORNING full of studying Dad's healthcare plan and running errands in Missoula for the ranch, I return to the house to find Frankie sitting on the guest bed. Her golden curls are in a wild, unkempt crown around her head, and her eyes pierce through me. The joyful, bubbly demeanor she generally carries is nowhere to be seen.

"Hey, Frank," I say, already rifling through the dresser for work clothes to wear so I can help Wells around the ranch.

I know what Frankie wants to say. It's been bubbling under the surface for the past forty-eight hours. But she just stares at me.

"Out with it," I groan. "Tell me what you're thinking."

Frankie squares her shoulders to me, lifting her chin. "Fine. I think you're a dumbass."

I scoff and throw the shirt in my hands at her. She blocks it, glaring. "Good morning to you too," I grumble, Frankie's somber mood rubbing off on me—not that my mood was particularly sunny beforehand.

"How could you let her go?" Frankie demands, standing

234

from the bed and crossing her arms over her chest. That unmistakable Davis fire is alive behind her sharp gaze.

My halfhearted laugh comes out shaky. "Didn't you hear what I said to everyone? We weren't actually dating."

"Don't be so technical." She sighs, tapping her fingers on her crossed arms. "I noticed the change in you after you met Laine. You were hopeful. Happy. You were giddy when you talked about her paying $300 for a date with you. Before you came, you told me that Laine was bright and bubbly. What I didn't expect was how much it rubbed off on you."

My skin prickles with heat, and I turn into the bathroom to dress. Frankie continues talking through the door.

"Fake relationship or not, you care about her, Sutton. I *know* you do."

Once dressed, I throw the door open, my lungs heaving with labored breaths. "I don't just care about her. I *love* her." As soon as the words are out, the air feels thinner, and I rub my chest with my palm, forcing air into it.

Frankie's quick laugh is pure delight. "I knew it!" After seeing my horrified reaction to my own declaration, she asks, "What did Laine say when you told her?"

I shake my head once.

"You dumbass!" Frankie says again, but this time with a grin still plastered on her face. "You have to tell her how you feel. I'm sure she wouldn't have left if she knew." The details of a grand gesture are already forming behind those eyes.

"That's exactly why I can't tell her. I don't want her here. I mean, yes, a selfish part of me does." Frankie opens her mouth to object, but I continue on. "You *know* how hard these last years with Dad will be. You've done your research. I love Laine too much to sentence her to that."

"Just because you're staying in Montana doesn't mean you two have to end things."

"Long distance wouldn't work. I won't be able to think about anything aside from Dad's health. And I refuse to subject Laine to a half-assed relationship. Not when she deserves all of me and more."

Frankie's eyes are wide, and I see her mentally mapping out options. I also see when each one hits a dead end. "Have you thought about Laine? Doesn't she deserve to know?" Frankie asks, unable to come up with a solution. "She looked at you the same way you looked at her. She must be heart-broken right now."

My shoulders drop, and I stare at my hands, red and raw from my week of working on the ranch. "Whatever Laine is feeling right now is nothing compared to the heartache she would face if she stayed here to watch me—watch us—go through hell. The heartache of trudging through hell right alongside us."

"Then maybe you shouldn't stay." Even as Frankie says it, I can tell she doesn't fully mean it. "We have it handled. You can still come visit."

"I didn't have any warning with Duke." My brother's name is acid in my mouth. "But I do have a warning with Dad. I'm not missing out on his final years, not for anything, not when I already wasted six years being mad at him. If things are meant to be with Laine, maybe we will find our way back to each other someday."

Frankie's mouth opens and closes a few times, but she chokes down her arguments. Instead, she leaves without another word, her steps defeated.

My chest still feels tight, so I turn to the same place I always have: a book. The green leather spine of *Peter Pan* sticks out from the others on the bookshelf. I pull it out to see a scrap piece of paper near the back, just barely sticking out from the pages. I open the book to that spot.

Laine was on the last chapter, just shy of finishing. At the top of the page, one line of the book stands out from the others. *When people grow up, they forget the way.*

The scrap piece of paper is a receipt from our night at the karaoke bar two weeks ago. The memory feels foreign to me, as if it's something I read in a book, not something I lived. Laine's messy handwriting on the receipt reads, *Don't grow up too fast.*

My legs feel weak. After placing the receipt back in the book, I stand and tuck it under my arm.

I don't realize I'm going outside until Hank calls to me. Determined to make the most of his body while he can, he's on horseback. Bill is on one side of him, Wells on the other. Both of them are pretending they're not keeping a watchful eye on my father.

"You alright?" Hank asks, his voice slightly kinder than usual.

"Fine," I mumble, lifting the corners of my mouth into an unconvincing smile.

Again, my body acts of its own accord, and I'm suddenly staring down at my phone, my text thread with Laine opened within seconds. I wince at the last messages we sent to each other.

> Hank wants me and Wells to help him with something on the ranch. I'll be back tonight. I miss you.

The sky is dark, so unless I'm mistaken, I think that means it's nighttime. Any update on when you'll be home?

Are you stuck in the storm?

Text me when you can.

Then the next day's.

> Can we talk, Laine?

> Bill said you're on your way back to the city. Can I call you before your flight?

> Will you text me when you get home so I know you're safe?

> I'm sorry for what I said.

My fingers barely move when I type and delete message after message. Nothing sounds right.

"Son!" Hank's voice snaps me out of my stupor. "You don't look so good."

All I can do is nod.

Wells rubs the back of his neck. "I'm headed out to check the trails, see if any got washed out by the storm. Come with me. You can—I don't know—get some fresh air or something."

I give another nod.

Duke's horse is on-edge while I saddle him, even more so than he was during my first ride with him last week. Not wanting to leave my copy of *Peter Pan* or, more importantly, the note inside, in the barn, I tuck it in the saddle bag, triple-checking that the straps are secured before swinging myself up onto the horse. As soon as I do so, something jabs in my thigh, and I pull out Laine's lipstick tube from my pocket. I hadn't realized I grabbed it this morning.

After opening the tube, just to see that familiar shade of red, I place it in the chest pocket of my snap-up work shirt, just below the embroidered "S" of our family's cattle brand.

As soon as I kick my stirrups, Duke's horse rears its head and lets out a harsh whicker.

"He's been like that ever since the storm," Wells explains.

I follow behind Wells' horse, hoping it'll keep Duke's in line. "What's the weather supposed to be today?"

Wells shrugs. "Little rain. Nothing bad."

Overhead, clouds kiss the mountaintops. They're white and as fluffy as cotton candy. "What's got you worried, bud?" I ask, patting the horse's shoulder.

35

LAINE

WHEN I GET to the restaurant Ophelia suggested, I find her already seated at one of the sidewalk tables. She's wearing a monochromatic outfit, a periwinkle turtleneck, a blazer, and a mini-skirt that shows off her mile-long legs. And though my wildly patterned outfit is a far cry from her put-together look, she gives mine an impressed nod after looking me up and down.

She hugs me, grinning. "Please tell me you dressed like that in rural Montana," Ophelia says, touching the arm of the yellow-and-green jacket I layered over my lavender tank top and orange pants.

"This, plus red cowgirl boots," I say, relief lightening my words. I spent all morning mentally preparing for the worst, but Ophelia's excitement calms my worries. For the first time in days, my smile feels natural.

She motions for me to take a seat, and I join her at the table. The street is bustling with people, and I try to ignore the overwhelm creeping into me. After just a week in West River, I somehow acclimated far too easily to it. Even in the throes of a fake relationship, the world felt serene there.

Now, every honking horn, every ring of a bike bell, and every clang of machinery feels like a needle stinging my skin. I refocus on Ophelia, pretending all the background noise isn't there.

"I've been going through the updated drafts you sent me. And I'm impressed. You've captured the essence of Montana in a way that's authentic and captivating," Ophelia commends, her eyes gleaming with genuine enthusiasm. "*That* was the voice we were looking for."

Another crashing wave of relief crashes over me. "I'm glad you liked them. Montana was inspiring, to say the least."

"Liked them? *Loved* them," Ophelia gushes. "I handle most of *Wonderings'* online presence, and I want to run all the stories on our website. And when I showed them to Adam, he was equally impressed. He is thinking about focusing an entire issue on the wonders of the west. We would probably hire some more freelancers, locals from other rural towns, but we want your articles to be the centerpiece."

I'm rarely rendered speechless, but Ophelia's suggestion does the trick.

She laughs, probably at my slightly agape mouth. "Your articles are...*fun*. I don't know how else to explain it. I rarely see people who can convey so much personality through writing. You described West River in a way that feels *magical*. That sounds cheesy, I know, but it's true."

"Then I must have described it accurately." My body feels like it's fighting itself. Hearing such high praise makes me feel like I could float. Maybe I could if not for that heavy sensation that settles in me as soon as I think about West River.

"And there's more. Adam and I both think your unique voice and storytelling ability is exactly what we want for *Wonderings*. I understand if you would prefer to stick to the freedom of freelancing, but if you're interested, we would love to have you on board permanently. Because we don't have an office, you could work from home or, if you're anything like Adam and me, from the road. And while we will want some input on your topics, you'll still have plenty of flexibility."

The sudden change from a terrible day yesterday to *this* today gives me whiplash. "I...I don't know what to say."

She chuckles. "Say yes, Laine. We need you."

Somewhere in the back of my mind, I hear snippets of the lectures I sat through during my career-prep classes at NYU. My professors taught to negotiate, to wait for official offers, to check the benefits. I ignore it all.

"I'd be honored, Ophelia."

"It might be too early for champagne, but how about a mimosa?" Ophelia asks, leaning over the table toward me.

"You read my mind."

After we give our orders to the server, Ophelia's mouth curls. "Tell me more about Sutton."

I choke on my water and start up in a coughing fit. "Sorry," I croak out, clearing my throat again and again. "What do you want to know?"

"Oh, don't be coy." Ophelia rolls her eyes playfully. "Did you know that Adam and I fell in love on a work trip? Now, I have a sixth sense for spotting the signs in others' writing. I suspected there was something going on between you and Sutton when we first met at karaoke. But after reading your article about him, I knew."

"I—I didn't write an article about Sutton," I stammer.

Ophelia gives me a *nice try* look. "'Cattle and Kin' was the name, wasn't it?"

"That was about the ranch as a whole. The entire Davis family," I stammer.

"Maybe that's what you *thought* you were writing about, but the way you talk about Sutton makes him stand out above the rest." She pulls her phone from her purse. "'His presence is like distant, rumbling thunder, quiet strength and determination.' That's how you described Sutton Davis, isn't it?" Ophelia recites, a knowing smile playing across her lips as she flashes her phone screen at me, showing me my own words.

I squirm in my chair, my cheeks burning hot. "I guess I may have mentioned him a bit more than the others." Apparently, I hadn't been as subtle as I thought. "It's just...he's a fascinating person. He's the antithesis of his father, and they have a nice contrast."

"That's the magic of it," Ophelia insists. "Your readers are going to be captivated by this family, but especially by Sutton. The first in line for his family's ranch dynasty, yet he would rather spend his days working on children's books? Readers are going to eat it up. I know I did."

After the server delivers our glasses of champagne, Ophelia raises hers in a toast. "To the newest member of the *Wonderings* family."

I tip my glass back with a bit too much fervor.

"Didn't you say that Montana is the farthest you've been from New York?" Ophelia asks. "How does it feel to be back in the city?"

"Weird," I confess. "I grew up here. I've never really left. And I thought I would miss it more. But West River was so calming, once I got used to it. It felt like I was living in meditation, especially on the ranch. Aside from the sounds of birds and streams and animals, it was silent. So perfectly still."

"It sounds amazing. Like I said...you don't have to stay in the city for this job." Again, that mischievous smile shines.

My faint laugh feels like I'm coughing up thumbtacks.

U

THE ADRENALINE of the job offer only lasts for about ten minutes after Ophelia and I part ways. Instead of taking the subway right away, I walk along the street. Closing my eyes, I try—I really try—to find some peace in the city, in this familiar soundscape. But despite my best efforts, my skin crawls. I never realized before how much there is to take in. So many sights, smells, sounds. Endless options and decisions that I need to make.

I know what I want to do. My hand is practically pulling itself toward my purse, toward my phone. I cross my arms to keep from obeying that silent desire. If I could just hear his voice. If I could tell him about my new, proper job, he would be so proud and not at all surprised.

Sutton's words ring through my head. *I don't need impulsiveness or indecisiveness right now.*

Well, that makes one of us.

In a snap decision, I turn on my heel and head in the opposite direction. Knowing the city like the back of my hand, I find my usual salon with ease, pushing through the tall glass doors.

The roar of blow dryers and the rhythmic beat of a carefully curated playlist welcome me in. Stylists, clad in chic black attire, wield scissors like artists' brushes. And the best part, along one wall, a massive collage of avant-garde hairstyles smiles down at me, every bit as beautiful as the Sistine Chapel to me in this moment.

"That better not be Laine Rodriguez," a familiar voice says from the washing station at the back.

"Hi, Paul," I say in a singsong voice.

Paul, a close friend of Dad's, has been cutting my hair since I was a toddler. In fact, he's been cutting my hair in the *exact* same bang-and-bob combo since I was a toddler. At every appointment, I start with twenty minutes of rambling about the endless possibilities I could do with my hair. Eventually, Paul gets sick of that and cuts it the same way he always has. He was the one to give me my first tube of lipstick, telling me that if I wear a red lip every day, it's one less decision I'll need to make.

"You know I won't do it," Paul says as I stalk up to him.

I smile innocently. "Do what?"

Paul points an accusing finger at me. "Whatever it is you want me to do. You were eight years old when you made me swear to never change your hair. And every few months, you come back in here, we have this conversation, and you end it by making me renew this vow."

I fold my hands together and hold them to my chest in a begging motion. "I just need a change. A change that won't alter my life, but that will distract me for at least an hour."

Paul narrows his eyes at me. "What exactly do you have in mind?"

"Dealer's choice."

"Not a chance!" Paul holds his arms out to the side in a wide gesture, drawing the attention of half the patrons in the salon. He goes back to rinsing his client's hair.

I smirk, shrugging. "If you don't do it, I'll just get the old rusty craft scissors I have in my junk drawer. Or maybe I'll buy clippers and really go to town. I'll look like that chick from *Mad Max*."

Turning my attention to the collage on the wall, I point at the first one that jumps out at me. "That one." In the picture, the model's bangs were cut to maybe an inch below her hairline. The sides of her hair were trimmed short, and the back is left longer. To top it all off, her hair is a vibrant cobalt blue.

"Sorry, no," Paul scoffs. "Those pictures are for art's sake, not for normal people. I'm not having you walk out of here with a futuristic mullet the shade of Cookie Monster's ass."

"You've got to give me something," I plead. "Something fresh, something to mark a new chapter in my life."

My puppy-dog eyes must have been pitiful enough, because Paul slumps his shoulders a touch. After a long groan, he concedes. "Baby bangs."

I nod my approval.

"And a pixie cut," he adds. "Very *Roman Holiday*."

"You're the visionary," I say, happy at the prospect of having my hands stuck under a big black cape soon. Because at least for an hour, during the cut, I can't be tempted to text Sutton.

"But I have appointments all day, kid," Paul says, looking pointedly at his hands, wrist-deep in the shampoo bowl amidst strips of discarded foil. "If you need this done today, you'll have to be patient. I might be able to fit you in while a client's color is processing."

"Beyond fair." I head toward the waiting area but turn back quickly, holding my phone up to Paul. "Do you mind if I stash this back here?"

Paul, too busy to bother asking why I don't want my phone during the wait, just gives me a go-ahead wave of his hand.

Time drags on. Paul's salon is too upscale to have TVs in the waiting area. In fact, there is only one thing to occupy my time with: fashion magazines in a perfect line on the coffee table. I wait around long enough to read through each one multiple times.

With every second that ticks by, I have to fight myself. Everything in me wants to grab my phone from the shelf in the back of the room. It sits among the shampoo bottles. I can almost hear it singing to me like a siren from a Greek myth.

I have to wait through one and a half appointments before Paul squeezes me in. He gives me a single tip of his head, calling me to the wash station in the back. As soon as I'm seated, he swishes the cape around me and finger-combs through my bob. The corners of his mouth twitch.

"You're absolutely certain about this?" His eyes are full of remorse, like he's personally mourning the loss of my trademark style.

"Come on, Paul. You know me better than that. I'm never absolutely certain about anything."

He gives my hair another longing stare, and then, probably remembering that he only has so much time, he goes to work. After a quick wash, we're at his station. Thanks to years of experience, Paul dives on in without wasting a second. The moment I hear the first snap of the shears, I drop my eyes to my lap and play with my rings under the black cape. And for the rest of the cut, I second-guess my choice.

That is, however, until Paul blow-dries my hair, styles it, and instructs me to—finally—look up.

U

"I CUT MY HAIR," I tell Mom over the phone, pacing down the street. I felt lighter immediately after the haircut, like I was shedding my old self. *This* Laine Rodriguez will be organized. Stable. Predictable. She will not tack up every poster and art print on her wall or clutter her calendar with nonsensical Post-it notes.

Mom chuckles. "And to think, you thought you would never get a 'real' job, and you thought you would never change your hair. And here you are, doing both in one day."

My laugh dies halfway through, like a car engine sputtering. I'm not entirely sure what I respond, but whatever it is, it isn't very convincing.

"Aren't you excited?"

I'm glad nobody around me on the sidewalk cares enough

to pay a second thought to my weak smile. "It is a big day. It's just...weird to not be telling Sutton about it."

Mom says nothing. I can perfectly picture her pursed lips as she bites down on her advice.

I, for the thousandth time in the past ten minutes, run my fingers through my hair. It feels alien, like it belongs to someone else entirely. "Do you think I should call him?"

"I think—" She cuts herself off and starts again, clearly trying to give me space to make my own decision. "I think you know what's best."

We talk for a minute longer, and I find my way to Washington Square Park. Somehow, it's even louder than it was on the street. I tuck myself into the corner of the park, the closest thing I can find to a secluded spot. After my mom hangs up, I stare at my phone. Then, with hesitant movements, I navigate to my contacts. Then to my starred favorites. There's only one name there aside from my parents, and I stare at those six letters for so long they blur into one terrifying shape. My thumb hovers over his name.

But right as I'm about to push down, another call comes on my screen. *Frankie*. Seeing it makes my heart both swell and crack, and I answer quickly, a feeling that I can only describe as homesickness settling in me.

Before I can greet her, Frankie's voice rings out so fast the words string together. "Sutton's been in an accident."

36

LAINE

I STAND, sit, and stand again. "What are you talking about?" My voice sounds distant, like I'm hearing it through a closed door.

Frankie takes three heavy breaths, and they feel like an eternity too long. "He and Wells went out today to check the trails. There was a flash flood. Nothing major, but Sutton's—Duke's—horse got scared. He took off, and Sutton was thrown from the saddle."

"But—but how is he doing? He's okay, right? I mean, he has to be okay," I say, trying to convince myself that if Sutton wasn't okay, if he was…gone, I would feel it.

"I think he'll be okay," she says, choking on her words. "He doesn't look great."

Thoughts whirl, ticking by so impossibly fast I can't register any individual one. "Is he seeing a doctor? How is he hurt? Did he hit his head? Where is he now?"

My panic seeps into Frankie, and her breathing shudders. "They're taking him to a hospital in Missloula. We won't know how bad it is until they run some tests."

"He'll be fine," I say, equally for Frankie's benefit and for mine. "He will be fine."

Frankie's dry swallow is loud enough for me to hear over the phone. "I hope so."

We turn into a chorus of "It'll be okay" and "He'll be fine" until a hush falls. It's clear neither of us is quite sure what else to say, so we mumble out our goodbyes. Then, in true Laine fashion, I open Uber without a second thought.

Just like the first time I flew to Missoula, there aren't any direct flights from New York City. But as a small sliver of grace, the ticketing agent at the airport finds me a route with only one layover. After I get through security, I barely have enough time to tell my parents about the accident—and my subsequent decision to check on Sutton myself—before boarding the first flight.

I only have my purse with me. Inside, I have my wallet, phone, loose change, single bills, and a scratched pair of sunglasses, the protective case for which I lost ages ago. I spend the entire first flight staring at the screen mounted in front of me. Even if I had headphones, I wouldn't want to watch a movie. Instead, I keep my eyes fixed on the live flight map, watching our little cartoon airplane make its painfully slow trek to Minneapolis.

My hope of getting an update from Frankie by the time I land is in vain. No word, no call or text from anyone in the Davis family. By the time I'm off the first plane and to my next gate, I have just enough time to grab a random armful of snacks. However, on my second three-hour flight, I don't eat any of them. I just sit, writhing, willing the plane to move faster.

It doesn't.

The Missoula airport is eerily quiet as I disembark from my final flight. That stillness I craved when I went back to New York feels haunting now. With it being just past midnight, the dimly lit terminal is nearly empty. The lights overhead cast long shadows, and for a moment, it feels like I'm the only person left in the world.

My phone buzzes in my pocket, and I snatch it out, my heart leaping into my throat. But it's not a message from Frankie, just a notification from the airline, letting me know my flight has landed. I stare at the screen, willing it to light up again with some news, anything that might give me a clue about what's happening with Sutton. When nothing happens, I shove the phone back into my pocket, fighting the urge to scream.

I head toward the exit, the automatic doors swishing open to a blast of cold air. The night is quiet—the kind of quiet that presses in, reminding me of just how alone I am.

The ride to the hospital is a blur. Before I can fully process it, my Uber parks outside the main doors. My stomach flips as I struggle with my seatbelt, my hands shaking so badly it takes me three tries to unbuckle it. Finally, I stumble out, glaring up at the building overhead, and let out a curse at the sight of it. How can a hospital this small possibly provide everything Sutton needs? If only we were at New York Presbyterian or Mount Sinai, where thousands of employees would be right within reach.

The hospital doors slide open with a soft whoosh, and I'm greeted by the smell of antiseptic and the harsh brightness of fluorescent lights. The receptionist looks up as I approach the desk, her eyes narrowing slightly as she takes in my disheveled appearance.

"I'm here to see Sutton Davis," I say, my voice hushed in the quiet space as if I'm in a church.

She nods understandingly, her fingers dancing across the keyboard. "Family?"

My answer is immediate. "Girlfriend."

The woman's brows crinkle. She grabs the guest check-in

sheet and reads it over. Then again. "*You're* dating Sutton Davis?"

"Yes?" I raise an eyebrow, wondering at the suspicious tone of her voice.

She raises an eyebrow right back. "Maybe it's best if you come back another time."

"Is he—is he in surgery or something? I can wait. I'll wait here."

"It's not that. It's… He already has a visitor right now."

I shake my head in question, because it seems nicer than shouting, *And your point is?*

"A girl is seeing him right now."

I shrug. "Probably his sister."

The woman clicks her tongue, looking like she's about ready to crawl out of her skin. "I'm sorry. But the girl said *she* was dating Sutton Davis."

"That must be a mistake." I twist the pendant on my necklace around on its chain, just to have something to do with my hands while this woman wastes my time. "What's her name?"

She holds the sign-in sheet's clipboard to her chest, as if afraid I would snatch it right from her hands. "Only one visitor at a time. We don't want to overwhelm him."

"I'm sure it's his sister." My voice is tight, patience waning.

The woman checks the sheet again. "She has a different last name."

Okay, now I get why the woman is shielding the clipboard from me. I'm about three seconds from reaching over the table and wrestling her for it. I huff, close my eyes, and allow all my feelings to flow, unbridled.

Almost immediately, I feel a stinging behind my eyelids. My nose crinkles. My heart lurches against my ribs. The mere thought of Sutton lying somewhere in this hospital, connected to monitors, enduring any amount of pain, sends tears streaming down my face. I blink rapidly, trying to hold them back, but they keep falling, unchecked.

"Please," I choke out, vaguely aware that I'm exploiting my own emotions to get what I need.

The receptionist's brows knit while she studies me. "Alright, but don't make a scene. He needs rest." She hands me a visitor's pass, and I follow her directions to Sutton's room, my steps quick and purposeful, nearly at a run.

The hospital corridor is eerily quiet, the only sound from hushed conversations between nurses, beeping machinery, and my hurried footsteps echoing against the sterile walls. The closer I get to Sutton's room, the shorter my breaths come. I can't shake the image of him being thrown from the saddle, my imagination playing out like a horror film.

I pause just outside the door, taking a moment to compose myself. The woman's words about another visitor linger in my mind, but I push them aside, too worried about Sutton to wonder who the girl might be. After a deep breath to steady my nerves, I open the door.

The room is dimly lit. In the shadows, I see Sutton lying motionless on the hospital bed. Everything in my body tenses, threatening to shatter. Machines surrounding him sound off, providing a steady beat to the stillness. Dead asleep, he doesn't move at the opening click of the door, but someone else does. Her brilliant red hair shines, even in near darkness.

"Hi, Laine," Cassidy whispers, those doe eyes glistening with tears. She's seated at Sutton's side, her hands wrapped around his.

Even in the shadows, I can see the blush rise to Cassidy's cheeks as she stands up. She beckons me out of the room and leads me down the hall to a sitting area. Aside from a couple of nurses meandering by the front desk, it's just us. Cassidy perches her tall, narrow frame on one of the stiff chairs and stares down at her wedding ring, a rock of a diamond atop a thin silver band.

She's upset, clearly. And I should probably be patient. Compassionate. But every second with Cassidy is a second spent away from Sutton, so I break the silence, ready to get whatever this is over with. "I was wondering who would have checked in as Sutton's girlfriend." My voice is lifeless.

Cassidy's chuckle has no trace of humor. "She asked if I was family. I said no. She said no friends were allowed in this late. So, I said I was Sutton's girlfriend. Well,"—she holds up her left hand, her diamond flashing at me—"I said I was his fiancée, actually."

Much like I have a habit of doing, Cassidy spins her ring around her finger. Her bottom lip pouts out while a stray tear streaks down her mascara-stained cheek.

I take a hesitant seat across from Cassidy, my eyes never leaving her face. A cocktail of emotions swirls within me—concern for Sutton, frustration at Cassidy's timing, and a prick of awkwardness. Why is she here, anyway?

"Wells is waiting for me in the parking lot," Cassidy says, as though she can read my mind. "He wanted to come visit Sutton, but...he didn't have the stomach for it. He asked me to come alone and report back."

"Is Sutton okay?" My voice is gentler this time, my concern for Sutton eclipsing my impatience. "How bad is he hurt?"

Cassidy looks up, her gaze meeting mine. "When he was thrown off his horse, he landed in the creek bed. And his collarbone..." She pauses, shuddering. "It was awful. It went right through the skin."

I close my eyes against the mental image that pops into my mind. My stomach heaves, ready to empty if I would allow it. But as sickening as the thought of his injury is, relief sits idly by, waiting for reassurance so it can wash over me fully. A break, even one that bad, couldn't be life threatening. "Was it just the broken collarbone?"

"Some broken ribs too. And he hit his head pretty hard. He was unconscious for a while. The doctors say there's some minor swelling. They said he should be fine, but…" She trails off.

"But what?" I press.

Cassidy sniffles loudly. "But I'm still scared." Then, she erupts into a sob so loud it startles me.

I shift uncomfortably in my seat. Instead of relief washing over me, there's more nausea, a distinct feeling that I'm intruding here. After another ragged whimper, I reach across the small table between us, patting her knee gently. "I'm sorry, Cassidy."

"No, I'm sorry," she heaves. "It's all my fault."

The nurses look over at us, eyebrows raised.

"It was an accident," I reassure Cassidy, hoping my quiet tone will prompt her to follow suit. We don't need to make any more of a scene than we already have. "You can't blame yourself."

Cassidy's eyes darken. "I'm like a curse to the Davis family. All I do is make life hell for them."

"That's not true," I insist. "Look how happy you make Wells."

A sour laugh slips between her clenched teeth. "And only at the expense of Sutton. The moment I realized I liked Wells, their entire family started this downward spiral. As if cheating on Sutton with his brother wasn't enough, Sutton also had to find out himself. Find us. And just after Duke died?" Cassidy brushes her trembling hands through her long copper hair. "What is *wrong* with me? Who does that?"

Because my mind is still caught up thinking about

Sutton's current state, I don't have the mental capacity to formulate any response to Cassidy.

"Sutton and Wells were never close," she continues, "but I tore them clear apart. Wells wouldn't even talk about him for the longest time, and Sutton stopped coming home for holidays. But then you..." Another tear falls past her lashes. "Frankie told me about you months ago. She said that from the first time Sutton spoke about you, she knew he had feelings for you. And when I found out you were coming to the wedding with him, I finally felt relief, relief I was craving for six years."

"You shouldn't feel so guilty," I say, still only half-listening. I peek down the hall longingly, as if I might see Sutton standing there.

Cassidy looks at me with self-condemnation. "I just wanted him to be happy. I thought maybe if he fell in love with you, he could move on. But now that I know you two were never really in love..."

"Well, it was my idea to fake the relationship, so you can just blame me. Deal?" I don't bother waiting for an answer before standing. "I need to go see him," I mumble, mostly to myself.

Thankfully, Cassidy doesn't follow.

The sterile smell of Sutton's hospital room makes my stomach turn again. Sutton lies in the bed, still and vulnerable, surrounded by the low light of monitors. My steps toward him are cautious. Every inch I near closer, I see something I wish I hadn't. His split lip, still not healed. The old bruise around his eye now dappled with yellow and maroon. His once tan face pale, lifeless. A raised bump on his forehead, like a golf ball shoved under the skin, marred by a line of stitches. Bandages and wrappings line the base of his neck, extending down below the line of his hospital gown. And on his arms, countless nicks and scratches broken up by splotches of purple.

Silently, I pull the chair Cassidy was in closer and sit down at Sutton's side, my gaze never leaving his face. I reach for his hand, taking it in mine with as much gentleness as I can muster. The contrast between his once warm, firm hand and the cold, lifeless feeling of it now sends a shock down my spine.

My throat is dry as I try to hold back tears. The reality of the situation crashes over me, making the room spin. I lean closer to him, as if my presence alone could bring him back to consciousness. "Sutton," I whisper, my voice barely audible. "I'm here. I don't know if you can hear me, but I'm here. Laine's here. Can you squeeze my hand if you hear me?"

No response, of course.

"I missed you," I croak.

The monitors continue their rhythmic dance, and I'm left with nothing but them and the darkness. My fingers trace over Sutton's hand, desperately wishing for any sign that he's okay.

The weight of an uncertain future presses down on me, and I speak again, more to myself than to Sutton. "I don't know what's going to happen, but I'm not leaving you."

The sleepless nights and hours of travel pile up, and it takes too much effort to even lift my head. Folding myself in half, I lay my face down on the side of Sutton's bed.

Just before I close my eyes, relenting to my body's begs for rest, I see something familiar on the table at Sutton's other side.

A tube of red lipstick.

∪

THE SOUND of lapping water and the vision of moonlight dancing on the edge of a lake fills my dreams. *The* lake.

Laine. Sutton's voice calls to me, but I can't see him anywhere around me. I spin in the rough sand along the shore, studying the tree line for any sign of him.

Sutton says my name again and again. Then, a steady tone accompanies his warm, soothing voice. In my dream, I look up at the sky, searching for the source. The moon becomes hazy, slipping away like water through cupped hands. I try to hold on to the dream, craving the sanctuary of the lake, but it fades.

The steady beeping of the hospital room fills the space as I stir, my cheek pressed against the itchy sheets of Sutton's hospital bed. The fog of sleep clings to me, and for a moment, I'm caught between the dream and reality. But then, a gentle pressure squeezes my hand, pulling me fully awake.

I blink, trying to clear the haze from my mind, and lift my head. Sutton's eyes are half-open, his gaze unfocused but undeniably aware. Relief floods through me so intensely that it almost knocks the breath out of my lungs.

"Sutton," I whisper, my voice cracking. I sit up straighter, my heart racing with a mix of joy and concern. His grip on my hand tightens slightly, the smallest gesture, but it feels like the most significant one in the world.

"Hey," says, his voice rough and weak, barely more than a whisper. It's the most beautiful sound I've ever heard. "You cut your hair."

I almost laugh, giddy to see him awake. "I did."

He nods slightly, his eyes softening as he looks at me. "You're here," he says, his voice a mix of surprise and something else—something that makes my heart skip. "I was scared I wouldn't see you again," he admits, his voice hoarse.

A smile tugs at the corners of my lips. "You're not getting rid of me that easily." I lean in, unable to resist the urge to be closer to him. "I'm not going anywhere, Sutton. Not unless you tell me to. And maybe not even then."

He chuckles then winces, clutching at his side, his broken ribs. "Laine," he murmurs, the corners of his mouth pinching. "I have to apologize. I have to be honest." Closing his eyes, as if to preserve what energy he has left, Sutton says, "I've hated being away from you, even just for a few days. Everything feels dull when you're not around. I wanted you to go for a reason. Just not the reasons I said."

I brush the curls away from Sutton's face, hating the pain in his expression. "Shh. Just rest for now."

Sutton opens his eyes again, determination hardening his gaze. "After that night at the lake, I figured we could make it work. I wanted to do whatever I could to make you happy."

I lean in closer. It takes everything in me to not brush my lips against his.

"When I found out about my father's diagnosis, I didn't want to burden you with it. I asked you to leave, but only because I hate the thought of seeing you suffer with us. That's why I wanted you to go, not because of anything you did. Not because of anything you are."

He closes his eyes again, exhaustion overtaking him. We're quiet for a few moments, long enough that I question whether or not he has fallen asleep.

When I speak, I whisper, just in case he really has slipped into a dream. "Sutton, you can't push me away like that. If I want to suffer with you, let me." I trace circles along the back of his hand. "I don't want you to face everything alone. You've been doing that for too long."

Just as I think Sutton is about to fall asleep, he whispers, "Can I kiss you?" He tries to sit up but falls right back down, grimacing with pain. "On second thought, can you kiss me?"

I stand, hover over Sutton, and his mouth lifts into a drowsy grin as mine melts against it.

"Feeling better already?" someone asks from behind me.

Jolting up, I turn to see a woman in a white coat walking in, a sideways smile tipping her mouth. "I figured it had been too long since a Davis kid was here." At my confused look, she says, "Those three kids had their fair share of emergency room visits growing up. All ranching kids do."

After the doctor checks Sutton's healing, jots some notes down, and gives him a few words of encouragement, I interrupt her departure. She patiently sits through my dozens of questions.

Yes, Sutton will make a full recovery. He will be in a sling for a while. He can go home later today.

"So, bottom line, he's okay?" I ask, no more worries left to express.

She smirks and gestures between me and Sutton. "Better than okay, by the looks of it."

Soon after Sutton falls back asleep, for real this time, the nurse comes in and tells me he won't be awake for a while, thanks to the pain medicine he's on. I take that as my sign to call yet another Uber—this one to Target. There, I load a basket with travel-size toiletries, two new shirts, a pair of stretchy pants, and a phone charger.

Even being away from Sutton for less than an hour has my anxiety spiking, so I don't waste any time before hurrying back to the hospital. In the hall bathroom, my own reflection startles me. I forgot about my last-minute decision to chop my hair off.

I wash up as best as I can with wet paper towels and apply a thick layer of deodorant. After dressing in fresh clothes, brushing my teeth, fixing my hair, and lathering my face in a much-needed moisturizer, I assess. I smell fine, but one night of unsteady sleep wasn't enough to fade the shadows under my eyes. This isn't exactly the way I would have wanted to show up when seeing Sutton again.

I'm almost back to Sutton's room when someone calls my name, halting me. Finally, it's exactly the person I want to see.

Frankie runs down the hallway, barreling into me so hard she nearly knocks me over. "I can't believe you're here!"

"Of course I'm here."

As soon as Frankie releases me, I'm pulled into another nearly identical hug. I hadn't even noticed Magnolia and Hank behind Frankie. Magnolia sniffles as she holds me, her emotions overflowing. "We missed you," she says as she lets me go.

Thoroughly *not* a hugger, Hank extends a trembling hand to me, and I shake it happily. Then, he leads us into Sutton's room.

Inside, Sutton is still sound asleep, a deep crease between his eyebrows. Even while bandaged and bruised, he looks painfully handsome. We all line up on the far side of the room, watching his every unconscious movement.

"What on earth are you doing here?" Magnolia whispers, holding me by my elbows as if I'll make a run for it.

"Frankie told me about the accident, so,"—I shrug—"here I am."

"And back for good, I hope," Frankie whispers, beaming.

It takes all my will to not groan. "Sutton still doesn't want to put me through,"—I pause, flicking my eyes to Hank as I clear my throat—"the hardships ahead."

"Fool," Hank grumbles under his breath, eyes narrowing slightly at Sutton. "He'll never be happy in West River if he has to sacrifice you to be there."

"Not to mention his dream job," I add, hoping Sutton's family realizes the gravity of his choice.

Magnolia laces her fingers between Hank's. "It wasn't a straightforward decision for him."

"Do *you* think he should stay in Montana?" Hank asks me, his jaw clenched.

I exhale slowly. "These next years are going to be hard on everyone. And for Sutton, giving up his career would make that all the more difficult. I think he should at least ask if there's a possibility of getting the best of both worlds."

Hank nods to himself. Then, his pale-blue eyes are on mine, cold and unreadable. "And you?"

It feels like I'm staring into the eyes of a wolf. "What about me?"

"He'll be miserable without you." Hank says it the same way he says everything else, matter-of-fact.

"Hell, I'd move to West River tomorrow if Sutton asked me to," I whisper with a smirk, not entirely joking.

Hank ruminates on that for a moment. "Then do. Move here."

I let out a disbelieving laugh. "Good luck pitching that idea to Sutton."

Frankie waves a dismissive hand. "Why does he need to be the one to approve? I do."

I roll my eyes playfully, trying to not read too much into their words.

37

SUTTON

EVEN THOUGH WE shared a bed our first week in Montana, Laine bunked with Frankie in the days following my return from the hospital, reminding me we didn't need to continue our charade any longer. Beyond that, however, Laine rarely left my side. And whenever we were apart, someone in my family would pounce on me, each of them with the same end goal.

"She makes you happy," Mom said.

Frankie was less direct. "Remember what I said about you being an idiot?"

At one point, even Wells mumbled an attempt at convincing me to change my mind. "Laine's good for you."

Tonight, the night before the wedding, Laine left to go help Frankie and Mom with the florals around the wedding arch. Within minutes, I see my father walking up to me, his steps slow. He has been watching me—me and Laine—from a distance since I returned home from the hospital. That constant stoic expression hid far more than it revealed.

He claps a hand on my shoulder, holding it there long enough to give the otherwise simple touch greater meaning.

For a moment, we stand in companionable silence, watching the bustle of the ranch hands and cattle.

"You have a hell of a catch," he says, his voice gruff but carrying a rare warmth. "She's got fire, that Laine. Reminds me a bit of your mother when we were young."

Taken off guard by my father expressing even a whisper of sentimentality, I stay motionless, worried anything I do or say might stop this train.

"I know you said you and Laine weren't an actual couple, but I don't know any fake girlfriends that would fly across the country at the drop of a hat."

"It's complicated," I say, rubbing at the immediate headache forming behind my temples.

"Tomorrow is her last day here, isn't it?"

I nod, trying to ignore the pressure suddenly hard against my lungs. "Laine's going back to the city to look for an apartment."

Hank clicks his tongue. "Maybe you should stop her."

My sigh is shaky. "We aren't actually dating. I can't ask Laine to give up her life, her career, to stay here—especially… under the circumstances."

Hank dips his chin a touch, his weathered face looking wise. "Your mother had dreams too, things she left behind when she chose to be with me. She never blamed me for it. Never made me feel bad about it. I don't think she has ever regretted her decision to come here." He huffs a laugh. "Or maybe that's just what I tell myself to avoid feeling too guilty."

I'm stunned. I don't think I've heard my father speak this much at one time.

He looks out at the emerald field again, the corners of his mouth twitching. "I appreciate you wanting to be here while…" He swallows the rest of the sentence, unable to talk about our harsh reality in too much detail. "I think you and I are more alike than we realized. We both try to bury our emotions. But if what you feel for Laine is even a sliver of what I feel for Mags, you don't want to hide from that. That kind of love makes life worth living."

It's only six in the evening, but my father excuses himself to head to bed, shuffling back to the house. I keep my eyes peeled on him, just in case he stumbles. Then I notice Wells on the back porch, doing the same. He offers me a half-smile.

Knowing Laine will be gone in less than forty-eight hours, there's nothing I want to do more than simply be at her side. So, because my doctor made me swear off horseback riding and driving for at least two weeks, I have no choice but to walk to her. I keep my body tensed, protective of my shoulder and ribs as I shamble down the dirt road toward the venue for tomorrow.

When I reach the last crest of the road, I'm not surprised at the beautiful view in front of me. The grassy field stretches toward the lavender that begins just beyond the wedding arch. The soft purple blooms sway in the evening breeze, their fragrant scent carried through the air. Everything looks exactly as it should for a perfect wedding—the rows of white chairs arranged neatly, the delicate floral arrangements entwined around the wooden arch, and the distant mountains framing the entire scene like a painting. Mom, Frankie, and Laine huddle together, making final adjustments to the space. Their laughter is like music.

Mom oversees the placement of each bloom with a discerning eye. Frankie is happy to follow her directions. Laine seems content just to be with them. She looks at ease —at home, even—moving naturally through the space as if she belongs here. And I can't shake the feeling that she does. It's not just about how she looks; it's about the way she fits. Like this place was always meant to have her in it.

A smile lights up Laine's face as she notices me on the

trail. Immediately, she abandons her task to walk toward me. Golden hour bathes her in a soft glow, making her dark, cropped hair shimmer. She closes the distance between us, and for a moment, the world narrows down to just her.

"How are you feeling?" she asks, the same greeting she gives every time she sees me.

"Better now," I murmur, stepping closer to her.

She twists the pendant of her necklace around, nervous but still grinning. "Still no memory loss?"

"Not a lick of it."

"Shame." Her full lips pout, their familiar red washing over my vision. "I was really hoping I could take some inspiration from *While You Were Sleeping*. You know, convince you we're *actually* madly in love and engaged."

"Wouldn't take too much convincing, I think." I suddenly miss Laine's longer hair, just for a moment, because I could have an excuse to touch her face if I could brush a strand from her face.

It's been like this for days, both of us trying to downplay our feelings without actually abandoning them. We haven't kissed again, and neither of us has brought up the one we shared at the hospital. All we've done is sneak in flirty comments and pretend they don't mean exactly what they do, in fact, mean. My selfish desires still battle with my guilt. Laine, meanwhile, told me that she wants me to focus on healing, not on her.

It was a pointless wish.

She occupies my every thought.

Mom and Frankie walk up behind us, giggling like teenagers.

"We were just heading out," Mom says, winking at me.

"You two have fun." The implication is clear in Frankie's voice, and I roll my eyes at her.

Laine looks up at me, perhaps waiting for me to tell them to stay.

I don't.

And Laine smiles.

Once Mom and Frankie are out of earshot, Laine steps close enough to brush a finger just outside the line of stitches on my forehead. My swelling has gone down a bit, but the goose egg is still visible, as is a hint of my black eye and my other bruises. Tired of resisting my impulses, I reach my hand up, laying it against the back of hers so I can hold it to my cheek. Closing my eyes, I drink in her closeness, breathe in her perfume.

"How are you feeling about the wedding tomorrow?" Laine asks.

I lift my good shoulder in a one-sided shrug.

"Not...jealous or anything?" Laine takes her hand back and folds her arms against the evening chill. Seeing my confusion, she explains, "When I went to see you at that hospital, Cassidy was there. She was pretty...emotional."

"Seeing as how we've known each other our whole lives, and she's about to be my sister-in-law,"—I say that title with more ease than ever before—"it makes sense."

Laine's brows knit. "Being back in West River hasn't stirred any of those old feelings up?"

I have to hold myself back from laughing. "I guess, in one regard, I am jealous of my little brother."

Laine's expression drops, and I rush to explain.

"When Wells wants to, he can love so easily. And when he does, it's a wholehearted love. Just look at this place." I wave a hand out to the lavender fields. "Five years in the making. He was so sure about Cassidy—no matter the complications—and he sure as hell wasn't giving her up."

Laine's mouth twists as if she can't decide whether to smile or frown.

"I'm not like Wells," I tell her. "Love hasn't been easy for me since Duke died. I've been too afraid of my grief to allow myself to open up to any big emotions."

Laine smiles out at the swishing purple fields. "Well, I feel *all* the big emotions, all at once. You've trained yourself to not feel them at all. We balance each other out."

"I hope you know I didn't mean any of what I said when I asked you to leave." I remember trying to explain this to Laine in the hospital, but on such heavy painkillers, I have no idea what I *actually* said. Now, I have the chance to say it again, say it right. "I hope you're always impulsive and excited and joyful. Those are things I *love* that about you. I just thought a little heartbreak now would be better than years of pent-up heartache—heartache you would face if you stayed with me and had to be here while everything goes downhill for my family."

"You shouldn't have pushed me away," Laine says, her arms drawn tight across her chest, gaze averted away from me.

"I agree." I'm unable to hide the pain in my voice.

She looks at me then, eyes searching for something in mine. The silence between us is palpable, thick like the air before a storm. I want to tell her everything—how the thought of her leaving feels like the ground will give way beneath me—but the words sit like stones in my throat, unmovable. I'm on the verge of shattering that silence, ready to say what's been weighing on my heart, when distant laughter and the sound of footsteps slice through the quiet, pulling me back to reality.

Cassidy and Wells appear, hand in hand, strolling along the trail. Their smiles are infectious, but I can't help but feel a pang of envy at their happiness. Not because I want to be in Wells' spot, of course, but because I want to hold Laine's hand with that much confidence.

"Hey, you two," Wells calls out.

Laine uncrosses her arms, her eyes glinting with amusement. "Isn't it bad luck for you two to see each other the night before the wedding?"

Wells shrugs. "I think we've had more than our share of bad luck already."

Cassidy looks at Wells with the brightness of the sun. "Plus, I'm going to have to share him with the guests tomorrow. This might be our last moment alone for a while."

Wells glances between Laine and me, his expression shifting as he picks up on our tension. "But we can have that moment somewhere else if we're…interrupting something."

"We were just about to head back," Laine says, eyes flicking to mine for just a moment.

She starts back up the trail toward home, and I feel my near-confession deflating within me. Wells grimaces and mouths, "Sorry," to me, reading the sense of defeat in my posture.

38

SUTTON

"WHY DIDN'T YOU TELL HER?" Frankie asks me in a whisper. "Last night would have been perfect."

All day, our family has been busy getting the final things in line in the hours before the wedding. Frankie was ready before any of the other bridesmaids and snuck away to the guest room to scold me.

"I was about to," I say as Frankie helps me slide my button-up over my injured shoulder. "Wells and Cassidy interrupted."

Frankie groans. "Then you should have found another moment."

"I *want* to," I insist. "But I want it to be the *right* moment."

"I think, at this point, she would settle for you saying you love her by writing it on a Post-it note."

Before I can say anything else, there's a knock at the door. Cassidy slides in, eyes already narrowed at me. Her wedding dress' shape is the only thing simple about it. Tiny flower embellishments cover the fabric, making Cassidy look like a living garden in white. She pinned half of her long red hair back, and the rest cascades down, nearly to her waist, in big curls. Her makeup, though more dramatic than usual, is sheer enough across her cheeks and nose to show her freckles.

"Hey, Cass. You look nice," I tell her, choosing my descriptor carefully so I don't inject any awkward tension into the conversation.

"Thanks." She waves a dismissive hand, her eyes still slits. She points an accusatory finger at me. "You haven't told Laine how you feel?"

I snap my head to Frankie. "You told her?"

"Oh please," Cassidy says, rolling her eyes. "Frankie didn't need to tell me you love Laine. Everyone knows it." She points a manicured finger at me. "But *I'll* tell Laine the truth if you don't hurry and do it yourself."

A knock at the door silences us again. This time, it's Laine who enters.

For a minute, I forget that Frankie and Cassidy are in the room too.

Laine's short hair needs minimal styling. It draws attention to her features, allowing them to shine, especially her deep eyes and the long, full lashes that frame them. There's a hint of blush on her cheeks and a sheer brush of red across her full lips. Her pink dress hugs along her soft curves.

I take an involuntary step closer to her. "You look...perfect."

Laine's eyes flick to Cassidy and Frankie, cheeks reddening. "I was just coming to see if you needed help with your tie—you know, with the shoulder and everything. But it looks like you have enough help."

Frankie and Cassidy practically trip over each other as they sprint to the door.

"We were just leaving," Frankie says.

Just before Cassidy closes the door behind her, she peeks

her head back in, glaring me down. "Remember, if you don't, I will."

The door closes, but I can still hear Frankie and Cassidy on the other side of the door, eavesdropping.

"What was that about?" Laine asks, fidgeting nervously.

I hope my smile looks nonchalant. "Don't worry about it."

"Do you want some help?" She gestures at my shirt, still unbuttoned, and blushes again. "It's almost time for the ceremony."

"Yeah, I could use a hand," I admit, grateful for the excuse to have her close.

Laine steps forward, fastening the buttons along my torso with a light touch. As she works, I catch her gaze, and there's something unspoken in the air. The atmosphere is charged with the emotions we've been dancing around for days. Laine's eyes, as rich as black coffee, meet mine. My breath catches.

"I like the scruff," she says, breaking the silence with a teasing smile. I've had a close-trimmed beard for years, but I've never let it grow past that until now. "Leaning into the cowboy aesthetic, are we?" Her comment, though not really a joke, draws a chuckle from me, and it's a relief to let out some of the tension that has been building.

"I can't trim it until the cuts heal."

"Let's hope they never heal, then," she says, one corner of her mouth flitting up.

With my shirt buttoned, Laine moves to the tie. She threads it around the collar of my shirt, sure to avoid touching around my collarbone. The sweep of her fingers along my neck is enough to send a shiver through me.

Once the tie is in place, Laine grabs my jacket from the bed. I wince as she guides my arm through. She waits for my face to return to normal and finishes the job with even more caution, hands tracing around me as she adjusts everything in place. The sling is next, and she studies my expression while helping me get it on, watching for any signs of discomfort.

She steps back just enough to look me up and down. "There. Handsome as ever," she declares, eyes sparkling.

"Even with the bruises?"

"Oh, *definitely*," Laine says, voice thick with sarcasm. "You look *so* badass, which is obviously the goal at a wedding. And finally, the finishing touch." Laine pins the boutonniere, a delicate arrangement of lavender, cut fresh from the field, onto my lapel.

Mere inches apart, we lock eyes again. Just like last night, Laine's gaze searches for something in mine. Even after the boutonniere is secure, she doesn't move away. Instead, she lingers, her hands still hovering over my chest. We stand in silence, just looking at each other. I almost say it, right here and now. I even open my mouth, but I'm silenced by Laine tiptoeing up toward me. Like the tide to the shore, I'm drawn to her, catching in a gentle kiss.

The kiss is somehow tender *and* urgent. Laine curls her fingers against my chest before gravitating to my hair, knotting her hands in my curls. I wrap my good arm around her back, holding her to me. A small gasp escapes her lips, passing between our mouths, and that little sound has my heart racing. Without thinking, I grab her fervently with both hands.

Shit.

Pain flashes through me, and I recoil against it, my body going into rigid self-preservation mode as I roll to catch my weight on my uninjured side.

Immediately, Laine shoots up, cursing. "Are you okay, Sutton?"

"I'm good," I force out between clipped breaths.

As soon as I regain composure, we roll into a round of laughter, both of us delirious.

"Alright, cowboy," Laine says, holding a hand out to me. "We have a wedding to get to. You are the best man, after all."

I groan, drawing her in with my good arm. "Can't we stay here?" I murmur in her ear.

Laine melts in my grasp, shaking her head to think clearly. "Not unless you want another beating from Wells."

39

LAINE

SUTTON DOESN'T TAKE his eyes off me during the entire ceremony. I, however, really try to not get lost in that yearning gaze of his. I watch the smiles spreading throughout the surprisingly large crowd; I study the lavender-accented bouquet in my hands; I appreciate the purple field giving way to the rolling green hills and pine-coated mountains beyond it; I stare at the back of Frankie's head, golden curls dancing together.

But no matter how beautiful the scenery, no matter the number of unfamiliar faces to learn, I can't keep my attention off Sutton for long. My eyes drift to him whenever I let my guard down, and I'm always met with that sideways smile I've loved since the first time I saw it. He looks more handsome than I've ever seen him, bruises, cuts, and all. A few curls fell out from where he pushed them away from his face, and they drop over the edges of his forehead, like little arrows pointing at his unyielding stare.

Fully occupied by my efforts to not gawk at Sutton, I don't realize the ceremony is over until the guests all erupt into a rowdy applause, standing from their chairs. Sutton told me

275

that, with Cassidy and Wells both being from West River, their wedding is the event of the season. That's undeniable now, as a massive crowd of guests whoop loudly, many holding their hands up in true celebration. And with that, comes a sense of community. Apparently, everyone from West River is just as excited about this wedding as Wells and Cassidy are.

The new couple joins in on the cheering as they walk back up the aisle. Sutton shoots me one more look before he and Cassidy's sister—best man and maid of honor—follow them. The rest of the wedding party trails behind with me and one of Wells' high school buddies at the tail-end.

Frankie looks back to wink at me, her curls bouncing with every step.

The line of horse-drawn, floral-adorned wagons that brought everyone to the ceremony waits to transport everyone back to the ranch house for the reception. Sutton is at the first wagon. He tips his head back, motioning for me to join him. Right as I'm about to, though, a yank at my arm pulls me away.

Even though Frankie is loading onto the wagon Sutton stands at, Cassidy's sister guides me to the one behind it. "All the bridesmaids are taking *this* one," she insists. Her mouth pinches in a failed attempt to hide her mischievous expression, and she tugs on my arm again. She must be able to tell that I'm about to object, because she demands, "Come on, it's a quick ride."

I follow the line of pink dresses onto the wagon. Immediately, the bridesmaids draw in close to me, conspiratorial smiles tilting.

"Spill," one of them says, her eyes gleaming with curiosity. I recognize her as the one who, at the bachelorette party, almost threw up after her mechanical bull ride. "We heard that everything between you and Sutton was fake."

I look back toward Frankie and Sutton's wagon, hoping I have a chance to jump off mine to join them. But theirs has already started back toward the house. Even as he gets farther away, Sutton keeps his gaze locked on me.

"You two fooled me," Cassidy's sister giggles. "I mean, that ride you two took on the mechanical bull? Real dating or not, *that* was something."

The others nod in agreement.

The wagon jolts into motion, making it clear there's no escape from the inquisitive bridesmaids.

I shake my head dismissively. "It was all a stupid lie. I didn't want him to have to come to the wedding solo. It just got out of hand."

Every single one of them gives me an unconvinced look.

"Really!" I insist, laughing awkwardly. "He's my best friend. We were just having fun."

One bridesmaids scoffs, "It sure *looked* like fun."

"Yeah, it did," another says, grinning wickedly. "How can I convince Sutton to 'fake' date me?"

"What I wouldn't give," another swoons. "It's just not fair that Cass claimed Sutton all those years, only to end up with his brother."

"So greedy," one adds, giggling. "At least this means Sutton is on the market."

I really try not to imagine what it will be like when Sutton is in West River, surrounded by these hungry, gorgeous women.

"You really aren't with him?" Cassidy's sister asks, looking seconds away from an eye roll.

"We're friends," I say, sure, at least, of that one truth. But even as I say it, my mind is back on our last kiss we shared, how neither of us wanted it to end.

Finally, we turn the last bend of trail, the reception space at the Davis home in view.

"Sanctuary," I plead to the house under my breath.

Sutton is waiting for me, offering a hand as I step down. Each bridesmaid gives me a pointed look before I descend, some smirking, some pouting in jealousy.

"*Don't* leave me alone with them again," I whisper, leading Sutton away.

He stifles a laugh.

Right after the engagement with Cassidy was official, Wells got to work transforming the barn. After completely gutting it and cleaning it from top to bottom, he poured a concrete floor, polished it, and even refinished the old wood walls. Yesterday, Wells took it a step further, wrapping the ceiling beams with lights, greenery, and florals.

We find our seats at a round table next to Frankie, Magnolia, Hank, and Cassidy's parents. With his good arm, Sutton pulls my chair out for me, catching the suspicious attention of Cassidy's parents. They, like apparently everyone in West River, must have heard about our fake relationship.

The barn is aglow with warm light. The air is filled with the undulating sounds of laughter and music. The fresh flowers scattered around are fragrant, making me wonder how this place ever housed animals. When I ignore the feeling of people's eyes on me, I can actually appreciate the dreamlike ambiance.

I hardly register anything during the dinner of wild, braised venison, roasted broccoli, and potatoes from the Davis' garden. I can hardly taste my meal when I notice the pointed looks passed between Sutton and his family.

At one point, I hear Frankie whisper to Sutton, "You *still* haven't?"

I act oblivious to their conversation going on at my side, instead watching Wells and Cassidy cut into their wedding cake.

"Haven't found the right moment," Sutton whispers back.

Cassidy shoves some cake in Wells' face, eliciting a roar of laughter and applause from the crowded barn, loud enough for me to not hear Frankie's next words to Sutton.

I lean back a bit, hoping to get close enough to hear again. I'm met with warm breath tickling my ear and Sutton's hand on my shoulder. "Want to dance?" he murmurs.

Sutton laces his fingers with mine, and all the stares are worth it when we stand together. He keeps his hand in mine, leading me along with the crowd to the outdoor dance floor. Overhead, sparkling string lights blur with the stars, a perfect backdrop for Wells and Cassidy's first dance. Heat radiates from where my hand rests in Sutton's. The heat works its way up my neck, arms, and finally settles as blush behind my cheeks.

When the newlyweds' first dance ends, we trickle onto the dance floor with the other couples. The melody of the new song is low and intimate. With his good arm, Sutton pulls me close against him. Everything else—the crowd, the whispers, the world—fades into the background as I rest my face against Sutton's chest, relishing the sound of his racing heartbeat in my ear.

"How relentless have the bridesmaids been?" Sutton asks.

I sneak a peek at the huddle of pink gowns. Sure enough, each bridesmaid stares unabashedly at us.

"You have no idea," I say under my breath.

"We *did* give them something to talk about," Sutton hums.

He leans down, resting his cheek atop my head. I close my eyes, soaking in the feeling of him close to me. Before he straightens back up, he presses a kiss against my forehead. Whispers ring toward us, fueled by speculation and, perhaps, a touch of jealousy.

"Okay, now you're just taunting them." A small laugh

escapes me. "They're all plotting how they can stake a claim on you."

Sutton dips lower, his breath brushing against my hair. "Let them try," he whispers. "Trust me, they're the last thing on my mind right now."

My heart skips. The space between us narrows until there's almost nothing left. My grip on Sutton's hand tightens, as if I can physically make the seconds stretch longer.

My exhale is shaky.

We sway in slow circles for a few more songs. "I swear I'm a decent dancer when I'm not sporting five cracked ribs," Sutton says. "My mom made sure of that."

"Dang ribs getting in the way," I mutter, skimming a hand across Sutton's injured side.

"It's a good thing, too. If not for this,"—he looks down at his sling—"I wouldn't be able to keep my hands off you."

Dang ribs.

That warmth in my cheeks spreads again, coursing through my body, down my torso, settling in my core. I tip my chin up, just seconds from giving the bridesmaids something even better to talk about, when Cassidy's grabs Sutton's shoulder.

"Hey, you're up." She places a champagne flute in Sutton's hand. "It's time for you to start the toasts."

Sutton lets out a groan, his jaw flexing. "I'll be right back," he murmurs in my ear, giving me one last smile before he goes to the microphone at the front of the dance floor.

Within a few heartbeats, Frankie is at my side, her expectant smile as contagious as ever. "*So,*" she says, bouncing on her toes once, "how's it going?"

I'm still watching Sutton when I mumble, "Good."

She loops her elbow with mine. "Nothing...exciting to report?"

"Is one of your brothers marrying your other brother's ex not enough excitement for one day?" I joke.

Magnolia, Hank, Wells, and Cassidy stand in a grouping near the front of the dance floor. Their attention turns toward Frankie and me. So discreetly I almost don't see it, Frankie lifts a downturned thumb at them. Before I have time to question her, microphone feedback sounds through the speakers.

"Ladies and gentlemen," Sutton's voice carries a warmth that matches the ambient glow of the string lights. "Thank you all for being here to celebrate this incredible day with Wells and Cassidy. I've been given the honor of saying a few words. I'm sure you're all wondering why I look like this, and you can thank Wells for that one." He pauses, grinning. "I probably deserved it, as you can imagine."

A ripple of laughter runs through the crowd.

"I've known Wells since his day one. We've shared our work, secrets, sadness, and, for a couple of awkward years, the same taste in girls."

Another wave of laugher. Sutton winks at Wells, who is laughing louder than anyone, aside from maybe Cassidy.

"When I heard Wells was getting married, I was thrilled. At least, *eventually* I was, after that initial shock wore off. Thrilled because I knew he was marrying the right woman. Like most of you here, I've known Cassidy a long time. We all know firsthand how powerful it is to have her in your corner. I'm so happy that Wells will have that honor for the rest of his life." Sutton's voice is certain, genuine.

"Wells and Cassidy prove that love isn't always a straight path. Sometimes, it's a wild, roaring river that leads you to places you would never expect. Sometimes…it feels like a big mess." He pauses, eyes snapping to me, and that sideways grin dimples one cheek. "But what a beautiful mess," he says, repeating the same words he said to me after we confessed our feelings at the lake last week.

There's a pause, the kind that makes the room lean in, the hum of quiet expectation palpable. His smile tilts, a little lopsided, but the warmth in his eyes remains steady. "Love challenges you. It changes you. It asks you to show up, to keep showing up, no matter how messy or imperfect it gets. And when it's real—when it's right—it's worth every ounce of chaos."

He clears his throat, shifting his weight, and the crowd hangs on to his every word. "Wells and Cassidy show that love doesn't have to be perfect. It just has to be true."

Sutton's eyes find mine again, clinging to me for a heartbeat longer than they should, and my breath catches. He lifts his glass, and his voice grows lighter but no less sincere. "To Wells and Cassidy. And to the messes that lead us to the best things in life."

40

LAINE

APPLAUSE COURSES through the crowd as Sutton lowers his glass, his words still hanging in soft glow of the string lights. Wells claps him on the shoulder, grinning, while Cassidy wipes a tear from the corner of her eye, laughing through it. Around us, people murmur about how touching and thoughtful the toast was, how Sutton's words seemed to resonate with everyone in some way.

I stay rooted to my spot, the glass of champagne in my hand forgotten. My heart is doing something strange, like it's caught between racing and stopping entirely. Sutton's voice keeps echoing in my head, but it's not the part about Wells or Cassidy that's sticking. It's everything he said about love: messy, unexpected, and worth the chaos.

When I look up, Sutton's already stepping off the small platform, weaving his way through the crowd with a polite smile here and a nod there. But then his eyes meet mine, and his face shifts into something softer, something undeniably just for me.

My breath hitches.

He doesn't break eye contact as he approaches, stopping

just close enough that I can feel the invisible tether between us, a stronger pull than gravity.

"You okay?" he asks, his voice low, almost teasing, but his expression gives away something more serious.

"Yeah," I manage, though I'm not sure if it's true. "That was…some speech."

"Glad you liked it." His grin is small but steady, and then he glances toward the trees, where the soft glow of the party gives way to shadows and quiet. "Come with me?"

"What?" My voice is barely above a whisper, and I glance around. "Why?"

His brow lifts, a hint of mischief dancing behind his eyes. "I have something I want to say. And I'd rather say this part without an audience."

I hesitate, but only for a second, because even with my brain shouting warnings, my feet are already following him as he leads me away from the noise, the lights, the crowd.

And into whatever this is.

The night air is thick with the scent of pine and wildflowers, a smell that—when I was back in the city earlier this week—I wished I had bottled up and carried with me everywhere. The festivities continue behind us, the reception reluctant to come to an end.

"That was quite the show," I murmur.

Even in the dim moonlight, I can see Sutton's cheeks redden. "That wasn't exactly in my comfort zone," he agrees.

He sighs, looking up at the sparkling blanket of stars overhead. The quiet stretches between us, but it's not the uncomfortable kind. It's heavy, charged with all the things we've left unsaid. The things I didn't realize how badly I've been needing to hear.

Sutton's jaw works for a moment, his hesitation making me ache. Then, finally, he speaks.

"I used to think love was simple," he begins, his voice

steady but carrying the weight of a confession. "I thought it was about finding someone who fit into your life—like checking off boxes. But I've realized something."

He steps closer, his eyes searching mine, like he's making sure I'm really listening. "You've turned my life upside down, Laine," he says, his voice dropping even lower. "And for the first time, I'm not scared to admit that. I've spent so long trying to stay in control, trying to avoid risks, avoid heartbreak. But you…you've made me realize that love is worth all of that. It's worth everything."

His words hang in the air, raw and honest, and all I can do is stare at him, my heart swelling and twisting all at once. He takes one more step, reaching his hand out to brush mine, the smallest touch sending sparks down my spine.

"I don't expect you to feel the same way, not after how I treated you last week," he says softly. "But I need you to know, Laine. I need you to know that you've changed everything for me."

The world seems to hold its breath, the stars above us blinking like they're listening in, waiting for my response. My chest feels too full, my ribs barely containing the rush of emotions crashing over me—hope, fear, longing. But when I look at him, standing there with his heart on the line, the words I can't seem to find don't matter. Slowly, deliberately, I reach out, my fingers slipping into his, our hands fitting together like they were always meant to. His breath stutters at the contact, and for a heartbeat, we just stand there, anchored by something fragile but unbreakable.

And in that still, moonlit space, there's nothing left between us but the truth.

My voice trembles when I finally speak, but the truth in it doesn't. "You've changed everything for me too," I whisper.

"Laine," he murmurs, my name soft on his lips, like a promise. "I love you."

The words settle between us, cradling this moment in their quiet embrace. The distant hum of the party becomes nothing more than background noise, insignificant compared to the weight of Sutton's gaze and the steady warmth of his hand in mine. It's just him and me, standing on the edge of something I've never dared to believe could be mine.

He lets out a shaky breath, like saying it has released something that's been building in him for years. "I've loved you for longer than I've let myself admit."

I blink, and tears spill over before I can stop them. His thumb brushes them away..

"I love you," he says again, his voice firmer now, a vow. "And I will, for as long as you'll let me."

"Sutton," I say, the truth steady in my chest, "I love you too."

The smile that spreads across his face is like nothing I've ever seen before—like the sun finally breaking through the clouds.

Before I can say anything else, he leans down, resting his forehead against mine, his voice light with relief. "Say it again."

I laugh, the sound bubbling up from somewhere deep inside me. "I love you."

He closes the last bit of space between us, taking me in a kiss that's soft and certain, like he's been waiting his whole life for this moment.

"This doesn't mean things are going to change, right?" I ask.

Sutton tilts away from me, and I rush to clarify.

"I mean, if we're together. We're still going to be best friends, don't you think? I won't get annoyed when you color code your closet, and you won't get annoyed that I have a new hyperfixation every three weeks?"

Sutton drags me into his chest with his good arm. "I do

wonder how long you'll be able to put up with me making a spreadsheet every time we go grocery shopping."

"And you'll tire of the way I simply refuse to stick to a recipe when I'm cooking."

"Which would make the whole grocery spreadsheet pointless."

I ruffle Sutton's curls. "Wouldn't that just drive you crazy?"

He thinks for a moment, a smile teasing at his mouth. "Doubtful."

"What about when I book us flights for a vacation we weren't planning on taking?"

Sutton shrugs, dimples hinting at his cheeks.

"Or when you see the hundreds of scrap-paper notes and little reminders I leave scattered around?"

"I'll still love you."

"What about when you realize I only finish one out of every ten books I start?"

"Even then."

"And what about—"

Instead of waiting for my next scenario, Sutton catches my mouth in a kiss, rendering me speechless. Sutton's lips crush against mine, curving with a smile. Somehow, he tastes like the ranch, like a cool creek and evergreens. I kiss him gingerly, mindful of his broken side as I fight every urge to wrap my arms around him and hold on with everything I have.

Sutton, however, seems to forget about his injuries. He squeezes me against him, stooping his tall frame down to kiss me deeper before hoisting me up with one arm. I'm only an inch off the ground before he drops me back down, wincing in pain.

Still not ready to completely give up my grasp, I graze my

finger lightly along his face, following the lines of healing cuts, the shadowed bruises, the growing beard.

How amazing it will be to memorize every detail of this face. How amazing it will be to watch it change over time.

Suddenly, Sutton's expression drops. With his good hand, he palms the back of mine, holding my hand against his cheek. "Your flight is tomorrow."

"Yes."

He nods, like he's trying to brace himself against something inevitable. "What happens then, Laine? Are we..." He trails off, his voice heavy with unspoken fear.

I lean in, close enough to feel his breath against my face. "I have to go back to New York, Sutton. But that doesn't mean I'm leaving this behind. Us behind."

His brow furrows, his gaze searching mine for answers I haven't fully figured out yet.

"I need to go back. My life, my parents—they're still there. But..." I take a steadying breath, my voice shaking with honesty. "But I'm not saying goodbye to this. I'm not saying goodbye to you."

His shoulders ease just slightly, relief softening the edges of his face.

"We'll figure it out," I continue. "I don't know how yet, but we will. Because you're worth figuring it out for."

Sutton exhales, his forehead resting lightly against mine as his grip on my hand tightens.

"I'll wait, Laine. However long it takes, I'll wait."

I let out a breathless laugh. "I don't think you'll have to wait too long, Sutton."

He grins, dimples cutting deep into his cheeks, and then he kisses me again—taking his time, like he's memorizing the moment.

EPILOGUE
SUTTON

STANDING BY THE LAKE, the water shimmering with the gold of the setting sun, memories of that fateful night flood my mind. Two years have passed since I stood here and told Laine that my feelings for her were genuine. And yet, the scene before me feels untouched by time—like the lake, the sky, and the smell of pine are holding their breath, waiting for something inevitable to unfold.

Life hasn't unfolded exactly as I planned. I held out hope that the job with Imagineer Books would be doable from Montana. It wasn't. And so, the final anchor to a life in New York slipped through my fingers. But instead of drowning, I reached for something steady—Laine.

For months, we built our lives on flights and FaceTime calls, on rushed weekends stolen from our calendars. She'd fly to Montana to sit with my father in the sunroom, wheeling him out to his favorite spot in the yard to watch the cows graze in the fields.

But somewhere between missed flights and tearful good-byes at airport gates, we realized we couldn't keep living in limbo. Laine moved to West River. Slowly, she built her world here—a small home on the outskirts of the ranch. Her laughter started to feel like part of the Montana wind, something that belonged here, with me.

Eventually, I found solace not just in Laine, but in something else—a new endeavor. I wrote a book. Something young Sutton would have needed. Something, I suppose, I still need.

From the tent pitched near the shore, Laine emerges, her hair tousled by the breeze and her grin wide enough to disarm the world. In her hands, she carries a gift wrapped in brown paper and tied with a red bow, the same shade as her lips.

As always, I gravitate toward her, drawn by that pull I still don't entirely understand but no longer question.

She holds the gift out to me. "To changed plans."

I unwrap it carefully, the paper crinkling under my fingers. Inside is a book—my book. I run my thumb across the title embossed on the cover: Echoes of Home.

"It's the first proof copy," Laine murmurs. "I convinced your agent to send it to me." Her hand cradles my jaw, her thumb brushing lightly over my cheek. "I'm proud of you, Sutton. You always said you wanted to write stories that helped people. And now you have. You've done it." Her voice catches. "Your dad would be so proud."

I swallow against the tightness in my throat and meet her gaze, unable to stop the grin spreading across my face. "Have you read the acknowledgments yet?"

She tilts her head, her brow arching in curiosity.

I hand her the book. "Last page. Last paragraph. Read it out loud."

She turns to the final page, clears her throat, and begins to read.

"'And last of all, thank you to the love of my life. Laine, this book wouldn't be what it is without you. I wouldn't be who I am without you. Falling in love with you wasn't according to my plan. But here we are. Will you…'"

Her voice falters, cracking on the last words. When she looks up at me, her eyes glisten with unshed tears, and her lips part slightly, as if she's trying to form a response but can't find the words.

I step closer, taking the book from her trembling hands and setting it gently on a nearby stump. "I had a big evening planned to a T," I admit, my voice low. "There were supposed to be fireworks, flowers, music. But this—right here, right now—feels better."

She exhales a sharp breath, a teary laugh escaping her lips.

"Laine, will you marry me?"

The world stills, even the crickets going silent. It's just her and me, nearing the edge of something vast and terrifying and beautiful.

Laine nods, her tears spilling over as a smile breaks across her face. "Yes, Sutton. Yes!"

Above us, the stars burn bright. The water laps gently at the shore—a quiet applause for a love that, against all odds, found its way home.

ACKNOWLEDGMENTS

First and foremost, to my amazing friends and family—thank you for being my constant support system. You've cheered me on through every plot twist, detour, and late-night writing session. I couldn't have done this without you in my corner.

To my readers, both new and returning—thank you from the bottom of my heart for your patience as I worked to get this book out. Your encouragement, excitement, and belief in this story have kept me going. You've been with me on this journey, and I hope *Untruly with You* has been worth the wait. You're the reason these characters exist on the page, and for that, I'm forever grateful.

Finally, I want to thank myself. For pushing through the challenges, for staying committed to this story even when life threw unexpected curveballs. The road to finishing this book wasn't always smooth, but I kept going, and that's something I'm truly proud of.

Thank you, all of you. This book is as much yours as it is mine.

ALSO BY FLORENCE FIELDS

@authorflorencefields

florencefields.com

www.ingramcontent.com/pod-product-compliance
Lightning Source LLC
Chambersburg PA
CBHW032153190626
46814CB00005BA/1979